1990, ARAMGANJ

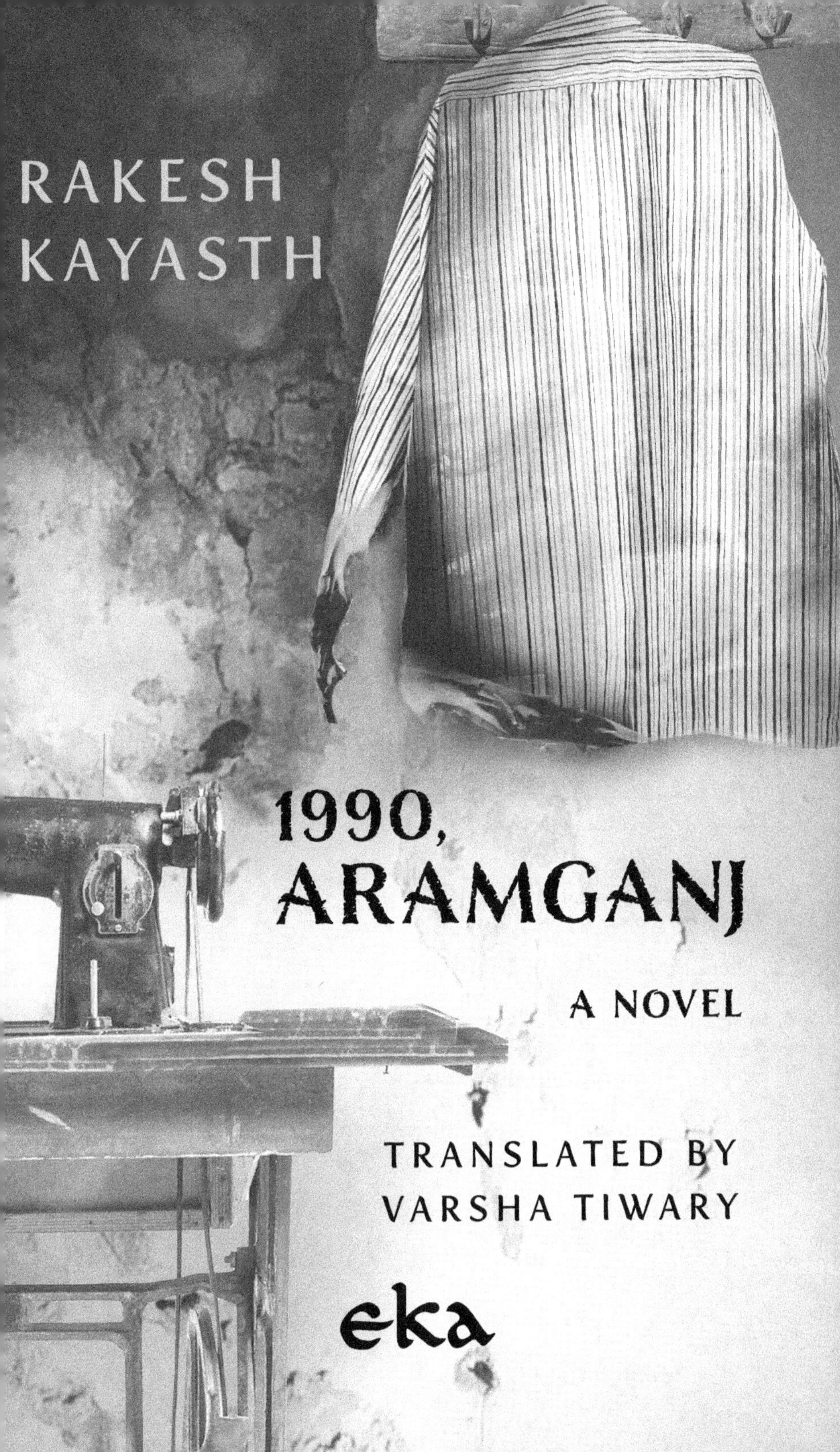
RAKESH
KAYASTH

1990,
ARAMGANJ

A NOVEL

TRANSLATED BY
VARSHA TIWARY

eka

eka

First published in Hindi as *Rambhakt Rangbaz* in 2021 by Hind Yugm

Published in English as *1990, Aramganj* in 2024 by Eka, an imprint of Westland Books, a division of Nasadiya Technologies Private Limited

No. 269/2B, First Floor, 'Irai Arul', Vimalraj Street, Nethaji Nagar, Alapakkam Main Road, Maduravoyal, Chennai 600095

Westland, the Westland logo, Eka and the Eka logo are the trademarks of Nasadiya Technologies Private Limited, or its affiliates.

ISBN: 9789360452506

10 9 8 7 6 5 4 3 2 1

Typeset by Jojy Philip, New Delhi

Printed at Thomson Press (India) Ltd

CONTENTS

1

THE STORY BEGINS

The watch ticks. The heart beats. What connects the two after all? The watch tells the time. And time sets the pace at which the heart will beat. Time ordains whether the heart will go on beating or come to a stop forever. Every watch in this world—whether on my wrist or yours—is, in fact, a time bomb. If not today, then tomorrow, if not tomorrow, then the day after—one day or the other, this bomb has to explode. That is why, every mother in this world is a sacrificial goat's mother—forever counting blessings, tying amulets, reciting invocations, chanting mantras.

Taking the watch to be a ticking time bomb might sound terrifying. But truths often tend to be terrifying. Still, the fact remains that the time in between—starting with the ticking of the timer and lasting until the hands touch the timer—is not always terrifying. This in-between time—when childhood blossoms into youth, weather changes, flowers bloom and people fall in love—is called life. And where there is life, there is always a story.

A good story is timeless. But when the story is true, it is crucial to mention the dates alongside the events it portrays. Hence I'll keep giving all the key dates related to this tale as we go along.

Right now, we are in the year 2020. The date is 30 January; a date no Indian can forget, it being the date on which the Mahatma was assassinated. But such is this year that in the times to come, no one would even want to remember it.

The story is an old one. But today, that is on 30 January 2020, a long-forgotten character of my story, has unexpectedly appeared before my eyes after ages. This handsome, strongly-built man checked in this morning at a hotel—Hotel Capital Heights in the very town of my story—and is now cruising along the lanes and neighbourhoods in a sedan. The only reason this man has returned is to be able to write the last page of this thirty-year-old story the way he wants it to be written.

But when you haven't even read the first page, what is the point of talking about the last one? So let us forget about this man for now. I too will set him aside. And get down to the task at hand. My job is to tell the story. I close my eyes, and see the hands of the clock turning anti-clockwise. The hands have now turned back to September 1990 where this story begins.

The September of 1990 was truly historical. Overnight, things were changing, not just in the country, but in the world. The debris of the wall pulled down in Berlin had not yet been cleared; news stories of the USSR's disintegration into bits and pieces were being heard every day. In India, the Mandal Commission's report had stormed in a month back, fuelling protests by upper-caste students against the proposal of greater job-quotas for lower castes. Amidst all this, Lal Krishna Advani, having pledged to unshackle the Hindus from a thousand-year slavery, embarked on a rath yatra—an expedition across India on a Toyota-truck designed to resemble a chariot—from Somnath on the western coast to Ayodhya, Lord Ram's birthplace in Uttar Pradesh. The symbol of Hindu valour, the saffron flag, fluttered in the sky. Leaping across pools of blood, the massive Ram Rath wheeled full-tilt ahead, cutting thick grooves over the land. Valour. Joy. Frenzy. Fear. Devotion. Curiosity. Countless such emotions floated in the air. So potent were the acclamations hailing the Ram Rath, that hearing or comprehending other voices above this din was beyond the capacity of most. The rath had already crossed many states, and was about to reach my town.

My town—where earlier, such fervour was displayed by folks only when waiting for a circus to arrive. Jumbo Circus, Apollo Circus, Jupiter Circus—all such circuses. That came with lions, elephants, monkeys, dwarves, jokers!

Brimming with curiosity, anxious groups of townsfolk strove to comprehend and explain the scenes to be expected upon the entry of Advani's rath into the town. Would it resemble the arrival of a circus or be somewhat different? The more serious among the townspeople could well understand that despite some elements of entertainment, the arrival of the rath was certainly not as innocuous as the arrival of a circus.

This town was like most other small or medium-sized towns in India. But my neighbourhood, Mohalla Aramganj? No, all mohallas were not like Aramganj. At least, I felt that my mohalla, Aramganj, was completely distinct from the rest of the town. Why the rest of the town? For me, Aramganj was the most unique place not just in the country but also the world. Why, you might ask. Now, how do I answer that? During that decade, between 1980 and 1990, neighbourhoods in every small town looked alike. The same crowded bazaars, the same sleepy intersections. The characters and their stories, too, were the same. How, then, to establish that Aramganj stood apart from Bakarganj in Patna or Keedganj in Allahabad?

But for Ashiq Miyan's presence, I would have doubtlessly concurred that Aramganj was like all other mohallas.

The most distinctive character of the tale I am relating to you is Ashiq Miyan. Whichever corner of the world he might inhabit, a man like Ashiq makes a place and its stories interesting. Stories truly are crafted at the hands of their characters—the job of the writer is only to take them to the people.

So, in all honesty, I accept that this story belongs not to me, but to Ashiq Miyan and Aramganj-walas. If any part of it seems weak, think of it as a failing of the writer's craft, and not of the story or its characters. Let me do one thing. I will take you to that September of 1990, and leave you at the Aramganj crossing, where our Ashiq Miyan makes his entry.

2

UP GOES THE SHUTTER,
OUT COMES THE HERO

The shutter goes up at exactly nine-thirty every morning. The shutter is inscribed with the words 'Mister India Gent's Tailor', next to which is a painted picture of a suited-booted Anil Kapoor, the reigning Bollywood hero. Today, on 20 September 1990 as well, the shutter goes up at nine-thirty. The man steps in, and the shutter of the adjacent shop too gets lifted up from the inside, this being 'Savitri Ladies Boutique'. Behind this second shutter lies a shiny glass door with a 'welcome' sign, and below it, the injunction—*'Yahaan shohdon ka khada hona manaa hai'.* Loafers, louts, scoundrels not to stand here. *Shohdon*, the word used in the edict, refers to not just any scoundrel but a smirking, winking, neck-craning embodiment of sleaze only to be found in mohallas like this one.

Now hear this—both shops, owned by the same man, with the same wall and veranda, but with two different sets of rules! The day before, Bhola babu had come here to give measurements for a pyjama. The festive season is on, and Mister India being jam-packed, he had shifted just a bit to the other side. At once, a voice rose to admonish him—*Aey! You. Mind where your feet go. Haven't you read this or what?*

One step to that side, and our dear retired Bhola babu turns from the most respectable man of the mohalla to a *shohda*! Just tell me, who acts like this!

Good or bad, decent or characterless—all things can get settled within the span of a single step. This is the philosophy of the owner of Mister India, Sheikh Nizamuddin Wali Ashiq—in short, Ashiq Miyan.

'You want the pant length kept forty, or forty and a half inches?' Ashiq asks while measuring a customer.

'Keep it whatever, yaar, what difference does half an inch make?'

'Think again, bhaiyya. The difference of half an inch can turn a man into a Hindu or a Musalman.'

Aramganj-walas don't want to forget this half-inch difference. And don't care to remember the two different shop names. Consequently, they have combined the two names, Savitri Ladies Boutique and Mister India, into one—Two-in-One Tailor. Just as a two-in-one can be a radio as well as a tape-recorder, our Ashiq Miyan can stitch salwar-suits and blouses for women with the same facility with which he makes shirt-pant and kurta-pyjama for men.

Mostly, our mohalla people like to say that Ashiq might be 'two-in-one' as a tailor, but as a man, he is four-in-one. Maybe even more than that. In the entire stretch from Aramganj Chowk to Pahadi Tola, and from Bada Talab to Main Road, many different stories are heard and known about Ashiq Miyan. When Ashiq Miyan flew kites, the sky would get emptied of rivals in a matter of minutes. Records for roadside games like marbles and gilli-danda are all in his name, and will remain in his name—because now these games are hardly played. Who knows how many things this man is a master of!

'Had he not been a tailor, Ashiq would have been a wonderful painter. The portrait of Anil Kapoor on his shop's shutter is his handiwork.'

'No, no, he would have been a top mechanic. The company repaired my TV, but after it was fixed, it conked off again. Who knows what Ashiq did after opening the thing, but within five minutes, it was working again.'

'In this entire town, you won't find another fellow who can drive every vehicle—from cycle to truck. Give an airplane to this guy, that too he would fly without any training.'

Among Ashiq's many exploits, the most famous is the incident when he jumped in the baoli at Sheetala temple and saved Peetambar's ten-year-old son. Peetambar sells garlands outside the temple. There is no dispute over the veracity of this story. The sole argument is over the exact duration of time for which Ashiq kept circling in the water with the drowning child on his shoulders. Some say at least fifteen minutes. But there are those who insist that he must have swum for not a minute less than an hour. Because, no rope being at hand, it was sent for from Jamuna's hardware shop, and that had taken a lot of time.

The stories of his exploits and talents may be slightly adulterated. But the truth as absolute as sixteen annas in a rupee is that Ashiq alone possesses a unique talent never seen before in these parts. This involves not just his ability to break-dance like Jaaved Jaaferi, the movie star. When Ashiq performs the breakdance, he also juggles lit torches in both hands, and filling his mouth with kerosene, blows such rings of fire in the air as he gyrates, that people watch with dropped jaws. Whether it is Dussehra, or Saraswati Puja, or the Kali Puja immersion procession, the crowning glory of any such evening is this feat of Ashiq Miyan.

It isn't as if Ashiq Miyan is well liked by everyone. Several young buggers of Aramganj say Ashiqwa *saala* is a top-notch bastard. Much like Lord Indra presiding over a gathering of celestial nymphs, he himself is always surrounded by women, but tells those who come for measurements that they must *never ever* turn their neck towards Savitri Ladies Boutique! He says, 'Turning the neck ruins both measurement and character. If you want to get your clothes tailored, stand up straight, give measurements, and get lost.'

As for him—the slightest stir of a lady customer at the boutique's door, and Ashiq at once rushes through the four-by-two inner door connecting Mister India to Savitri. Now watch Ashiq Miyan's demeanour! How he laughs and smiles, calling this one his sister-in-law, and asking the *bhabhi* how the visit to the maternal home is going. Every older woman is his aunt—if not bua, then chachi. The younger ones are all sisters, didis. Now he is divulging to chachi a cure for arthritis, as swift and sure as Ram-ji's arrow. And promising young Chutki that he will stitch such a salwar-suit for her that the boy's side will at once say yes upon seeing her. And then what? Quick engagement, express wedding! And chachi can then breathe easy, as after taking a dip in the Ganga-ji ... Isn't that so, chachi?

The 'gents' customers might keep waiting, but would Ashiq Miyan free himself up before at least an hour or hour-and-a-half of attending to these buas and didis? Such a magical sweetness in his words! As for the ambience of the boutique—don't even ask! To put it together, Ashiq has poured in not just money but the very contents of his heart. Man-sized mirrors on three sides, and towards the front, a huge wardrobe, where stitched garments are arranged tastefully. There is a tiny trial room as well, outside which stands a marble-bodied mannequin clad in a salwar-suit.

Loafers-louts-scoundrels are not allowed inside, but nothing can stop stories from coming outside. Arguments go on and on. Over whether the mannequin's face is more like Sudha's or

Puja's. Women past their prime go to Ashiq's shop less to give measurements and more to keep an eye on the younger girls. No, there is no risk inside the shop itself. But on stepping out, one has to walk down the streets of this mohalla. The times are very bad, and on top of it, this mohalla! Because of the goings-on in this mohalla, Sarvdaman Singh keeps crying to this day.

Ashiq Miyan is fair-complexioned, with a taut and well-exercised body and eyes full of light. His thick moustache tapers and thins on the sides, just like Anil Kapoor's. His age must be around thirty-two, but he looks even younger. In ladies' circles, some difference of opinion prevails about his looks. Some women say, 'No, no, he does not resemble Anil Kapoor, he looks more like Jackie Shroff.'

Ashiq's popularity among the chowk women gives many a heartburn. But the truth is, Ashiq is a lover boy, or *ashiq*, only in name. This householder has one caring but quarrelsome wife, two children and an old mother. Not a hint of scandal around him as far as can be seen. Yes, one thing though needs to be said. Ashiq's words bear a nectar of sorts. Maybe that is why people are drawn towards him. Women are his admirers because he has infinite patience to listen to their happy or sad stories.

Such is the magic in his words that the dramatis personae of Ashiq's tales come alive, and the incidents seem to unfold right before the eyes of the listeners. The wise men of the mohalla say Ashiq lives off his ability to talk and not off his ability to wield the needle and thread. Hearing this, Ashiq grows serious and replies in a philosophical tone—'I live off whatever my Ram-ji gives me.'

And this indeed is the most unique feature of Ashiq's personality. Saying this is not merely tall talk or Bollywood style dialogue-baazi for Ashiq. Things really are like this. The lone Musalman in this mohalla of Hindus—like a tongue surrounded by thirty-two teeth. And not even a shadow of fear! Where, after all, does he get this courage from? Don't ask Ashiq Miyan. Or he will immediately turn into Ramanand Sagar, of the TV show *Ramayan* fame, and nail a four-line *chaupai* on you. But seriously speaking, it was on the strength of his knowledge of Ramayan quatrains that Ashiq was able to get the shop next to Mister India on rent.

For many years after his father's death, Ashiq ran only the gent's tailoring shop. But when the houseowner Triveni Mishra, that is Pandi-ji, carved out another biggish shop from a portion of his courtyard, many started hovering around him to get it on rent. Ashiq too went to talk, with his expansion plan—the ladies tailoring shop idea—but Pandi-ji almost shooed him off. 'You can barely manage the trade you already have, what will you do with a new shop? You won't be able to afford such high rent.'

Ashiq's face fell. Pandi-ji thought for a few moments and then said, 'Nine hundred a month is the rent. If you have the will to take it, tell me.'

Ashiq replied that he had no dearth of will, 'But, chacha, hasn't Goswami Tulsidas said in Ramcharitmanas, "*Aawat hiye harshe nahin ...*" Tulsi says, "Don't let gold lure you into going/ Where no one is happy to see you."'

When Ashiq quoted this *chaupai* in Awadhi to make the point that more than money, it was his regard for Pandi-ji that made him approach him, Pandi-ji's jaw dropped. Now see Ram-ji's miracle—a week later, Pandi-ji himself summoned Ashiq and said, 'You father was an honest man. Take the shop. I would have charged others nine hundred, you pay eight.'

Ashiq is a straight talker. 'The rent is fine. But I won't be able to manage any *pugree-vagree*,' he said, demurring on the matter of the high security-deposit required to be paid.

Pandi-ji laughed. 'You are a genuine man. Don't pay the *pugree*. Just keep paying the rent on time, like you do for the other shop.'

Pandi-ji's decision irked the mohalla-walas a lot. To have given such a fine shop to a Musalman, overlooking people from one's own caste and community!

Pandi-ji's reply was, 'Ashiqwa is a Musalman only in name. Knows religion and piety better than you folks.'

Ashiq Miyan is reaping the rewards of his piety-religiosity in this Hindu mohalla. Fathers and mothers of Aramganj often tell their children, 'Look at him and learn a thing or two. One, he is a tailor, and on top of it, a Musalman. Still so full of all the right values.'

Without being told, he hunts for and obtains the best *singhada* flour for the neighbourhood chachis' grain-free fasting—that's our Ashiq. From Nag Panchami to Anant Chaturdashi, which sacred Hindu-calendar date falls when, he remembers them all by heart. In recommending the right measures and ways to invite auspicious omens, he is a step ahead of Radha pandit. *If you ever misplace something in the house, no need to take tension.* 'Just tie a knot in your sari-pallu reciting Ram-ji's name, and if the lost object is not found soon, keep a pet dog in my name,' Ashiq once advised Bimla bua with absolute confidence.

The whole mohalla has now tested this recipe successfully. Whether he is a low-caste *dom*, or a polluted *maleccha* of another religion, who can really tell when and on whom God's divine grace will be bestowed? Really, truly, he is blessed by Ram-ji. That is why Ashiqwa is also one of the highest earners in this shabby, dilapidated bazaar. Had Ram-ji not favoured him, could a Musalman have run a shop so fearlessly in a Hindu mohalla, that too in current times! Apart from 'Ram-bhakt', the other adjective associated with Ashiq's name is 'Rangbaaz', a many-hued, colourful personality. Many fellow shopkeepers in the bazaar call him by this name.

Ashiq's walk has a carefree, joyful lilt. Quick repartee comes naturally to him. While ever ready to do anything for friends, he never pointlessly yields or succumbs to anyone. But are such things enough for him to earn a medal for boldness and sass, and be called a Rangbaaz?

I think the name must have stuck because back then, the word 'swag' had not yet been coined. Anyway, now that you have come to Aramganj, you will have a proper lowdown on everything about Ashiq Miyan and others in this mohalla.

3

WHY DO VULTURES COME HERE?

Abha is not troubled by the tick-tocking clock. But the *tnnn-tnnn* of the pendulum makes her get up with a jerk. She had lain down after sending off Guddu for tuition and God knows when fallen asleep. And then this sound. To check the hour, she goes to the drawing room. The hands are at seven and twelve, and the pendulum is still swinging.

Abha peers down the balcony. Like every other day, hawkers have set up shop on both sides of the road. The office closes at 5.30, and at exactly 5.45 every day, Abha puts tea and water on the stove. By the time it boils, her husband arrives. But who knows what happened today. It is not just seven, but five past seven now. Abha returns to her room. Through the window she sees the same sad peepul, half its branches dead since forever.

There used to be a time when this tree would turn into a colony of vultures every evening. Abha has a childhood fear of vultures. Her grandma would tell tales—of how in the old days, flocks of vultures would start coming on their own at the time of an epidemic or a battle.

The empty lot near the cremation ground, where they throw dead animals, was about two kilometres away. Still, who knew why the vultures picked this tree to roost in.

Abha had only heard tales of vultures. Only upon coming here after her wedding, did she actually see them. Back then, out of fear, she would keep the windows shut. She had naively asked her husband: 'Why do vultures flock to this tree?' Her husband had laughed and replied, 'I haven't called them. And what harm do they do to you? They live in their house, and you in yours.' But Abha couldn't get rid of the feeling that the vultures kept gazing unblinkingly at her window.

Soon after marriage came the good news. But Abha fell sick one morning in the fourth month. Upon reaching the hospital, the doctor said that she had aborted. Abha fell deep into depression. Even after staying in her mother's home for months, this sadness refused to leave her. When her husband came to take her back, she became adamant: 'I will not live with the vultures.' What could the poor husband have done? Neither could the tree growing on government land be cut down, nor could the location of his ancestral house be changed. After all, it wasn't just any house—it was a double-storey house right on Aramganj Chowk.

So, after bringing Abha back from her mother's house, the husband shifted their bedroom to the small room next to his mother's room. From there, the dead peepul with vultures on its branches could not be seen. Time flew. Guddu was born. Then, Guddu, who used to crawl on his knees, grew big enough for his father to think that he should have his own room. So it was decided that they would shift back to the old bedroom. But Abha was still not ready. Her husband tried to reason with her: 'Where are the poor vultures left now? They are all gone.' But Abha remained perturbed. *Could the eaters of dead bodies ever die?*

Now back in that old bedroom, Abha complains every third day. 'You know, the vultures still come here.' Earlier her husband would smile upon hearing this, now he pays no attention.

The husband hasn't arrived. It is twenty past seven now. Guddu, back home from tuition, is reading comics in his room. Abha paces restlessly. These days the newspapers are full of troubling news. News of riots in Rajasthan and Gujarat. Even in this town, it is not as if things are fine. Yesterday Umesh told them about an incident of knifing in Urdu Bazaar—the police had to order closure of all the shops. Her husband's office is not on that side, but then who knows when and where something untoward might happen these days!

'Yes, didi, I too agree, the world is turning bad. But nothing bad can happen to the folks of Aramganj. After all, Ram-ji had passed through our mohalla on his way to the forest.' Ashiq's voice echoes in Abha's ears from nowhere, and picking an old kurti, she quickly goes down the stairs.

Ashiq is good at darning as well. He picks out matching threads while carrying on the conversation. But today his words do not amuse Abha. Ashiq notices the lack of colour on her face, the slight dampness in the corner of her eyes. He takes the conversation further. 'Just the touch of Ram-ji's foot, and Ahilya turned from stone into a woman—such is Ram-ji's power. Once anyone seeks refuge in Him, Ram-ji protects them forever.'

Suddenly Ashiq shouts, 'There he is! Bhaisaheb is returning after loads of shopping from the *haat*.'

Abha jerks her neck back and spots her husband moving homewards through the crowded street on his Bajaj Chetak, the scooter basket laden with green vegetables.

'*Arre* didi, this is nearly done ... it will only take two more minutes,' Ashiq calls out after her. But why would didi stop now! Saying that she will collect the kurti tomorrow, she runs home, thinking, Ashiq truly has the gift of Ma Saraswati, whatever he says comes true. He is right to say that Ram-ji had passed by this street when he went to the forest, and that's why nothing bad can possibly happen to the residents here. Ashiq watches Abha go. He knows why she had come to his shop with that never-to-be-worn old kurti.

In this mohalla of gossipy, snitching, jealous folks, people might differ over a thousand things, but there is one thing everyone agrees on—that Ashiq's proclamation of Ram-ji's divine grace being upon Aramganj is absolutely correct. Throughout the day, vehicles roar past this street. The footpaths on either side are so crowded, it's tough to squeeze a foot in. Amidst all this, children create a ruckus, crossing the street at will. But see Ram-ji's grace—till today, not even one has been crushed under the wheels.

Once, a bullock lifted Manohar babu by the horns and hurled him to the ground. But despite rheumatism and piles, he simply stood up dusting himself, like some football player. Not a scratch on him! Similarly, a pig came before Lallan's bike all of a sudden, and the bike got tossed up, sending Lallan straight into Bajrangi's dhaba, and neck down into a bucket. An inch here or there, and Lallan's head would have been in a wok full of frying oil.

Dataram Jaiswal's one and only son had got an LML Vespa in dowry. Once, he was coming back from somewhere late at night on that scooter. At Devi Mandap turning, two goondas brandishing a country-made pistol snatched the scooter and fired as they took off. But the bullet merely grazed past Jaiswal-ji's son's shoulder. Only mild scratches, nothing else. On the other hand, the rascals taking off crashed into a telephone pole and, abandoning the scooter, ran away in panic. Point being, both life and scooter stayed intact.

All this—does it not prove Ram-ji's miracle? Due to Ram-ji's grace, no one has heard of an untimely death in this mohalla. Who cares whether this town falls on the path leading to Ayodhya, Chitrakoot, Dandakaranya, or not! Who knows where this town was during Ram-ji's time. That is why, what Ashiqwa says is totally correct. Right now, the whole country is debating as to which corner of Ayodhya Ram-ji was born in. Advani-ji is out on his rath to tell the entire nation that Ram-ji was born 'there', and hence, the temple, too, will be built 'there'. But Aramganj-walas already know without Advani-ji telling them, that Ram-ji had gone to the forest from 'here'.

Will Advani-ji come to this street to pay his respects, to do *darshan*? As per convention, he should. When he has got on the rath in the name of Ram-ji, why shouldn't he visit the place Ram-ji had passed through? The logical people in the mohalla feel that Aramganj must have been named after Lord Ram's name. The bhakts must have said, '*Aa* Ram—Come, Ram. And Ram-ji must have appeared before them. Where comes Ram, comes comfort, *Aram*.

4

THIS IS ARAMGANJ CHOWK

The special thing about Aramganj is this: if you are not alert when you step out in the morning, without you realising, it will be noon by the time you manage to get past the corner. Someone or the other will waylay you, hold you by the hand, and prevent you from moving forward. Each time you escape and move a couple of steps ahead, another will intercept you. So many people! So many characters! Such talk, as you cannot imagine. We often follow a story through its characters. But I warn you, don't even try to do that in this case. The characters being such, they themselves will start following you. This mohalla is teeming with rambling talkers, clingers and weirdos who will bore you to tears. My endeavour will be to steer clear of them and keep moving. If I get caught up in their tales and talks, this story will never end. I have no intention of turning Ashiq Miyan's tale into *Arabian Nights*.

Aramganj is part of a leading industrial city developed by the British in Eastern India. It was called the 'summer capital' of the province. So it has a decent-sized railway station, a functional airport, and a high court building as well. Laid out over a length of thirty kilometres, this town has many parallel roads. One of the roads emerging behind the *kutchery* goes right up to the plateau of the Poorna river. On both sides of this road are small mohallas. The shared identity of Aramganj comes from variously named gali-mohallas spread over a radius of four kilometres.

The road going towards the Poorna river becomes wider and livelier at one place. That place is Aramganj Chowk, *chowk* meaning 'square'. If we think of Aramganj as a republic then the chowk is its capital. For outsiders, the chowk is Aramganj. But the chowk-walas are extremely conscious of their singular identity.

'Not in Aramganj, but right on the Aramganj Chowk we have our house.'

'This is Aramganj Chowk. The houses here are mostly double-storeyed.'

'This is Aramganj Chowk. No shop rents for less than eight-hundred to a thousand here.'

'This is Aramganj Chowk' rolls off people's tongues in a tone exactly like 'This is BBC London'.

Settling the boundaries of this chowk was as complicated as the settling of the Indo-China border dispute. Customarily, only the thirty or forty houses falling between the Aramganj crossing roundabout and Jangilal Coal Depot enjoy the status of being 'chowk houses'. The houseowners with houses on the wide road ahead of the coal depot were also claimants to this status. But the entrance to the Dalit basti, Valmiki Nagar, lies in between the coal depot and the wide road. The matter got stuck at this point. Giving 'chowk-dweller' status to those living in houses ahead of the coal depot would imply that Valmiki Nagar was also a part of the chowk. Valmiki Nagar, a part of the chowk? No chowk-wala would ever step inside the basti in full consciousness. That's why the all-knowing intellectuals of the mohalla ordained that Jangilal Coal Depot be considered the final frontier of the chowk.

If to the south lies Valmiki Nagar, then a right turn northwards takes one to the Muslim settlement known as Rayyat Toli. Here the narrow lanes to the right and left were settled by gradual extension over reclaimed marshlands and agricultural lands. While the plots on the other side of the chowk were carved in British times, and all houses built on them belong to the upper-castes—the savarnas—Singh-jis, Pandi-jis, Lala-jis. There are a few savarna houses in the inner galis too, but mostly the houses in them belong to the backward castes—Sahu-ji, Mahto-ji, Yadav-ji type of people. No wonder the chowk gentleman sweeping his gaze around feels as powerful as the leaders of the great Indian nation feel when looking at the SAARC nations.

The fifties—when Nehru-ji gave the slogan, *'Aram haram hai',* calling laziness sinful—was the golden era of repose as far as the chowk-walas were concerned. Modern India required government employees in huge numbers. Several first-generation chowk-walas were employed by the British Indian government. The era after Independence was such that any literate man from the second generation could obtain government employment merely by applying. An application and routine recommendation could land one a permanent job.

The second generation breezed leisurely through their government duty, earning huge bribes and finally retiring into complete relaxation. The auspicious inception of 'the double-storey revolution' on the chowk took place in that era. This generation energetically expanded their families as well. Radhe babu fathered nine offsprings between 1963 and 1980. Jagdish babu and Murli babu eight each. There is no count of those with four or five. I mean, Aramganj Chowk has a solid demographic dividend.

The third generation chowk-walas came of age watching the 'angry-young-man' movies. This generation is clearly very annoyed with the 'System', but they love their traditions, hence they have never compromised on relaxation. As a result, the sixty-year-old record of zero-migration from the chowk is still intact. Why would anyone leave their home and go to some other town to take up some useless two-paisa job? 'Private job' was a pejorative term for the previous generations, and it remains thus even now.

Currently public employment levels have gone down by fifty percent as compared to those of the previous two generations. Even so, there are four bank clerks, one probationary officer, one engineer, one confirmed and a half-a-dozen ad-hoc lecturers on sarkari payrolls among those below thirty. The rest are subscribers of *Competition Success Review* and *Pratiyogita Darpan*—magazines for aspiring public servants. In the entire radius of Aramganj, the highest population is that of lawyers. The neatness with which a black coat can cover up the stain of unemployment cannot be matched by anything else in this world.

There are other benefits to being a lawyer. The biggest being that proposals start arriving from marriageable girls without necessitating any clarifications from the boy's father about how the household runs on pension and rental income alone. The first generation had built such huge houses, that even after the division of parental property among siblings, almost everyone has a shop or two at least. The basement and ground floor have been let out on rent, and the first and second floors—with overhanging balconies that elbow electricity poles—are occupied by the houseowners. Many useless sons of these households have been made to sit behind the counter in shops. Though these shops have been funded by dowry money or with provident fund money, the community of fathers is not really comfortable with this decision. They lament—what was the point of educating them then?

Padhe Farsi beche tel
Dekh bhaiyya karam ka khel!

Learnt Persian, sells oil
Karma can make anyone toil!

'These days even Pandi-jis and Lala-jis have to set up grocery shops. But whatever it may be, at least it is better than loitering about aimlessly.'

'Merit matters mostest, who is saying otherwise! But tell me, what is achieved on merit alone these days?' Nityanand Tiwari's favourite dialogue is like life-support for the sinking hearts of the community of fathers.

Aramganj Chowk-walas were aggrieved, but in their familiar laidback manner. Then something happened so abruptly that the chowk was shaken up. This was a month prior to the beginning of this story. On 7 August 1990, Prime Minister V.P. Singh announced the implementation of the Mandal Commission's affirmative action recommendations to extend reservations for the lower and backward castes in government jobs to fifty per cent. From the very next day, along with the nation, Aramganj Chowk and the rest of the town began to seethe with resentment.

BA–MA pass karenge
Lalu–V.P. baans karenge

BA–MA we will do
Lalu–V.P. we will screw

The slogans bouncing on the streets flew in through the windows and began echoing inside homes. The youth breaking bulbs and streetlights wanted their voice to reach not just the government's ears, but also the ears of 'those low-castes' who would now start dreaming of becoming officers. Thakur

Sarvdaman Singh made an open announcement: 'The young man who burns down a government bus will be given a reward of eleven thousand in cash.'

The elderly say that at the age of fifty-five, Sarvdaman Singh, also famously known at the chowk as Sarvdaman babu or Babu sahib, has more guts than any of these agitating youths. Poor man—he has been deceived so much in his life. A zamindar from Kanakpuri, rolling in ancestral wealth. A much celebrated contractor of the town, too. And *his* daughter had eloped with a low-caste Lohar! In mortal rage, Babu sahib had marched out to finish off the boy's entire clan with his double-barrel. But, after all, who was there in that clan? The boy had been staying with a distant relative for studies. He won over the girl, and disappeared. The poor distant relative would have been killed for no reason. Luckily, the gun misfired. It became a police case though. Somehow, after some 'give and take', the matter got settled, or the disgraced Babu sahib would have had to serve jail time. The daughter is out of his hands anyway. For a long time now, no one even knows where she is. In a way, that's good. Had she come before his eyes ...

Sometime ago, a rumour flew that Sarvdaman babu's son-in-law had become a big officer somewhere. But what son-in-law? When the daughter who blackened his face is to be treated as dead for good, why have anything to do with that lowlife? To this day, once every month, Sarvdaman babu fires twice in the air. One shot for that lowlife Lohar, and the other for that accursed girl whom he raised with such care. If dishonour wasn't avenged, then a man wasn't fit to be called a true Thakur.

Revenge is something many youth of Aramganj Chowk want to take. '*Ye log*—these people—have begun climbing too high.'

'Earlier, never would they dare to wag their tongues. Now look, how they hold forth on politics!'

'If we keep sitting—one hand over the other—they will climb on to our heads and piss all over us. What *will*? They already *are*. Pissing on us.'

The Mandal storm instantly reminded the chowk youth of the grandeur of their dreams. All of them now straightaway aspired to be IAS officers, and nothing but IAS officers. Nothing less. But then V.P. Singh's firm and final green signal came, snuffing out the flame of their dreams. The black-coated lawyers, the bangle-sellers and grocers—everyone—readily accepted that all the misfortune in their lives was solely due to the antics of the government.

The elderly community went into a different sort of depression. In Lakshmikant Sahay's house, they sat and recalled their heyday—when the area in which the lower-caste galis are now, had been full of Adivasi bastis. The chowk people could easily find labour willing to work for nothing. The tribals were so simple that they wouldn't even ask for wages. And their women would collect priceless stuff like honey and chironji-seeds from the jungle and hand it over to the chowk people in exchange for salt or sugar. But those who settled in their place could only be called *patidars,* or landowners.

The elderly condemned themselves for not having purchased the land selling for peanuts back then and letting the lesser castes settle there. For quite some time, 'these people' had been trying to act like equals. Now they would even strive to become Collector–SP and rule! Who knew what was in store for this mohalla!

5

TOO MUCH POLITICS

Neutral observer Nirmal Jain (being a chowk tenant and not an owner) is of the opinion that a man who fails to yawn at least once between every two sentences cannot but be an outsider. Certainly not anyone from Aramgamj Chowk. In the time betel-leaf spittle takes to land from the mouth to the drain here, a decent man will reach from one crossing to the next in any other part of the town.

These days, the whole country is electrified by Mandal. But this current has fizzled into a mild shock upon reaching Aramganj Chowk. The poor chowk-walas are having trouble handling even this. The 'ishtudent cumnooty' is hot-blooded everywhere. So it is in Aramganj too. But exactly how much hotter their blood is, as compared to the blood of students from other places, is a moot question. Six odd broken tube-lights and ten or twelve shattered bulbs is the sum total of the achievements of Aramganj's anti-reservation agitation. Add to that some deflated tyres of an odd tempo or truck too. Sudama had inserted a thread-bomb inside an old letterbox, causing a loud explosion, but the letterbox itself continued standing upright. Had it even fallen down, exactly what would have been dislodged by dislodging it? Letters had ceased being taken out of that box ages ago.

'The chowk-walas are masters of tall talk. If actually asked to do something, their hands start trembling,' remarked Minku's grandfather, shaking with toothless laughter over the fate of the chowk's anti-Mandal agitation. Minku's grandfather, meaning Sakaldeep Sahay, doyen of the chowk's first generation. He often tells a story. When the country became free, news of the tricolour's hoisting started coming in from various parts of the town. But Jagannath Pandey held the chowk-walas back saying that unless they had the express permission of the district administration, they would all be straightaway put in jail. Later on, God only knows how, that very Jagannath Pandey managed to get his name inserted in the list of freedom fighters, and coolly kept drawing pension till the day he died.

If not the actual agitation, then arguments and counter-arguments about the agitation! All kinds of theories and a variety of stories are floating from Mangal's paan-shop to Ojha-ji's paan-shop. The anti-reservation agitation at the chowk would have been the best in the entire district, but what were the poor volunteers to do when there was no unity among the forward castes. 'Really, too much politics here!'

On the day of the Bharat Bandh shutter-down strike, Munna and Pappu, with a couple of followers in tow, had marched, enthusiastically raising slogans: *'Lalu–V.P., let us screw.'*

Munna arrived early that morning at the tailoring shop, just as the market was opening up, and began bellowing, *'Abey* Rangbaz! Don't you know Bharat is bandh today?'

A voice replied from inside, 'If Bharat is shut, then why are you out on the street? Go back to your house.'

Rebuking loudly, Munna told Ashiq to pull down the shutter at once and go home. Agitators raised fervent cries.

STOP RESERVATIONS!
BA–MA WE WILL DO
LALU–V.P. WE WILL SCREW ...

The reply came, 'I am very scared of you, Munna, that's why I pulled down the shutter in advance. Now you also go home. Chachi must be waiting.'

How cunning Ashiq was. He had pulled Mr India's shutter down, but the sewing machines could be heard running inside. Munna stepped forth, roughly pushing the glass door of Savitri Ladies Boutique. The very next moment, an angry female voice arose, hurling non-stop abuses.

'Who the hell is this burnt-face *re* ... who walks into a ladies' shop like this? *Aai-hai!* Is he blind? Don't you have a mother and sisters at home? Someone ... is there anyone here ...? CALL the POLICE *re*. Tell them to put him in jail!'

She was a Valmiki Nagar customer, stepping out of Savitri Ladies Boutique with a heap of darned and repaired clothes in her arms. Her single collision with Munna led to the untimely death of the chowk's anti-reservation agitation. Munna was quick to guess that to continue standing there for a moment more would invite allegations of eve-teasing. He, and his gang of merit-seekers, disappeared at once.

That day, the chowk-walas realised another thing about Ashiq aka Rangbaz. Not only did Ram-ji shower him with divine grace, even Goddess Kali stood ready, sceptre in hand, to defend him. Two-in-One tailoring shop stayed open, and emulating him, other rented shops too remained open for business. The owner of Manish Cloth Store told the property-owner's son Lallan straight up, 'Okay, I will shut the shop. But whatever loss of sales I suffer, please adjust it against the rent. If you agree, say so.'

Such audacity in a mere tenant! Daring to talk this way to a landlord's face! Really, Mandal has changed everything! Sudama brought this news—'Jadojee Professor from gali no. 3 is inciting people in Ramavtar's saloon, saying, the days of Pandits are past, the time of the Backwards is coming.'

This is August 1990. Mark Zuckerberg, born in New York, is just six years old. Jack Dorsey's groupies, too, are still roaming about in half-pants. Despite Twitter and Facebook being decades away, without any technical aid, the hashtag '#Toomuchpolitics' is going viral on Aramganj Chowk.

Among the many worth-mentioning things about Vinod bhaiyya—an ad-hoc lecturer conferred with the honorary title of 'Professor sahib' by the citizens of Aramganj—the most important is that his engagement to a girl barely escaped getting broken off recently. Someone had squealed to the future father-in-law that the boy did not have a permanent job. Vinod bhaiyya was supposed to get a Maruti 800 in dowry, but the matter finally had to be settled on a Bajaj-Priya scooter. Only by a bit of luck he somehow managed to get married.

This incident traumatised not just the chowk elders but all potential grooms as well. '*Saala*, what kind of times are these! People just can't tolerate the happiness of others. Bloody wedding wreckers like these must be caught and made to drink piss before everyone at the chowk.' Many such revolutionary proposals are heard at Aramganj Chowk, but seldom put into practice. Every morning, people make big resolutions. But by evening, the cud gets chewed out of the idea.

Right now, Vinod bhaiyya, i.e. Professor sahib, is slowly chewing the cud out of a Bangali paan smeared with tobacco-lime paste in two flavours: *kala-peela teen sau zarda* and *Tulsi zarda*. Attired in the fast-disappearing official gear of Aramganj—a shirt over pyjamas—the black spectacles perched on his head lend him gravitas. The 'trending' hashtag '#Toomuchpolitics' has his approval. His one-member fact-finding committee has got to the bottom of 'the real reason behind the failure of the mohalla's anti-reservation agitation' and has grabbed it by the tail. His report is now being made public at Ojha-ji's paan-kiosk.

'Matters got bungled because we relied on Kamlesh Singh. That bugger played a double game. Despite being from a forward caste, he neither sent any men nor himself took to the streets on the day of the Bharat Bandh. When questioned, he simply said that Munna and Pappu, too, are like his own boys. Tell me, can two people ever make a Bharat Bandh? The chowk-walas said, "What's the point in making us shut shop when we already are against Mandal? It's the gali-walas who support Mandal. Go there and get the shops shut down." Now, can anyone make low-caste localities like Gwala Toli and Teli Mohalla shut shop without volunteers?'

The public starts assembling at the paan-shop to discuss this matter. The simple question is, what made Kamlesh Singh do this? Throwing light on this, Professor sahib presents a deep analysis: 'Kamleshwa, a Rajput, is a follower of that Bhumihar, Jatashankar Sharma. And half the time, his mind works like that of a wily Kayasth. Even though he belongs to the Brahmin-Baniya party, he has maintained his hold over the low-castes. Such a complicated man will do nothing that anyone can easily comprehend. But surely, he's playing some big game, and the chowk's Bharat Bandh got ruined due to his murky politics.'

The public gets the point that this convoluted politics is beyond their comprehension. The one-line conclusion is that 'too much politics' turned the Bharat Bandh into a flop show.

Akhilesh is not ready to accept that the anti-reservation agitation is a dud. The youngsters coming of age first heard the phrase 'tit for tat' from Akhilesh's mouth. This proverb is now on everyone's lips. An example of its usage: '*Bahut tentiya raha hai, chalo chalke iska "tit for tat" kar dete hain.'* He is twatting too much, let's go and do his 'tit for tat'. Akhilesh is a distant relative of Sarvdaman babu, and his sentiments got badly hurt by the 'Rajput-Lohar' love story. The Mandal cyclone has now given him a pretext to settle scores with the gali-walas.

Akhilesh is proud of the fact that he spearheaded the secret activities of his revolutionary group in the anti-Mandal agitation. This group had taken many steps in the last four or five days. After locking Phuleshwar Mahto's door from the outside, and sticking Sellotape all over the call bell, the revolutionaries pressed his bell at 12.30 in the night and ran off. In the potters colony, the Kumhar Toli, they shattered unbaked clay pots left out to dry on the road, and scrawled all over a wall, 'Now Kallu potter will turn collector'.

By any yardstick, Akhilesh has a genuine claim over the eleven-thousand-rupee prize announced by Sarvdaman babu. But no one knows why, despite his diligent, detailed and repeated recounting of his feats in every shop on the chowk, Sarvdaman babu is not taking note of Akhilesh's revolutionary activities. Receiving the prize money remains a distant dream. Truly, there is '#Toomuchpolitics' at Aramganj Chowk!

Things are heating up in the galis as well. The gali-walas never had a quarrel with the chowk people to begin with. But the equation changed the day, double-barrel in hand, Sarvdaman babu entered the Lohar gali, hurling mother-sister abuses at the low-castes. And now, Mandal has taken away whatever little cordiality was left.

The carrom club in Ranjit's courtyard has become the hub for discussion on political and social issues.

'The swagger of these high castes will vanish the minute they lose monopoly over government jobs. That's why the chowk-walas are quaking in their boots.'

'Harijalwa had gone to deliver milk early that morning, and the chowk-walas surrounded and began ragging him. Now tell me, has *he* implemented Mandal? There is a limit to goondaism.'

'They only have their caste-status to preen over. Otherwise, in which field are they better than us? In studies, look at Dilip bhaiyya. If you want to look at goondaism, can they match Prem Boss and Muneshwar Sahu? No chowk-lout is worth even the pubes of these two.'

'Mind your language, *bey*!' Ranjit signals, seeing Harendra Yadav coming. Harendra Yadav is also a 'professor', who teaches political science in some non-descript college. The college is non-constituent, and the post is ad-hoc. But in no way does this make him any less respectable than the 'chowk' professors. From the days of Lok Dal to those of Janata Dal, he has always been active in town politics. Harendra Yadav gives them good news. An IAS coaching centre will come up in Sadhna Puri—in gali no. 3! Putting his arms around the shoulders of the most intelligent boy of the new generation, Vipin, Harendra Yadav says, 'Recognise the talent within. If you try clearing the UPSC, then getting the State Commission is possible; and if not that, the Staff Selection Commission is there. Meaning, somewhere or the other, you will get in.'

Harish is also ready to go somewhere else. The day after the news on Mandal, he told his father, 'I am going to America.' Harish's father, Girish babu, went around the mohalla announcing in Magahi garnished with English, 'Hariswa ijj not going to isstay here now ... He ijj going to America, becoj, seeing what's what, anyone can make out that this country haj already sinked.'

Girish babu is probably the only father in Aramganj Chowk who is not only worry-free but also over-confident about his son's future. Harish got good marks in Matriculation. In ISC, he fell sick, hence got a second division. He is now in his final year of Chemistry Honours. Luck deserted him in the engineering entrance test, but does talent ever diminish due to vagaries like failing and passing? The parents have full faith in their darling son.

Girish babu is an overseer in the municipality. But neither his face, nor scooter bear the shabbiness that is the hallmark of the municipality. Always in tip-top attire, he keeps his nose scrunched, as if he has sniffed a bad smell. It remains to be researched whether this has some physiological basis, or merely reflects his contempt for everyone.

Girish babu likes to stuff in a line of English after every ten-twelve sentences of Hindi or Magahi. He pulls out these special English phrases and idioms the way, on special occasions, he takes out one of his two nicely pressed suits stowed away in his almirah. For the last three days, only one phrase has been coming out of his blessed mouth—'enough is enough'.

'*Aayeine?* What was the Overseer sahib saying?' the grocer Bhola Chowdhary asks a customer after Girish babu leaves. Bhola had observed that Girish babu's nose was scrunched even more than usual when he said 'enough is enough'.

'He meant to say that too much has happened. This government has done *ekdum* limitless limit-crossing.'

'Oh! All right then! It sounded like he was hurling abuses at me.'

Girish babu has a lot to feel proud of. A Kayasth man. That too a Shrivastav. Meaning, of Rajendra Prasad and Lal Bahadur Shastri's caste. His brother-in-law sahib is an IAS officer. Every time he arrives riding on his official car with the red beacon swirling on top, it becomes a topic for a whole day's discussion in Aramganj.

Meanwhile, Harish's proposed migration to America is also on the list of trending topics alongside '#Toomuchpolitics'. This news is selling like hot cakes from Mangal Paan Bhandar as well as from Ojha-ji's kiosk.

'Hariswa has got *bheeja* (visa). As soon as he gets the passport, he ijj going to fly away on a plane. Let us accept now that this country ijj already drowned and done for.'

'Yes, bhai, let him go. His IAS mamaji must have arranged to send him there.'

'No, not the maternal uncle, it must be the paternal uncle, his phoopha, who's calling him. He lives there only, you know.'

'Big people, fancy talk. God does not give such relatives to everyone.'

Suresh and Prahlad too have hopes. Harish has assured them that as soon as he settles down in America, he will call them over. Suresh has already purchased a *Rapidex English Speaking Course*, and is augmenting his knowledge of English from other sources as well. He is also coaching Prahlad. '"Sit" and "fuck", these are two of the main English abujess.' In the manner of roots and forms of Sanskrit verbs, Prahlad has made a list of all such useful nuggets to mug up. These two are immersed in their plans. But for the rest, Harish's terrible pledge to go to America has ushered in a wave of depression.

Sandeep Shrivastav, aka Chintu, is causing the depression levels of the youth of his generation to soar in a different way. Chintu is sixth among Radhey babu's nine offspring. It is important to mention the serial number, because since childhood, Chintu is accustomed to being referred to thus. As a child, every time he went around the neighbourhood, people asked, 'You are on which number, son?'

By their looks, the houses in this mohalla reveal the government departments their owners work in. If the house belongs to an electricity department official, you will see three separate line-connections coming with full pomp and show from three different poles, so that the house will see darkness only if all three phases are down. In the house of a forest department man, even the latrine door will be made of teak wood. Radhey Shyam Shrivastav had been in the public works department. No wonder his house is the tallest and the most impressive of 'personal works' in entire Aramganj. Radhey babu's house is superior to even Sarvdaman babu's triple-storey house, because a giant concrete water tank on the roof makes it taller by a few feet.

Chintu possesses not just this skyscraper but also the ability to see far. Owing to the binoculars purchased in Calcutta's Dharamtalla mela, his life is now so full of colour as to make his Aramganj peers sigh enviously. The scope of his binoculars extends to the surrounding low-caste localities. From Valmiki Nagar in the south to Gwala Toli in the west, from Lohar Gali in Shivganj to Ram Nihor Singh's house in the north—all are within the range of Chintua's radar. He can look wherever he wants to his heart's content. But these days, he is looking only towards the east.

A month back, his eyes had fallen on a colourful bra-panty pair hung out to dry on Siddheshwar Verma's terrace. On zooming in with his binoculars, the two undergarments blossomed so hugely in his eyes that he almost fell off the water tank. Binoculars in hand, Chintua now lies draped over the water tank at all times, like some botanist engaged in research in the deep forest. All he can see through the window of the bathroom built on Verma-ji's terrace are two hands, taking off the hair-band, and then ... one after the other ...

Because of the celestial vision provided by his equipment, or *maal* as he has termed it, Radhey-ji's sixth offspring has acquired in his group a status akin to Sanjay from the Mahabharat, who was blessed with divine vision to see things happening far away.

In Aramganj lexicon, the term 'equipment' has many meanings. Equipment can mean an 'infallible' weapon like a Rampuri knife, or a country-made revolver, whatever befits a person's status. Equipment can also mean some *patakha-chhap* or firework-type girl, and equipment can also imply some firework-type girl's boobs. Chintua's equipment, however, has powers far more impressive than even a country-made revolver.

Friends wheedle and press, *someday show us too, just once.* But Chintu flatly refuses, making them swallow their disappointment. Luck like Chintua's is not for everyone! But as of now, these luckless ones do not know that they are standing on that turn in history, round the corner from which, a newly liberalised India will witness the auspicious beginning of the *Bold and Beautiful* era piggy-backing on the cable television revolution.

In this period of flux, Shalabhmani Tripathi worries constantly, on account of the news regarding tensions brewing between the chowk savarnas and the backward castes from the galis. This way, Hindu society would get divided! Tripathi-ji, a recently retired professor from the university's Sanskrit department, is active in the Hindu party's think tank, and his name will always be taken among the worthies of chowk's history, to be remembered with pride.

Advani-ji, it seems, has heard what is in Shalabhmani's heart. Hardly a month has gone by since Mandal's imposition, when the Rath Yatra, with its avowed mission to bring unity among the Hindus, is announced. This is the chariot of the same Ram-ji who, in the mythological *Treta Yug,* had taken on Raavan without the help of any rath. But the Hindu consciousness is now stretching itself awake, and Ram-ji will no more be rath-less. The charioteer of this Ram Rath is Lal Krishna, much like Bhagwan Shri Krishna, Arjun's charioteer in the Mahabharat. Like the horses let loose to gallop unchallenged through territories to be annexed in the ancient ritual of Ashvamedha Yajna, this Ram Rath is gathering strength and gaining speed as it advances towards Ayodhya.

6

HERE COMES THE RAM RATH

After Dussehra, a special variety of midges crops up all at once, swarming every light source en masse, hassling the shopkeepers of Aramganj. Most of them tie a bunch of green leaves around the bulbs and tube-lights so that the midges perch on them and don't block the light. But midges, after all, are midges.

The public, too, is public. The crowds today on Aramganj Chowk are larger than those over bulbs and tube-lights. The chowk dwellers have assembled on terraces, while all the gali-walas are out on the chowk. The people of Aramganj never skip a spectacle, and today the occasion is indeed big. News has spread like wildfire and the crowd is no smaller than that on Dussehra eve.

There are several 'butterflies' in the throng. When Aramganj elders proudly assert that none of their girls are of 'that type', they are referring to these girls. Daughters of Sindhi, Punjabi, Rajasthani tenants, 'these girls' are quite different from the rest of Aramganj daughters who step out of their homes only with a brother by their side. Most of 'these girls' go to college. Some are very good at studies. There are some who, after failing or passing Matriculation, have started working in a showroom or a beauty parlour on the Main Road. These girls ride cycles and mopeds, and, every evening, descend in flocks to eat chaat on the streets. The task of administering the biggest culture shock to chowk dwellers was performed by one of these girls: Shalu. Marching into the crowded Vinayak Pharmacy during peak business hours, without the least hesitation, she had inquired, 'Bhaiyya, do you have Stayfree?' It was the first instance of its kind in the history of Aramganj that a young woman had marched on her own into a mohalla shop to buy sanitary pads. Shalu stayed in people's minds for long, as a shiver of pleasure, tickling the pickle of random young men standing about the chemist's shop. According to Lallan, had Shalu not left the mohalla, he would for sure have succeeded in landing 'a setting' with her—because you know, such girls are easy to persuade.

The chowk people suspect that one of these girls had a hand in leading Puja—Sarvdaman babu's daughter—astray. Otherwise, it is just not possible for a girl from the mohalla to get corrupted like this. But those who know Puja well say she needed no help from anyone in staying a step ahead of all these girls. How could they have led her astray?

So proud of her looks had Puja been! A complexion so fair had never been seen before. Like a marble statue she looked; and her heart too was made of stone. Quick to take offence, she never gave the slightest encouragement to anyone. Once, she had poured boiling water over a fellow standing below her balcony, singing, *main prem pujari, mujhe pyar chahiye,* I'm a devotee of love, I yearn for your love.

Any nice boy from the best of Rajput clans would have gladly taken her hand in marriage. But God only knows what she saw in that damned low-caste Lohar! Not only was the fellow from the caste of ironmongers, but also elder to her by five or six years. When this galling incident occurred, it thrilled some black-hearted mohalla characters so much that they scrawled on Sarvdaman babu's wall: 'One bang of the ironmonger equals a hundred of the goldsmith's'. Hot-headed as he is, Sarvdaman babu took it quite literally. He would have fired his gun at the three Sonar—Goldsmith-caste—houses in gali no. 5 as well, but by then, having got entangled in the police case, thanks to Puja's elopement, he got busy making the rounds of the police station. Thus, the remaining suspects on his hit list were spared his ire.

Laying the blame for Puja's elopement on 'these types of girls' is futile. But one thing is certainly true. The arid desert of the chowk youth's life now shimmers with greenery, thanks to 'these types of girls'. Otherwise, for years, Aramganj-walas had to subsist only on the single story of Madhu and Chanda's immortal love. Ever since tenant families started settling at the chowk, balconies, walls, sit-outs, galis—all have turned romantic. Many budding and disintegrating love stories are witnessed all around. Right now, eyes filled with eager interest, the girls are watching the faraway lights that are slowly moving in their direction. The louts standing on the verandas are watching the girls. The rest of the crowd has its ears perked up for the slogans growing louder by the minute.

> Ram-Lakshman-Janaki, let us hail Hanuman-ji
> Every child born of Ram, will battle for the birthplace of Ram
> Beloved Ram-ji, here we come, to build over there a temple for you

The sky is atremble with these chants. Suddenly, a whining voice is heard at the chowk. 'Admaani-ji haj come ... we will build the tempil heeyal.'

'Here? Where will you build the temple here, you fool?'

'Heeyal only, we will build,' Baiju says, pointing at the roundabout. Everyone starts laughing.

Among Aramganj's half-a-dozen crazies, Baiju is the junior-most. No other backward caste person in the area owns land on the main street. But this property is of no use to Baiju. After Baiju's parents died, his uncle grabbed the property, and now, poor 'loony' Baiju roams adrift. This Baiju isn't exactly crazy. But a more respectable and nuanced terminology for certain disabilities isn't in currency yet. So Aramganj-walas refer to people like Baiju as 'loony' or 'crazy'.

Baiju is a punching bag for Aramganj's 'ishtudent' and 'bijness' community. Every Holi, he is made to impersonate Anarkali and dance. When they want to bother any mohalla elder, the loiterers and scoundrels of the chowk set Baiju to stalk him. The show then is worth watching.

Once Alok saw the circus for himself. It's an old incident. He was returning home through one of the deserted inner galis. On the way lies the pump-house enclosure with two small office-like rooms in very dilapidated condition. Alok heard a strange sound coming from inside the rooms. As if someone was being strangled. As if an animal was being butchered. He looked inside. Baiju's hands were tied with a rope. Nakulwa was zipping his pants and Bulbulwa was zipping Baiju's.

The handle of a broken chair in hand, Alok had charged at them shouting, 'You motherfuckers—' The boys scampered away.

Alok knows that even today Baiju is made 'use of' by some people in this mohalla. This is a town of sickos. Poor Baiju is like a blank slate. Whatever is proposed, he agrees, whatever he is asked to repeat, he repeats. Had he been elsewhere, he might have learnt to make a living through some vocational training. But this is Aramganj.

Alok himself is quite the character. Most people haven't been able to decide whether to call him a studious guy or a *dada*—a don of the gali. Even though he belongs to an upper caste, Alok's house is away from the chowk, in a gali with houses of low-caste people all around. His social relations are also mostly with such people. He is perhaps the only savarna who mixes so much with the Valmiki Nagar boys.

Alok's nemesis is Kamlesh, who wants to make it big in politics. They are like two warring brothers. Back in the day, their respective gangs would challenge one another, hockey sticks and iron rods in hand. But both have mellowed over time. Kamlesh has his finger not just in the politics-pie, but also in building contractorship. While our poor Alok is still sweating it out to obtain gainful employment post his Masters' degree.

The truck-turned-rath is nearing the Aramganj crossing. The knowledgeable elders have lifted the curtain on the fact that this is not Advani-ji's rath. Advani-ji is coming on 20 October, and today is only the 1ˢᵗ of October. This rath is merely a tableau travelling ahead of the real one, to raise consciousness about the Ayodhya movement, and to collect funds for the construction of the temple. This procession is worth seeing. Two richly decorated elephants lead the front, and behind them is a truck displaying a model of the Ram temple, next to which stand artistes dressed up as Ram, Lakhan and Janaki. On this truck, one can see a heavily garlanded Jagdhari Singh, the MLA of this area, who is likely to reach the Lok Sabha soon. Somehow squeezing into the little remaining space at the back of the truck, a man has planted his feet with great difficulty and is displaying extreme fervour. He is waving at the crowds as if everyone has come only to see him. This is Jatashankar Sharma, aka Kaka-ji—Aramganj's biggest leader. Although he is from the gali, he is revered by many on the chowk.

Loafers and louts are filching spinach and tomatoes from the carts of vegetable vendors to give offerings to the sacred elephants leading the procession. Volunteers with saffron headbands tied around their heads are controlling the traffic with hand gestures. Women with folded hands stand on terraces. Pinki tugs at the pallu of her mother's sari, pointing ahead, again and again: 'Mummy, look, there's *Daayan*-dadi!' Chaube-ji's eighty-year-old mother is referred to thus behind her back. To the young brides, she is the '*Daayan*-aunty', or Witch-aunty. And along the same lines, kids call her the Granny witch.

The huge black wart on her face and her rasping voice are not the only reasons behind this moniker. Many years ago, the conference of daughters-in-law passed a unanimous motion, stating—no daughters-in-law in Mohalla Aramganj could ever live in happiness so long as Witch-aunty was alive.

The theories propounded by Witch-aunty are referred to by the daughters-in-law as the 'Witch Doctrines'. Witch-aunty is notorious for thinking up fitting punishments for any and every sin—from not covering the head to serving cold tea to one's mother-in-law. Whenever an aggrieved mother-in-law comes to her court, the witch mulls over the karma of the daughter-in-law, and passes a judgement. A copy of her decision reaches every house through the mother-in-law association.

'Ram-ram, she insisted on separating the kitchen. She did not cook breakfast today! Such a daughter-in-law will have lice infest her hair.' But if the complainant mother-in-law is not satisfied with mere bug infestation, she might mention two or three other major sins committed by the daughter-in-law. Witch-aunty, after deliberating over this review petition, revises the judgement, meting out punishments commensurate with the extra sins. 'Don't cry! Not just lice, leprosy will break out on her skin.'

But today, this 'Lalita Pawar' (quite in the image of the notoriously evil Bollywood mother-in-law) stands on her balcony, head covered and heart full of worship! Looking unblinkingly at the street, folding her hands and bowing low again and again. Today, for the first time, Pinki's mother feels a little respect for Witch-aunty. If this is not Ram-ji's miracle, then what is it?

The procession moves ahead slowly. There is an amazing fervour among the elderly of Aramganj. This fervour is more than a thrill. Two or three rickshaw-pullers ply on the turning towards Prem Nagar gali. Tiwari-ji makes a sweet, smiling personal request to the policeman on duty there. 'Sipahi sahib, please give these fools two of your choicest thrashings with your lathi as a favour to me.'

MLA Jagdhari Singh gives an impassioned speech from atop the truck, which, to sum up, asserts that without Hindu unity, this country cannot better itself. This is the time to recognise the enemy. The enemies of Hindus are the enemies of the nation. All Hindus are brothers. No one is bigger, nor is anyone smaller.

Durga Pandit notices some characters with tilaks on their foreheads standing on his veranda. He recognises the young man who is wearing a huge badge on his kurta: 'This one is Teliya, from the low-caste gali no. six, whose brother works in the AG office. *Sasura!* This rascal has become a leader!'

When the low-caste Rameshwar Mallah climbs onto the truck to perform the ritual worship, with incense and lit lamps, of the artistes dressed up as Ram-Lakhan-Janaki, Verma-ji, standing on his terrace, asks his neighbour, 'Do you see this new game?'

'Oh yes, bhai! They will take the government jobs and they will become leaders too.'

'The time has come to recognise the enemy ...' Jagdhari Singh's monologue echoes in people's ears.

Halting his Yamaha on one side, Manojwa spits out a huge gob of chewing tobacco, *fchacchakk,* right in front of Two-in-One Tailor.

'Give with an open heart in the name of Lord Ram. Hanuman-ji always helps the ones who work for Ram. Don't be miserly in giving. Lakshmikant Sahay from the chowk has given twenty-one rupees. Vibhuti Mishra has given fifty-one rupees.' A running commentary is going on on the mic. 'Rajnarain and Shrikanth Singh have also given fifty-one rupees each. Two-in-One tailoring shop's Ashiq bhaisahib has given one-hundred-and-one rupees. He is the first person to give more than hundred rupees. Take some inspiration from the love this Muslim brother has for Ram-ji.' The announcer can barely keep a check on his emotions.

'Ashiq and sahib?'

'Anyone can become a sahib these days by throwing money at people.'

'No, no, Ashiq is truly a man with a big heart. No matter how much they cry Hindu-Hindu, everyone gets scared when asked to dip into their pockets.'

Om-ji is watching the whole scene standing outside Mithilesh's grocery shop. Looks like he will fall down laughing. Controlling his laughter, Om-ji intones:

> *Na lutne ka dar, na pitne ka gham*
> *Jaisa tha mera baap, waise nikle hum*
>
> Beatings scare not, nor looting hurts
> Tough like my old man, I've turned

Om-ji is such a character!

People change course the minute they see him coming. Best not to cross his path!

7

MANDAL IN KAMANDAL

The whole of Aramganj is in a state of frenzy. All of a sudden, not only have the topics of discourse altered, but the past, the present and the future of the country, all seem to be undergoing a transition of sorts. The chowk youngsters are no more dejected over their inability to join the administrative or the police services. All the angst over Mandal reservations has faded like the colours of Holi. Only one thing is being heard now: the one who upholds the rights of Hindus will win the electoral fight!

'But what are these Hindu rights, who will tell?'

'*Arre*, didn't you hear what Jagdhari babu said? If there is any confusion, erudite men like Shalabhmani Tripathi are also there in the mohalla. You may go to him to clear your doubts. Jatashankar Sharma and Kamlesh, too, work day and night to spread awareness among the youth.'

Only the wise have divined the big game played by Kamlesh Singh, which Professor Vinod had been talking of while standing at Ojha-ji's paan-kiosk.

'The Mandal game was played by 'Beepiya' the Prime Minister to divide Hindu society. Now Advani-ji is on a rath yatra to unite it. Had Kamleshwa openly come out in support of the anti-Mandal Bharat Bandh, he would have antagonised the low-castes of his galis, and then, would they have come forward for Hindu unity? See how they cry themselves hoarse now! Chanting, "there itself the temple will be built"! I can give it to you in writing—this Kamleshwa will go very far.' This perceptive analysis by Advocate Prakash bhaiyya had the chowk audience in thrall.

When Professor Harendra Yadav went to distribute pamphlets, with follower Godhan Mahto in tow, in the low-caste Bhuiyan Toli so that its people would 'become literate, unite and struggle', he found that someone had already been giving them lessons. Saffron flags fluttered everywhere. The walls of huts and tenements, painted thus far with the sickle and hammer sign of the Communist party, now proclaim in bold letters—THERE ITSELF THE TEMPLE WE WILL BUILD.

All the galis to the left of the Main Road converge in Bhuiyan Toli, which has a Backward-caste and Dalit population of four to five thousand. Vipin, the young intellectual icon of Sadhna Puri, has brought news: 'The Yuva Shakti Sangh folks are roaming in every gali, enlisting volunteers to go to Ayodhya. Mandal has been trounced by the Kamandal.'

For the chowk-dwellers, the Ram Mandir is a new discovery, like it is for many others. There is a birthplace of Lord Ram in Ayodhya, and, till now, Muslims had been occupying it, and had even built a mosque over it! And this had been concealed from us for years! The reactions are typical of Aramganj Chowk.

'Advani-ji is right. It must be pulled down with a bulldozer.'

Arre, when did Advani-ji say anything about bringing it down? That poor guy is saying it should be lifted and placed elsewhere.'

'Come on! As if it is not a mosque but some Diwali toy house that can be lifted and put elsewhere. *Arre maharaj*, let us bombard it and settle the matter once and for all.'

'No, no. Breaking won't be right. And it is strongly built. We should cover it with marble, and if the idol is indeed there, we can just worship it.' Gupta-ji is a practical man. He hates any kind of spendthrift behaviour.

'We should settle Mathura and Kashi, too, while we are at it.'

'What? What happened in Mathura and Kashi?'

'Just hear this. This one does not know a thing. Such is the state of a Hindu's general knowledge! Just look at those people—from Mecca-Medina to Iran-Iraq—everything is one for them. And he is asking what happened in Mathura and Kashi!' Vibhuti Mishra says, looking contemptuously at Kamta babu.

Everyone has a different viewpoint on the issue. Many innovative ideas are cropping up in the minds of the younger generation. 'Is it not possible, that on Jumma, when they are all kneeling together and praying—at that very moment ...'

The Pablo Escobar of the mohalla, Prabhat Dayal is a man of many talents. Apart from dealing in pot, and running a banjo drum group, he also has a deep interest in real estate. Yesterday he was telling someone, 'The Ram Mandir plot is very big. The outer side should be made fully commercial. It can easily accommodate forty-fifty shops.'

'No, brother, at the very least, two hundred shops can be carved out. Every shop inside the Ram Mandir complex would have a turnover of at least thousands per day. Put money in a shop or two if you have the clout.'

When the subject at hand is shops, whichever corner of the world they may be in, Prabhat Dayal takes it seriously. He will speak to Tripathi uncle urgently.

Om-ji is taking long strides. Seeing him come, more than half the people start slinking away. Complexion black as coal, eyes always red, big moustache. People say, had he tried, he would have easily got a role in the television series Ramayan. But the truly frightening thing about him is not his appearance. If he catches hold of anyone, he clings fast like a leech.

Jaiswal likes to say, the Kashmiris must be dealt such a thrashing as to make them forget all their mugged-up nonsense on human rights.

Om-ji once caught hold of him in the wholesale market. That too at the moment when Jaiswal was swiftly and purposefully moving towards his goal, one hand on the pyjama-cord.

Om-ji started by asking, 'So you were saying something about human rights that day?'

'*Arre,* what are you doing, maharaj? Leave my hand. Can't you see where I am going?'

'*Arre*, you can go at leisure, bhai ... first let us think of where the country is going. You were saying something about human rights that day.' Om-ji tightened his python-like grip on Jaiswal's hand.

Witnesses reported that when the dam of the diabetes-afflicted Jaiswal's patience breached, and the torrent gushed past his girdle, Om-ji said, 'Now, see the outcome of human rights violations.'

There are many types of crazies in Aramganj. But the thirty-seven-year-old Om-ji is unique. In this mohalla of self-styled professors, he is totally genuine. He used to teach logic and philosophy at Paramanand Memorial College. But once, instead of using reason, he used muscle, and flung the vice-principal down. He is under suspension now. Om-ji is fond of telling youngsters that he wrote his entire Matriculation exam after consuming bhang, and his scores broke all records. By the time he was in MA, things progressed to drags of weed—but did that ever impact his results!

People know that it is impossible to win an argument with Om-ji. If the person opposite him is from the Hindu party,

Om-ji becomes an ultra-leftist. If the person is the progressive type, Om-ji turns into a true Hindu believer, a Sanatani. If you disagree, he will demolish you with his arguments. But even bigger trouble awaits those who try to escape by agreeing. Hence, it is best to change your path upon seeing him. Though his craziness is tinged with an intellectual flavour, he is a rascal of the highest order—totally repulsive. He is the main inspiration behind the Holi ritual of random passers-by getting a 'purifying bath', with a mixture of water from open drains and the liquid gold of septic tanks, that has been practised for many years in Aramganj. Last Holi, he caught hold of an emaciated black bitch that used to roam about the mohalla, and with the poor animal in his arms—wrapped in a bright red cloth, vermilion smeared all over its nose—he went around telling any elder who crossed his path, 'See, uncle, I have met your dearest wish. You wanted me to marry, no? Here is your daughter-in-law. Please give *munh-dikhai* to the new bride', forcibly extracting from them the customary cash gift given on seeing a bride's face for the first time. And in the name and spirit of this *munh-dikhai* and *'bura na mano Holi hai!'*—don't feel bad, it's only Holi—he made who knows how many pockets lighter.

Every year after Dussehra, the Yuva Shakti Sangh club members collect a donation to rent a VCR. As per tradition, the programme begins with the screening of great family movies, with mothers and sisters in the audience.

Last year, once the family-viewing segment was over, Om-ji nabbed Pankaj Jain. 'What are *you* doing here? Now it's time for a massacre to commence. Go away.' Implying that for a true follower of a non-violent sect like Jainism, it was time to clear off.

That poor gentleman had also contributed to the funds. But Om-ji would not budge. 'Don't you know what will happen in the next hour? Lakhs of sperms will be mercilessly butchered and dunked in drains. Masturbation is nothing but mass murder on a colossal scale. Go, run! Or I will tell your father.'

And this very Om-ji often advises the younger generation on the benefits of errr ... self-reliance. Because, according to him, the best results of this reliance on the self are directly reflected in the 'length'. Om-ji has chewed and digested all types of literature, from O. Henry to Ibne Safi, and from Maupassant to Indian porn king Mastram. Most of the time, his references are such that they fly over the heads of more than half of Aramganj's residents. Neutral observer Nirmal Jain insists that his words often have deep content, and if someone were to constantly take notes, a book could be made out of Om-ji's one-liners. But then who would undertake such a risky project?

An acharya-ji who came from Haridwar for a three-day ceremony in the Sheetla mandir compound, made everyone chant, 'When we reform ourselves, the world will get reformed.' Om-ji stood up and asked with great civility, 'When will you get reformed?' Without getting flustered, the wise acharya called him on stage and said, 'I do not take offense at your words because as a human being, it's my duty to go on improving and purifying myself.' Om-ji replied with folded hands, 'Acharya-ji, I really like what you say. I simply asked the date, so that I will know that when you are reformed, I too will automatically get reformed.'

The conversation did not end here. Displaying his love for knowledge, Om-ji asked the next question. 'Why do people always conceal their good and expensive stuff? No one ever discloses how much money or gold they own. If religion is such a valuable thing why don't people keep it to themselves? Why do they keep throwing it at others for free?'

Acharya-ji looked flabbergasted. And Om-ji began explaining by giving an example. 'Think of it this way—if I have an excellent bottle of Scotch, what will I do? I will sit in peace somewhere, and drink it sip by sip. But what if I get some illegal *tharra* or hooch? I will call all my friends and make a jolly night of it because, if I die, like the hooch-drinkers in the sura-kaand incident, I will at least die in the company of friends. Religion is cheap liquor—that's why those who get drunk on it, constantly invite others to share in it. For the fact is that they want to halve the risk it poses to them. The propagators of religion themselves don't know the path they are on, and constantly want to drag others along. Because, if they have to lament later, they won't be alone.'

The ins and outs of this man's thought process are beyond comprehension. At many religious gatherings, Om-ji is also sometimes seen sitting quietly, eyes closed in devotion. Often sacred red threads are seen tied around his wrist. Today, the people notice that Om-ji has come to the chowk, attired in a pair of green striped pyjamas and a saffron T-shirt.

8

ALI, BAJRANG BALI AND SPIDERMAN

Marigold plants laden with dazzling yellow flowers, a short row of sunflowers, and next to it, a thicket of jasmine. Butterflies flit from this flower only to land on that one. Shami has been running after these butterflies for around an hour without any success. A large-winged butterfly sits on a sunflower. Shami inches closer, holding his breath, when Ayesha's lisping voice rings out from nowhere.

Ud re titli ud, tere ammi-abbu royenge
Ud re titli ud, tere ammi-abbu royenge

Fly away butterfly, fly, or your abbu-ammi will cry
Fly away butterfly, fly, your ammi-abbu will cry

Shami looks back angrily, his hand shifts slightly and the butterfly flies off. Shami runs after his sister to thrash her. Ayesha makes for the door. Ashiq picks up his beloved daughter at once. The princess complains to her father, who is the king of kings, a *Shahanshah*, for her. 'Abbu, Bhai hit me again.'

'When did I hit her? She lies so much. She made my butterfly fly off.'

'Dadi says butterflies shouldn't be caught. It makes their abbu-ammi cry.'

Ashiq plonks himself down with the kids. He notes that little Ayesha's eyes have welled up talking of butterflies. No one should be separated from their ammi-abbu. Seeing his father sitting so close, Shami forgets the butterflies for a while. When was the last time his abbu gave him so much time? He isn't free even on Sundays. Taking advantage of the opportunity, Shami fires a question. 'Abbu, is Ali more powerful or Bajrangbali?' Shami wants a quick answer. 'Tell, no, Abbu. Mohsin said our Ali is more powerful than *their* Bajrangbali.'

A frown appears on Ashiq's forehead. One less, the other more. One good, and the other bad. These questions are not new. But these days, from morning till evening, they are heard all across Aramganj. Some days back, Shami came asking about the difference between Allah and Bhagwan. Ashiq replied, 'You call your mother ammi, and I call my mother, meaning your dadi, amma. But whichever name you call her by, a mother will remain a mother. Bhagwan and Allah, too, are like that.'

But how can Ashiq find an apt answer every time? Shami is now jumping, holding on to his shoulders. 'Tell, no, Abbu. Is Ali really more powerful than Bajrangbali?'

Ashiq replies after thinking for a while. 'These days, Spiderman is the most powerful of all. He flies like Bajrangbali, and if some innocent faces any danger while going on *Hijrat,* Spiderman at once weaves his web to save them.'

Hearing him talk about Spiderman, both the kids are thrilled. Shami starts singing 'Spiderman Spiderman ...' Marked by a tall antenna on the thatched roof, Ashiq Miyan's house in the basti can be seen from afar. The first TV in the basti was Ashiq Miyan's. Now, many other houses have a television. Ashiq's Amma says, 'Earlier, there was a contest as to who would have the tallest *tazia* in the Muharram procession, but now the competition is over the TV antenna.'

When an antenna is considered a status symbol at Aramganj Chowk, then why not here? Mufti sahib says that owning a television is *haraam*. But Ashiq knows how useful a television is. Since its arrival, there has been peace in the house. Now Zulekha Bano does not petition him about not taking Sundays off. Zulekha Bano is both Ashiq's better and bitter half. She has taken care of him and the household through tough times. Even now, her eyes hold a deep love for her film-hero-like husband.

When she was a new bride, every time her mother-in-law left the house to visit someone in the neighbourhood, Zulekha would start humming the movie song—*Karte hain hum pyar Mr India se*—I'm in love with Mr India—as she lined her eyes with kohl.

Even now, when in a good mood, she sometimes tells Ashiq Miyan, 'Listen, earlier I thought you looked exactly like Anil Kapoor.'

'What do you mean earlier? Don't I look like him now?'

Zulekha says *'Dhatt!'* by way of reply, laughing shyly. Two kids, an old and ill mother-in-law, a husband, who is busy day and night with work and only work—all these have ensured the fizzling of all romance out of her life. Her man never has the time to even throw a loving glance at her. For Zulekha, romance now exists only in the weekly TV programme of Bollywood songs, *Chitrahaar*.

Today, too, the same thing happened. Zulekha Bano brought the aluminium tiffin, Ashiq at once set Ayesha down from his lap, took the tiffin without saying a word, and strode out of the house. Zulekha quietly watched her husband go. Which clay has he been fashioned from? Only comes back to the house to eat and sleep, that's it! His heart and mind are always at Aramganj

Chowk. Zulekha has no major complaints. And despite the minor complaints, this little household of Zulekha and Ashiq's is beautiful. After all, which relationship does not have a little indifference, a little bickering? The only thing is, there should be no infidelity. And, in Ashiq and Zulekha Bano's case, there is no dearth of fidelity.

Ashiq's house is another world. But the minute he lifts his feet to go out, he feels he has stepped into a different universe. It would have been better if such a world did not exist. On government papers, this place is called Rayyat Toli. For the lumpen youth of Aramganj, this place is 'Katua Toli', the colony of cut pricks. For the older folk, this is 'Miyan Toli'. In addition to these three names, of late a fourth name has started sprouting on people's tongues: 'Mini Pakistan'.

The name 'Katua Toli' is not to be uttered in decent company—before one's parents for instance—within one's house. However, calling Rayyat Toli 'Mini Pakistan' elicits no objection from any quarter. Even if someone were to object, what difference would it make? Ashiq has a relationship of ongoing banter with the people of Aramganj Chowk, he never takes offence. He knows that the right to mock is not distributed equally.

Sometimes Ashiq wonders why the people of Hindustan can't do without Pakistan. Everywhere they must find or build a Pakistan. If they can't find a Pakistan in their town, near their houses or in the bazaars, they call the place where they go to relieve themselves in the morning Pakistan. For the denizens of Aramganj, Rayyat Toli is Mini Pakistan. By that logic, what would those living in Rayyat Toli call Aramganj?

The people of Rayyat Toli treat Ashiq as the resident commissioner of Aramganj. He is not just a resident, but 'a cent percent Hindu'. He is used to being called 'Misir', as he passes by. 'How is the Misir? All well?' These days, a new question has been added to these questions. 'Misir-ji, when are you going to Ayodhya?' By way of answering, Ashiq at times smiles, and at times, keeps walking without meeting the eyes of the questioner.

Rayyat Toli is an untidy cluster of forty houses—some proper pucca ones, and some with thatched roofs—on the road that connects Aramganj Chowk to Kutchery Road. One part of Rayyat Toli abuts the dilapidated walls of the sixty-year-old Kashinath Middle School, which looks as doomed as the settlement.

The chowk people use the lanes of Rayyat Toli as a short-cut to Kutchery Road or Main Road. As these decent folk gingerly step around bleating goats, hopping chickens, children defecating by the roadside and half-asleep stray dogs, they shake their heads at what 'these people' have reduced India to. During the rainy season, water pools up to the knees in this neighbourhood. Only one government tap exists here for water supply. Electricity connections are low on voltage. Even then so many people live here. As a matter of fact, 'these people' are suited to all this.

On the border between Aramganj and Mini Pakistan grows a centuries-old peepul tree, around whose trunk are tied countless red threads for wish-fulfilment. Some say that Brahma baba lives on this tree. Some say, the grave of a crazy fakir lies under the cemented platform around it. A four-roomed house that looks haunted lies to the right of the tree. Two small trees of ber and lemon, thickly smothered with spider web stand in its compound. Next to them, stands a dust-encrusted, giant old cactus, the size of a grown man.

The windows of this house have remained shut for ages. Bricks peek through torn plaster, and the walls have layers of moss on them. Not a sign of life anywhere. Only old-timers know that this house once belonged to Inderdev Pandey, who was also called Pandey baba. He used to run a small school from this house after retiring from his job at a high school.

His only son, Mannu or Markandeya, had been good in studies but deranged otherwise. He began smoking ganja at a young age. As soon as he came of age, he left home and ran away. No one knew whether he became a sadhu, an Anandmargi or a Naxal. With great difficulty, Pandey baba located him, brought him back, and put him to work at his school. But off he ran again, never to come back. Pining for the lost son, Pandey baba's wife passed away. Pandey baba bore this loss somehow and kept the school going. No one knows as much as Ashiq about this haunted house. Every day, as he comes out of the gali, he hesitates for a few moments, staring unblinkingly at this house before moving on. This is a part of his daily routine.

Most people don't know how this one-and-a-half-acre basti called Rayyat Toli came into being, erupting like some leprous sore halfway between Kutchery and Aramganj Chowk. The old-timers of the chowk had no issues with the overflowing drains or the buffalo meat being cooked in the houses in Rayyat Toli, for they well knew that the best re-tinners of brass vessels, the best weavers of rope-beds, the best cotton-carders, the best white-washers came from there.

However, as times changed, the need for most such traditional services ended, and Rayyat Toli lost its claim to fame. Unable to find work in Aramganj, the new generations of Rayyat Toli began looking towards areas in Kaanta Toli, Islam Nagar and Kunjada mohalla, where there was a large population of affluent Muslims. Many migrated to industrial towns like Calcutta and Jamshedpur. Today, most Rayyat Toli people don't venture towards Aramganj even if asked to.

The only exception to this rule is Ashiq Miyan. He is the sole man here, whose relations with the residents of Aramganj

Chowk have not lost colour or soured, but, on the contrary, become consistently stronger over time. He owns a fridge and a television, thanks to his earnings from the shop in Aramganj. His children go to an English medium school. Why should he not be called Misir-ji by the Rayyat Toli residents? If asked about his unusual relationship with Aramganj, Ashiq Miyan will have only one answer to give. It's all because of Ram-ji's grace.

9

WHO ON EARTH ARE YOU?

The impending arrival of the Ram Rath has turned into a strength-testing contest of sorts for various party leaders in town. Jagdhari Singh has emerged as the star so far. After a lot of push and pull, he has succeeded in getting the charge of the Ram Rath Reception Committee. Jagdhari babu has the blessings of the Member of Parliament Ram Pyare Chowdhary too. The High Command has directed that come what may, a crowd of minimum one lakh must be arranged for the 20th of October.

Jagdhari Singh is receiving orders directly from the state president himself, and in turn, directing small-timers like Jatashankar Sharma. Jatashankar received this *brahm-gyan* from him—'Learn how to organise. If you cannot rally crowds around a common cause and raise a people's movement in your area, stop dreaming of becoming a leader.' Jatashankar Sharma is trying hard, but how on earth can a people's movement be raised among Aramganj's half-asleep masses?

Since its departure from Somnath a week ago, the Ram Rath has been rolling forth, splitting the nation into two halves. Though this town isn't divided in that way yet, the possibility is plentiful. While localities like Aramganj are unaware of all this so far, many other areas of the town are already smouldering. A riot almost occurred when the procession calling for donations passed through Meerganj.

In the compound of the shining new Taufeeq Mosque, the office of the Janata Dal minority committee—the Aqliyat Committee—is abuzz with activity. Leaders like Hussain Tamboli, Faiyyaz Malik and Faheem Ansari are deep in discussion day and night, telling the *Qaum*, the people of Islam, that though the state government has promised to provide security, a calamity might strike anytime. Hence, every mohalla should form a security committee.

The Congress party district secretary, Roshan Lal Chhabra, is recouping from a fistula surgery. He plans to start a newspaper because it won't be possible to sustain political power without gaining control over information. As regards the present situation, he says that everyone has already seen what the fate of this nation would be without the Congress. This government is already on oxygen support. As soon as Rajiv-ji returns to power, everything will be fine—there's no need for anxiety.

But the townsfolk, who witnessed the communal riots of 1967, '73, '79, '81 and '84 are on edge. Those who saw ravaged settlements and corpses lining the roads know that it takes but the blink of an eye for a small spark to turn into a raging fire. Efforts at a modest level are being made to ensure the town's safety. Today, a meeting has been called in the state library hall to expand the scale of these efforts. Present at this meeting are cultural activists, writers and conscious citizens. Young men like Parag and Rajesh can also be seen—proof that even in a mohalla as laidback as Aramganj, the youth have a presence beyond the chowk. Under discussion are the routes and neighbourhoods to be covered by the proposed goodwill rally to foster peace. The

Aramganj youth look at each other smilingly, because they know that their mohalla has no need for a peace-rally.

Howsoever may times change, nothing will really change in Aramganj Chowk, Ashiq Miyan knows this well enough. But even he has noticed in the last few days that with changing times, the nature of questions asked of him is changing too. Akhilesh had asked to his face, 'We all think of you as a Hindu. Who do *you* think you are, *bey*?'

The answer came, 'Whatever my Ram-ji has made me, I am that only. Why do you worry about it?'

Akhilesh taunted, 'Meaning, Ram-ji made you a *mulla?*'

'Yes, think that if you please.'

'Incredible, the things you say! Is that even possible?'

'When a *chutiya* like you can be made by Ram-ji, then why not me?'

It isn't easy to trap Ashiq with mere questions. Even so, why are these questions being asked at all? Why has their frequency gone up all of a sudden? Aramganj-walas don't know why, but indeed they have too many questions about Muslims in their minds. Whether he be only half a Muslim or a Muslim just in name, for the chowk, Ashiq represents all Muslims.

If Anil Kapoor's picture is outside Mr India Tailoring Shop, then inside can be seen a picture of Arun Govil, the actor who played Ram in the TV series Ramayan. A blown-up poster from the series—of Ram, Lakshman and Sita going to the forest—is pasted on the wall. Lallan comes to the shop often, but today he suddenly notices that a mirror hangs on the almirah in front of the picture, on which there's a 786 sticker, a number sacred to a true believer of Allah.

'*Waah re* Rangbaz,' he exclaims. 'All this Ram-ji, Ram-ji is only for getting business, is it?'

'Why, do you think that Ram-ji and Allah Miyan are like Chajju and Bechu from gali no. 3 that they cannot stay together?' Ashiq at once cites the two brothers whose joint kitchen saw regular head-banging fights till they finally separated.

Lallan still wants to tease. '*O teri*! How immense is Lord Ram and how tiny Allah!'

Without missing a beat, Ashiq retorts, 'Allah lives in Lord Ram's heart.'

Lallan notices that indeed the 786 sticker is so stuck on the mirror that it occupies the spot where Ram-ji's heart lies in the poster's reflection. Who indeed is this man?

Even if someone mocks him in the name of religion, he does not take offence. These attempts to 'tease' are not new. *Katua, kattan, kate-bhai*—pejoratives referring to the Islamic custom of circumcision—are now so worn out and banal that even teasers and mockers have stopped relishing them. For Ashiq, these monikers are like sweet abuses, imbued with a strange intimacy. Something would be oddly lacking in his life if he did not hear such words.

Loafer and louts cannot stand outside Savitri Ladies Boutique. But Ashiq is often seen surrounded by the same louts across the road from his shop, in Mithilesh Grocery Store's veranda, happily striking the queen on the carrom-board. These *shohdas* are dear friends—his grouse is only with their antics. That's why he has, without mincing words, told them many times, 'Tease and flirt to your heart's content, brother—who am I to stop you? But not outside my shop. Even a witch skips seven houses when seeking prey.'

Only on rare occasions, when the 'skip seven houses' warning is turned a deaf ear to, does Ashiq the Rangbaz assert his *rangbazi* to dispense justice. Once, Manoj, peering into Savitri Ladies Boutique through the small hole in the two-by-four door, got caught by the collar and kicked out. Mahesh of gali no. 6 got such a resounding slap after snatching a girl's chunni in the bazaar, that for months he did not dare show his face at the chowk.

Ashiq has again conquered the queen. Is there scope for anyone else to win when Ashiq is playing!

In the gathering of carrom players, the question pops up from nowhere. 'Tell me this, Ashiqwa, why is it that a man cannot be a Muslim unless he is snipped?' The reference to circumcision comes up yet again.

'That varies from man to man. There are many who cannot become Muslim even after being snipped.'

'Really?'

'If you don't believe me, let me take you to the wielder of the knife. We can then see for ourselves whether you turn into a Muslim or a eunuch who goes about beating drums and dispensing blessings for cash.'

'Don't try to sidestep, Ashiq. Honestly, tell us why it is necessary to *cut* in your religion?'

'The thing, beta, is this: whether you get a slight cut, or keep the whole *thing* intact, the real "thing" is that to which water and coconut are offered. Whatever be the religion, the "thing" itself has equal importance everywhere. Do you get it?'

'And look at *him*, he hasn't understood the importance of the "thing" itself. That is why his sword is still in the scabbard. Lying unused, it will catch rust, Mukesh bhaiyya,' quips another carrom player, leaving the thirty-three-year-old bachelor Mukesh embarrassed.

'That's not the case, Ashiq. He sharpens the blade with his own hands morning and night.'

'If you say so, I will have to accept it. Keep that blade sharp, Mukesh bhaiyya! The stars are auspiciously aligned this year, you will cross over for sure. A hundred per cent!'

The collective laughter rising from the veranda of Mithilesh Grocery Store is such that the sound reaches across the road to Two-in-One tailoring shop. When Hanif gestures from there, Ashiq remembers these are business hours. Who knows how much time has gone by in carrom and idle talk.

Hanif is a distant relative, and now, under Ashiq's tutelage, is fast acquiring stitching skills. Ever since Hanif arrived, Ashiq Miyan gets more time for social activities. But now he gets up and crosses the street like an arrow, entering through the glass door of Savitri Ladies Boutique.

'Are you going to send me off empty-handed again?' A lady customer complains on seeing him.

'Don't you worry, bhabhi, your clothes are absolutely ready.' Ashiq takes out a packet from the cupboard and hands it to the woman. The woman pays and leaves.

'Chachi, *parnam* ...' Ashiq greets Basanti chachi who is here with her daughter Payal. 'I did not see you, when did you come?'

'Of course, son. Why would you even look at me when the sweeper-queen is here?

'*Arre* chachi, let it go na,' Ashiq tries to placate her.

'Look, son, let me tell you something. Don't you try slotting a Pandit's wife with a lowborn sweeper, or I will stop coming to your shop.'

'*Arre*, chachi, why do you get angry? She pays the same amount as everyone else. How can I refuse to stitch her clothes? The law treats everyone as equal these days. If I refuse, the government might put me in jail. These people go everywhere in the market. Will you stop buying stuff from all those shops because of that?'

'You even keep that scavenger woman's clothes and my clothes in the same almirah.'

'*Arre* chachi, times have changed. Who believes in untouchability these days? When Ram-ji himself sat in the low-caste Kevat's boat, and ate berries that Shabari had bitten into and tasted first, who am I to discriminate?'

'*Tum ho kaun re? Auqat bhula gayee*? Who do you think you are ... sermonising away about Ram-ji ... Forgotten your place, have you?' Hissing in rage, Basanti chachi lashes out in Bhojpuri.

'Not at all, chachi. I remember my place,' Ashiq replies softly.

Basanti chachi catches Payal by the arm, and marches out of the shop fuming. 'Not once, but twice I did the chaar-dham pilgrimage! Now this Miyan will tell me what Ram-ji said? You aren't the only one here, there are a thousand other tailors, from Main Road to Bada Bazaar.

'Pandit-ji committed a grave mistake by letting a Musalman settle here, and as if that wasn't enough, there is the entire sweeper colony too here ... Ram Ram!' Only then Payal covers her mother's mouth with her hand, looking beseechingly at Ashiq as if saying, forgive my mother.

Ashiq keeps sitting quietly, without any expression on his face. The words 'Musalman', '*auqat*', 'sweeper colony' ring in his ears.

Valmiki Nagar is a British-era settlement of scavengers who migrated from Rajasthan. The story goes that the chowk people had protested against this settlement. But the British officer in charge was a bully. He declared that not taking in the scavengers meant that they wanted Muslim butchers to settle in the area. Seeing no way out, people were forced to accept the scavengers. The primitive latrines of those days were the livelihood of scavengers. For years Valmiki Nagar folks carried night-soil on their heads. But now times have changed.

During the daytime, more than half of Valmiki Nagar folks are not to be seen. They are employed as sanitation workers in the municipal corporation, the university, the airport, as well as the railway station. The settlement is still congested, but now there is no dearth of food. Poultry, pigs and goats provide additional sources of income. Mithilesh the grocer says that the maximum order for Amul butter and Maggie noodles packets comes from Valmiki Nagar. Ashiq, too, gets at least seven or eight orders per day from there.

For Valmiki Nagar's women, Ashiq's shop is a window to the fascinating world of Aramganj. A wondrous, funny, weird world that forbids their entry. Yet the stories of this middle-class world delight them in the same way as stories about the lives of celebrities delight the middle-class living in the metros.

Ashiq's affinity with the Valmiki Nagar women is the same as that with the chowk women. The only difference being, Valmiki Nagar is the only area in the entire geography of the chowk whose women are addressed as 'bhabhis', or sisters-in-law, by Ashiq. The young women from other areas are *didis*, or sisters, to Ashiq. What exactly does this difference signify? Ashiq himself has never given it any thought, but it's certainly true that while sisters are treated strictly with deference, a man can share a joke or two with a sister-in-law.

Valmiki Nagar is making progress on most development parameters. Even though the whole colony makes do with just three public toilets, a few kids from there take the bus to schools like St. Francis or St. Louis every day. On the colony leader Pawan Hatwal's initiative, they even have a cricket team now that plays in the 'B' division league of the town. Om-ji calls this team Valmikshire on the lines of Yorkshire and Warwickshire.

The Valmiki Nagar residents walk their own path, and no one dares mess with them, for that would be like sticking one's hand in a wasp's nest. Payal understands this. That's why she covered her mother's mouth.

'Now this Miyan will tell me what Ram-ji had said?' The words are like molten lead poured into Ashiq's ears. It is past midnight now, but he is still tossing and turning in bed.

He was just seven or eight when he first went with his father to the shop. Back then, Aramganj Chowk did not have this kind of bustle. Ashiq could count the number of vehicles that went past the shop as he threaded the bobbin, and upon returning home at night, he would tell everyone, 'You know how many vehicles crossed the shop today? A full sixty!'

When his cousins, his phoophi or khala's kids, came to visit, he would bring them to the shop and proudly point out the things on the street. A shop right on the chowk! Right from childhood, this alone was his core identity, what he was recognised by. But there is another, bigger identity. It's so big that even if he wants, it won't leave him alone: he is a Muslim plying his trade in a Hindu area.

No, tonight he won't be able to sleep. Ashiq quietly opens the door and sits outside. His heart seems to be far away. Beyond the rows of flowers in his courtyard, beyond even the half moon in the sky, Ashiq's heart is still strung on Aramganj Chowk. The word *auqat*—knowing one's place—lashes at his heart like a whip, again and again. A man's place, his *auqat* is measured by his identity, by what he is known and recognised for. But what after all is a man's true identity? Is it what he believes about himself? Or is it what others decide for him? In a flash, memory transports him to who knows how long back in time.

Abbu sat inside the shop, and Ashiq stood quietly, right next to him.

'Every time this blighted festival season arrives, it feels as if some moneylending mahajan is sitting on one's chest, trying to extract the debts of one's past life,' Mahto-ji said, collecting the order of three identical shirt-pant sets cut from the same length of cloth.

'Yes, you are right. Only children get to enjoy the festivals, not adults,' Ashiq's father, Gani Miyan, replied.

'My mother and father stay in the village. I have a family of five here. New clothes are essential for Holi and Dussehra. It's tough to afford all this. How many do you have in your family?'

'Five of us in our home too. My eldest daughter is no more, so there are two girls, and this son, Ashiq.'

'All are from one wife?'

'I don't quite follow your question.'

'*Arre*, you people can keep four wives, no? I have heard so. That's why I am asking.'

'Oh, I see!' Gani Miyan laughed out loud and summoned his son. 'Tell chacha how many mothers you have.'

Ashiq kept staring at the floor at first. Then he slowly raised his finger to indicate one. The doubt in the shop got cleared. But who knew why, word spread among the mohalla kids that Master-ji had four wives. Whenever Ashiq was found walking alone to the shop, his peers would start singing:

> *Bappa ek maiyya chaar*
> *Ashiqwa ghoome beech bazaar*
>
> Father one, mothers four
> Ashiqwa wanders door to door

One day, a taunt like this made Ashiq pick up a stone and hurl it with full force. The flying stone hit a child on the head. Ashiq ran off, but Gani Miyan was held to account. 'So, Master-ji, have you people been allowed to settle here in order to breed terrorists? Do you see your rascal boy's handiwork?'

When Gani Miyan returned from the shop that night, he didn't say a word to Ashiq. He also did not eat. When Ashiq's mother asked, he said he was feeling under the weather.

Ashiq could tolerate everything, except his Abbu and Ammi's humiliation. It has been years, but he still remembers the night before Holi. There was a lot of work at the shop. To take a break from the stitching, Gani Miyan had stepped out to smoke a beedi when Ashiq heard him scream.

Alarmed, Ashiq ran out, a pair of big scissors still in hand. He saw some boys restraining Gani Miyan and forcibly trying to smear Mobil oil on his face. When people from the neighbouring shops began to scream and shout, the attackers ran off. They made Gani Miyan sit on the stool outside Manish Cloth Store so he could wash his face. But the Mobil oil clung to his beard. Thankfully it hadn't got into his eyes.

Ashiq kept thinking how good sinking the scissors into the belly of one of those scoundrels would have felt. Even after Holi, people kept asking after Gani Miyan's well-being. Gani Miyan never talked about that incident on his own, but Ashiq once heard him tell a customer that bad memories were worse than any debt—one must straightaway cast them off.

From another customer, they came to know that the fellow who had chased the miscreants away was one Muntu bhaiyya, a known criminal from one of the galis of the mohalla. On hearing this, Gani Miyan had said, 'However bad a man may seem on the outside, he is always good inside.'

Gani Miyan is no longer in this world, but from time to time, his words echo in Ashiq's ears. Ashiq's Abbu could swallow any insult like a gulp of water. He had seen many ups and downs in his lifetime, but never let a frown cross his face. The riots of 1967 had ended up transforming the town's appearance. Most Muslim shops in Hindu areas had to fold up. Riots broke out after 1967 too, but Gani Miyan remained where he was. Only due to his goodwill Ashiq runs not one but two shops today. Savitri Ladies Boutique even gives stiff competition to the ladies tailoring shops on Main Road.

Whenever Ashiq feels furious, he recalls his father's words, 'however bad a man may seem on the outside, he is always good inside' and his rage starts dissipating. He is doing that now too. For no reason, Basanti chachi called him this and that, showed him his place, even declared that Pandit-ji had made a mistake by allowing a Musalman to settle in Aramganj. But who after all is this chachi?

This is the same chachi who, through her doctor brother-in-law, had arranged for his mother's cataract surgery, absolutely free of cost. When Shami was about to be born, she would frequently ask after his wife, 'Ask your wife if she has a craving for something special, I will cook it with my own hands and send it.'

Kisna and Chandu would often pussyfoot up to Ashiq and press a bundle of five or ten thousand rupees into his palms. 'Keep it—it will stay safe with you, give it back in your own time.' Once or twice, Ashiq had kept the cash, but later, realising that it must be ill-gotten money, probably from gambling or some small crime, he balked. One day, he flatly refused to take the cash. The two wheedled, but when Ashiq could not be persuaded, they went away with long faces. Even so, they speak respectfully whenever they cross paths with him. Even when a man is bad, his heart has respect for good people, is what Ashiq thinks.

These days, the town is in the grip of a stupendous bomb and country-revolver revolution. Just as displaying cleavage is fashionable in rich society, young buggers roaming on the streets here display country-revolvers tucked in the gap between their shirts and jeans. But when the same louts discuss a romantic song from *Chitrahaar*, a startling softness flushes their faces. A just-released petty criminal buying balloons for his children in the chowk-bazaar looks no less than the purest, most spiritual man on earth.

Ashiq keeps thinking, but no face worth hating comes to his mind. It is simply not possible to hate someone whose idea of teasing is to call him 'Mishra-ji'. Rayyat Toli is a settlement of poor, powerless folk weighed down by worries of gathering the daily oil, salt and wood. Illiterate, destitute folk sometimes do make trouble for others. But why hate such people? With the same stealth with which he had opened the door to step out, Ashiq creeps back into his house and lies down. Maybe now he will sleep.

10

THE PATH TO RAM IS PAVED
WITH HARDSHIPS

Ashiq does not remember the last time he had such a long conversation with himself. Suddenly, Baba's face flashes in his eye. Baba, meaning Inderdev Pandey. Baba, in a one-room school, making children recite Kabir's couplets:

> *Bura jo dekhan main chala, bura na miliya koi*
> *Jo dil dhoonda aapna, mujhse bura na koi*

> Went looking for sinners, didn't find a single one
> Looked within, found myself worse than everyone

All the *dohas* and *chaupais* Ashiq knows by heart are due to Baba. When Ashiq grew up a bit, his father broached the subject of whether or not to send him to school. In the future, he would have to carry forward the family trade. But a six- or seven-year-old child could hardly be apprenticed as a tailor. What if he poked himself with the needle, or, instead of cloth, cut his finger with the scissors! Could there be any objection if, till the time his professional training commenced, he received a little formal education?

Even otherwise, a working knowledge of the alphabet and some addition–subtraction is essential to survive in this world. Neighbours advised Gani Miyan that Ashiq be sent to Moti Nagar madrasa. But who would risk sending one's only son so far away? Gani Miyan quietly handed Ashiq over to Inderdev Pandey, aka Baba, who ran a school in the neighbourhood, paying a monthly fee of twenty rupees. Every morning in Baba's school, they recited a prayer.

Eko Ram, dujo Shyam
Teen trilok, chaaron dhaam

First comes Ram, second, Shyam
In three worlds, four realms

In this vein, the prayer ended on nine planets and ten directions. Like the rest of the children, Ashiq would sing and sway to this song and later take a seat next to Pawan on a gunny sack in a corner. Eight other children sat to one side, while Pawan and Ashiq sat on the other. Pawan came from Valmiki Nagar. Had Pandey baba made him sit with the rest of the students, the school would have emptied out. Thanks to Ashiq's enrollment, Pawan found company. Pandey baba taught everything—Hindi alphabet, counting, multiplication. He even taught a little bit of History, Geography and General Knowledge. Like, when did India get independence, on which continent we live, what were the names of our prime minister, the president, and so on. Within a week, Pandey baba recognised Ashiq's talent. 'Without doubt, this son of the Julaha Gani Miyan is sharp.' Ashiq's father was not a Julaha or weaver, yet in common parlance, a Muslim and a weaver were synonymous.

Ashiq was indeed the brightest among Pandey baba's students. From multiplication tables up to seventeen, to Sanskrit chants, whatever Baba taught, the boy would repeat like a parrot. So obedient was he, that after school got over, even before Baba could ask, he would roll up the floor mat and keep it on one side. He would pick up the broom of his own accord and sweep leaves off the veranda. Giving his progress report at the end of the year, Pandey baba told Gani Miyan, 'The boy is very bright. Let him study, don't put him in tailoring.'

Gani Miyan replied, 'Reading–writing will not make a collector out of him. He ought to learn some skill to fill the belly. His training in tailoring must begin next month onwards.'

Pandey baba thought for some time. He then proposed that Ashiq come to the school early in the morning, help him with chores before classes began, and in exchange get an education. No fees would be charged. He could go and learn tailoring at his father's shop after school. If kept engaged thus for the whole day, he would also not fall into bad company. This suggestion felt right to Gani Miyan, and so from age eight onwards, Ashiq began doing double duty.

Like the mythological figure Aruni, Ashiq was devoted to his teacher and worshipped him, but Pandey baba's wife did not like having a Musalman in her house. Initially, the rules were very strict. His feet were not to fall anywhere except in the tiny classroom. He was not to lay hands on the rope and bucket used to pull water from the well, or step into the sitting room. Ashiq obeyed every such order as if an injunction from Lord Brahma himself had been imposed on him. Once during the winter season, Pandey baba and his wife sat sunning themselves on the veranda, snacking on chooda-matar and sipping tea. The wife's eyes fell on the hungry child sitting in a corner. Ashiq's eyes were restless in anticipation of Baba's nod of permission so he could go home. Going home meant he could fill his stomach.

Waves of compassion began roiling in the wife's heart. She told Pandey baba in Maithili, 'See how he looks like a wide-eyed kitten!'

The next day, a porcelain plate and cup were bought for the kitten. Ashiq started getting a portion of whatever was made in the house. Even fruits and sweets. The only rule was to rinse his plate and cup and keep them in a separate corner. Owing to him, sometimes even Pawan got to taste fruits and sweets from the same plate.

As Ashiq ate out of these specially bought utensils, Inderdev Pandey's wife would watch him with maternal adoration, which was much like the adoration lavished on a beloved pet. For the pandit's wife, this was the highest level of contemporary morality, compassion and humanity. As of now, it wasn't possible for her to go any further.

When tales of Krishna–Sudama, Kalia–Naag, Bali–Sugreev and Shravan Kumar began floating around in Rayyat Toli, some people came to Gani Miyan to complain. Kamruddin was foremost among the complainers. A peon in Anjuman Islamia, he thought of himself as no less than a mufti, an Islamic judge. As a matter of fact, the people of Rayyat Toli addressed him as 'Mufti sahib'.

'Your young sahibzada is ruining the faith and character of our children. *Arre*, what was the need to send him to a pandit's school?' Kamruddin complained in chaste Urdu.

'*Arre* Mufti sahib, what has Ashiqwa done now?' Gani Miyan replied in Bhojpuri.

'Just listen to the things that our children here are talking about. Is it sensible to propagate the practices of another faith here?'

'If Shravan Kumar takes his blind parents on a holy *ziyarat*, carrying them aloft on his shoulders, what is so bad about it, Mufti sahib?' Gani Miyan said in a low voice.

'You don't understand the impact of that pandit's company on your son. You can take it from me in writing that he will abandon his own faith one day and become a staunch Hindu.'

'And those who sit around gambling here and there in our galis, who openly puff on beedi-cigarettes, will they become theologians and Mecca-goers, Mufti sahib? Listen, Pandey baba is not teaching anything wrong. Ashiq will keep going there, and you better tell your boy that Ashiq is a faithless *kafir* and he should stay away from him.' Gani Miyan announced his decision.

Ashiq has turned into a kafir! The word slowly spread throughout Rayyat Toli. But his father alone knew the truth. Did he not get his son circumcised? He did. He may or may not have fasted during Ramzan, but he always offered the namaz on Eid–Bakrid. And the most important thing was that he worked diligently and honestly. By the time he turned sixteen, Ashiq had begun looking after the entire shop. Even in Gani Miyan's absence work carried on as usual.

Once, Ashiq had gone to his maternal uncle's place to attend a wedding. He came back having acquired a unique new skill. His mother was in tears when he stitched a kurti for her in two hours flat. Ashiq's uncle ran a ladies' tailoring shop in Patna. In big towns, there was a huge demand for ladies' tailors. Ashiq now began to dream of becoming a successful ladies' tailor like his uncle. He wanted to open a new shop; the old one would be looked after by Gani Miyan. They would earn a lot, and their house would be filled with prosperity and happiness.

The arrangement with Inderdev Pandey continued even after Ashiq grew older. He continued going to school. Not to study, but to lend a hand. Baba, it seemed, existed only to bear sorrows. His wayward son had run off again, and his wife had passed away. But look at Baba's courage! Even with his back bent, he ran the school as he used to ten years ago.

He offered hope to countless grief-stricken people who came to him to show their birth-charts and ask for divine solutions. He gave them special mantras, chants, cures and a lot else. If the person was very poor, he gave them some grains and small amounts of money as well. But for himself? Ashiq often heard him muttering these words when he was alone.

> *Karo raksha vippatti se, na aisi prarthana meri*
> *Vippatti se bhay nahin paaun, Prabhu ye prarthana meri*
> *Mile dukh-taap se shanti, na aisi prarthana meri*
> *Sabhi dukh se vijay paaun, Prabhu yah prarthana meri*

> Not freedom from trouble, free me from terror
> Not eternal peace, give me victory over grief and error

Baba never mentioned his troubles, even by mistake. Only once, he said to an elderly man who had come to see him—'The path to Ram is paved with hardships. When Ramchandra-ji himself faced so many challenges, how could his true devotees remain happy? This is how Ram tests his bhakts.'

Ashiq saw something of his Abbu in Baba—he too was a believer, like Abbu. Never would he utter a sigh, even in the direst of circumstances. Inderdev Pandey had taught Ashiq everything he knew. Although he was a Hindi and Sanskrit teacher, he had also tutored Ashiq in passable English. In Baba's company, Ashiq acquired so much knowledge of Hindu rituals and practices that had he been a brahmin, he could have earned enough to run the house on earnings from priestly work alone. Yes, this Sunni Muslim knew how to draw up birth-charts, how to read and decode astrological signs.

Baba insisted that Ashiq finish higher secondary education. 'Fill out the form to write the matriculation exam privately.'

Swaying between a yes and a no, Ashiq filled out the form and even cleared the exam in the third division. Baba then said, 'Likewise, by and by get a bachelor's degree as well.' But Ashiq was reluctant; after all, he had to eventually pursue his Abbu's vocation. Besides, he loved tailoring. But unable to sidestep Baba's word, he enrolled himself in an evening college. Time kept moving at its pace, until early one morning his Abbu began to vomit blood. Ashiq rushed him to the hospital, where they found out that Gani Miyan had lung cancer.

As luck would have it, his health deteriorated rapidly, and within a month, Gani Miyan passed away. Ashiq alone knows how he calmed his Ammi and sisters. The shop stayed shut for days. When Ashiq finally managed to get over this shock and stepped out to reopen his shop, like always, he stopped over at the school. The sight of the locked gate sent alarm bells ringing.

He discovered that Baba, too, had left for the other world. After going to sleep one night, he had never woken up. For a while, his body lay unclaimed. Somehow, distant kin arrived and his last rites were performed. The keys to his house had been taken away by some relatives who the neighbours said they were not acquainted with.

Ashiq had not cried so much on his Abbu's death as he did upon hearing that his teacher had passed away. But this time, except for the peepul tree, there was no one to share his grief with. Countless scenes from their shared past swam up in his tear-filled eyes.

'Ram lives in every heart. Ram is in every grain of this creation,' Baba would often say.

'Really? Is that so? Does this mean Lord Ram is right here, in Rayyat Toli, and at the chowk?' Eight-year-old Ashiq had asked him in utter amazement.

In reply, Pandey baba smiled and nodded.

'*O teri!* Meaning Ram-ji must be actually coming and going along this way? Meaning sometimes past the front of my house and sometimes past the front of the shop, is it?'

In reply, Baba would simply keep smiling.

As a child, whenever Ashiq went to play near the river and looked at the huge semal, imli, banyan and sheesham trees by the riverside, he felt Ram-ji must have lived in these dense forests during his exile. One day he asked, 'Baba, Chitrakoot is ahead of Aramganj, on the other side of the river, no?'

Pandey baba looked at his wife, and both had a good laugh. 'No, son, Chitrakoot is very far from here. Who told you this?'

Ashiq remained quiet for a while, then asked, 'Tell me, Baba, is it not possible that Ram-ji went to the forest beyond the river?'

'Anything is possible! Ram's maya, Ram's magic is known only to him.'

What kind of magic was this, that within ten days, Ashiq was orphaned twice!

Gani Miyan had taught him that even the worst man could be good deep within. But Ashiq's own experience has made him realise that it is not at all necessary that good things happen to those who are good. His Abbu was Allah's true follower. He was barely fifty when he passed away after struggling with intense pain. Pandey baba had always followed the righteous path, but, in the course of it, faced extreme hardship. He was perhaps right in saying, 'The path to Ram is paved with hardships.'

Why does God act so mercilessly towards his people? Who knows if He exists only in religious books, in tales and stories alone, or if He really is there? Who can answer these questions for Ashiq now? The one of whom he could ask such questions is not in this world any more.

11

WHAT ARE YOU IN FOR, GOPAL?

The racket outside jerks Ashiq out of his sleep. Getting up he goes out in his vest. A crowd has gathered at the municipal tap in front of his house. In one corner Gopal the cobbler stands trembling. Chakkan's eldest son, Salim, is on the other side, bringing up, one by one, every woman in Gopal's clan, using the choicest of abuses. 'If from tomorrow, I see you here, you rascal, I will break both your legs and deposit them in your hands. If you want water, go to some Hindu basti. Your mother here—'

It is evident from the mud plastered over Gopal's clothes that Salim has given him a thrashing. Eyes brimming with tears, he holds a bucket in each hand, a fear-filled beseeching expression clouding his face. A man can survive a thrashing, but can he survive without water?

From the spectacle, it does not seem that the quarrel is only about water. By now—at 7.30 in the morning—water has been stocked up by most residents. If a fellow living close by takes two buckets from the government tap at this hour—is he snatching anything from anyone? Gopal does not even dare to speak loudly to anyone; the question of him quarrelling does not arise.

Gopal's shanty is around the corner from here, on the path that goes from Inderdev Pandey's house to Aramganj Chowk.

An expert in making shoes for people with polio, he had once worked in a factory. But since the factory's closure, he stays at home. The demand for polio-shoes is meagre. When the rare customer finds his way to Gopal's house, he seeks a discount lamenting his bleak fate. So Gopal barely makes do with the measly sum he earns from repairing and polishing shoes.

Whenever Gopal sees Ashiq passing by, he respectfully folds his hands in greeting. This is his daily routine with everyone, not just with Ashiq. His age must be around fifty. Whatever children God gave him were taken back one by one. Somehow or the other, Gopal and his sick wife pass their days in his shanty.

The bystanders are watching mutely. Clutching the buckets, Gopal once more, like a Satyagrahi, wordlessly turns towards the tap in his muddied clothes. Everyone holds their breath. Salim at once grabs Gopal's kurta. 'The fucker will not learn like this. I will bury him here ...'

People see Gopal tighten his fists over the two buckets. Ashiq steps forth at lightning speed, and roughly pushes Salim aside, making him almost fall on his face.

'*Aey* Misir, don't try this smartness with me. Limit your *rangbazi* to Aramganj Chowk.' So saying, Salim leaps at Ashiq, but two or three neighbours pull them apart and drag Salim to one side. One of them pleadingly looks at Ashiq, as if requesting him to take it easy. Ashiq silently places Gopal's bucket under the tap.

Salim roars, 'If anyone so much as taps an electric wire in Rayyat Toli, such is *their* grudge that *they* at once lodge complaints with the electricity department. And look at us— we act like ultimate *chutiyas* and let *their* low-castes fill their pots here! Sisterfuckers! Even that Valmiki Nagar has got three government taps. And we? Only one! Worse than even the colony of Bhangi-Chamaars ... Just because it's in front of his house, does it mean the tap belongs to Ashiqwa's father? The company of upper-caste Hindus has made not just his body fat, but his mind as well. Let me tell you, one day I am going to strip all that fat off him.'

Constant challenges keep issuing from the adjoining gali. This is not unique to Aramganj or Rayyat Toli. This is the way of life in all small towns. In a fight, the man most liable to get beaten up displays the maximum hot-headedness before those trying to calm things down.

On his way to the shop, Ashiq keeps thinking about Gopal the cobbler. He has told Gopal that if he does not get water anywhere, he should come and fill up from his well without hesitation. But Ashiq also knows that the water in the well would become smelly and unfit to use after the rains as drain water will seep into it, and Gopal will once more be forced to approach some government tap or the other.

Om-ji calls Gopal 'Nepal'. Nepal, meaning the buffer state between India and China, which cannot afford to annoy either of them. While passing by, Om-ji likes to forecast that 'Nepal' will get himself killed one day—slaughtered by the Cold War. Had Gopal been Nepal, it still would have been something. But the truth is—to the Rayyat Toli residents, permanently seething with frustration, irritation, helplessness and pain, Gopal is just a punching bag. A low-caste Hindu living at the mouth of a Muslim basti, he can be made to pay, that too with interest, for the many alleged and real injustices done to them.

But is Gopal really a Hindu?

If he had gone asking for water in Aramganj, would anyone have let him fill water from their house taps? Forget Aramganj, even the fair-skinned Marwari manual scavengers from Rajasthan look down upon him. Once Gopal got thrashed even in their area for the alleged theft of water. Ashiq had then brokered peace with the help of his childhood friend, Valmiki Nagar leader Pawan Hatwal, to ensure a safe passage for Gopal.

As a result, no one beats Gopal now at least in Valmiki Nagar. But getting water from there requires at least half an hour to go and come back. Add to it the back-breaking labour of lugging water over such a long distance. So for Gopal, simpering before the Rayyat Toli people and swallowing their abuses is a better option. Even if he gets beaten up once or twice, it is hardly a calamity. Right from the time he began walking on his own two feet, he is habituated to thrashings. The only thing is, now his ageing body can't take it anymore.

A weird question pops up in Ashiq's mind: after all, what is the difference between him and Gopal? Abbu would say that along with giving us a life, Allah also grants us a way to live. To save one's own life is every man's right, as well as his duty. Gopal is performing this duty in his own way and Ashiq in his own. The minute it strikes Ashiq that in some matters he is very much like Gopal, he is filled with disgust. Who knows why since yesterday, his mind is being preyed upon by many such strange thoughts.

Hanif has already swept both sides of Two-in-One tailoring shop, and is sitting in a corner, hemming. Ashiq is perched on a stool. Looking attentively at the shop walls is his habit. He gazes at the old pair of scissors lying on the table. These ordinary-looking scissors would turn into a magic wand in his Abbu's hands. The old measuring-scale leaning against a corner looks back at him, as if saying—don't ever get rid of me. Clothes heaped under the counter look like his Abbu is bent over a mat, offering namaz. Every speck in the shop is full of such intimacy. No matter how bone-tired or morose Ashiq might be, as soon as he comes to the shop, he livens up. Why should he go to the mosque when his Khuda resides here?

12

CONGRATULATIONS AND CELEBRATIONS!

Who knows after how long the three-storeyed mansion has seen such a stir. A Fiat arrived early in the morning. After that, a Maruti 800. And now, a Contessa is blowing its horn. The three-storeyed house, meaning the '7, Lok Kalyan Marg' or '10, Downing Street' of Aramganj Chowk. The official residence of the first citizen, and No. 1 PWD contractor of the chowk, Sarvdaman Singh. Wonder what's up today.

The news comes from Mangal's paan-shop: 'A compromise has been reached.'

'Really?'

'Yes, there's been a compromise.' Someone at Ojha-ji's kiosk seconds this. From Mithilesh Grocery Store to Pappu Chai-wala, from Hari Sweets to Bajrangi Dhaba, only one thing is being discussed—that a compromise has been reached.

'Sarvdaman babu will now take off his turban and keep it at his low-caste Lohar son-in-law's feet, haha … haha.'

'Ram-Ram, old age has addled his brains. The girl was a gone case already, now the father too—'

'Hadn't he once gone charging to finish him off, rifle in hand? What changed all of a sudden? Seems to have gone totally senile, our Sarvdaman babu!'

'Not senile, he is extremely canny and calculating. The Lohar has cleared the civil services exam, so quietly, Sarvdaman babu has changed his stand. His own son is totally useless. Now courtesy the son-in-law's officerhood, he will live life king-size in old age.'

'By God, an IAS?'

'Of course! Dilip is an IAS officer now.'

Whoever hears this goes into a swoon. It is not as if there have been no officers in Aramganj before this. The preceding generation had many officers big and small—like Radhey babu, Sahay-ji and Verma-ji. Shrikanth Singh's younger brother Nilkanth Singh is a judge in the Allahabad High Court. But no one cleared the UPSC before Dilip. Thanks to Dilip, once more, a new thrill courses through Aramganj Chowk.

Harish, who had gone to buy bread and butter, hears the news and comes back half-dazed. Only after gulping down a glass or two of water does he gain a bit of control over his senses, and tells his mother, 'It will prove to be a rumour, just wait and see.' But after sometime, an invitation arrives from the three-storeyed house to partake of *prasad* at the Satyanarayan katha being performed to seek blessings for the bride and groom. Harish's mother cross-checks with the emissary if the groom is indeed an IAS officer. After the courier leaves, she says with a long sigh, 'He may have lots of money, but Sarvdaman babu is such a cheapskate. If he is accepting the daughter and son-in-law, shouldn't he at least arrange a proper banquet dinner? Wants to get away merely by distributing a spoonful of *panjiri* and water washed down from Lord Satyanarayan's feet.'

'Sarvdaman babu is a practical man. In these times, all men should be as practical as him,' people gathering at the three-storeyed house say to one another sotto voce.

Adjoining the veranda is Sarvdaman babu's huge sitting area. A hay-stuffed tiger, once hunted by his grandfather, stands by the door. Actually, it's a leopard—but is called a tiger. Just as Sarvdaman babu, a small-time zamindar, is called 'Raja sahib' by his servants. And just as his son-in-law, selected for the Indian Revenue Service (IRS), will now be called an IAS officer.

The senior citizens of the chowk are occupying eight to ten chairs on the veranda. The rest are standing. It looks like, finding the door open, some uninvited guests, too, have walked in, most of them menials. Who can stop people from coming in to partake of Lord Satyanarayan's prasad!

Looking at the guests, it's clear that this Rajput–Lohar compromise has in no way altered the social equations of Aramganj. The gali-walas have not been invited. The few exceptions hanging around have been invited under compulsion. Banana leaves have come from Sahu-ji's house, the mango branches and wood for ritual offerings made to the sacred havan fire are from Yadav-ji's garden—so how could they not get an invitation? Dilip's distant uncle at whom Sarvdaman babu had fired his double-barrel is not visible anywhere. Whether he wasn't extended an invitation or he himself chose not to come out of fear, is not known—who will ask after all?

The chief guest of this function—Shalabhmani Tripathi—is seated in a special armchair kept right next to the stuffed tiger. To his left sits Jatashankar Sharma. Around them, stand a couple of hangers-on. Tripathi-ji is clad in a silk dhoti-kurta, with a green stole draped around his shoulders. Sporting three thick lines of sandalwood paste on the forehead, he looks exactly like the scholarly leader Murli Manohar Joshi.

Seeing Tripathi-ji, the guests seek to quell their curiosity. Chaube-ji says, 'Lalu Yadav is saying he will not let Advani-ji enter Bihar, the rath will be stopped and sent off to Delhi.'

Smiling gently, Tripathi-ji replies, 'The one holding the reins of power might even manage to stop the rath, but the chariot of Hindu consciousness has taken off and cannot be stopped by anyone.' The public breaks into applause.

Had he been in Patna or Delhi, Tripathi-ji would have been a towering leader. Even here, he is hardly a small fry! MPs and MLAs all come to him for counsel. Verma-ji was telling someone that the compromise was facilitated by none other than Tripathi-ji.

Reading out a mantra dedicated to Lord Vishwakarma, the patron god of all craftsmen, Tripathi-ji explained to Sarvdaman babu that Lohar—the caste of ironsmiths—wasn't such a bad caste. In a way these people were also Rajputs. What would a Rajput warrior wield if the sword had not been hewn by the ironsmith? The lineage of Lohars was no less glorious than that of the Rajputs. Once they gave their word, these people never backtracked.

The Lohars had pledged to Maharana Pratap, the sixteenth-century ruler of Mewar, that until their motherland wasn't freed from the clutches of Mughals, they would not build houses for themselves. The Gadiya Lohars of Rajasthan honour that pledge to this day. The nomadic people who make and sell iron goods, travelling on bullock carts, are the descendants of those Lohars. 'Not a son-in-law, you've got a real gem. Had you hunted for an IAS groom within your caste and clan, you would have had to part with at least twenty to twenty-five lakh.' Tripathi-ji's words worked like magic on Sarvdaman babu, and made him abandon his vow of sinking bullets in the chests of that blot-on-the-clan of a daughter and the lowlife son-in-law.

But Sarvdaman babu's nephew Akhilesh is still enraged. 'Chacha turned out to be a bigger blot on the glorious reputation of Rajputs than V.P. Singh. Here, I roam around like a stupid fucker, on the ready to lay down my life to avenge his honour, and there, he is bent upon chopping not just his, but the entire community's nose. The reason behind this laxness in his stand is Tripathia's Lavan Bhaskar bowel-loosening chooran-like influence on him.

'Let him marry his own daughter to a low-caste Kahar or Dhobi, then we will see. Only yesterday, he was telling someone—if a Brahmin is not pure-blooded, all rituals, prayers and recitation are rendered profane. But other Hindus should inter-marry! This would make Hindu-jati strong! The lying, thieving fucker! He is stuffing Chacha with all this nonsense only to showcase his politics; and Chacha, being the simple *gobar-ganesh* that he is, has readily accepted all this. *Arre*, whether a collector or director, can a low-caste ever equal a Rajput?'

Akhilesh and his entire family boycotted the function. But emerging Rajput leader Kamlesh Singh is present. Sarvdaman babu has given a special directive to Kamlesh: 'Under no circumstance, must Om *pagalwa*—that lunatic Om—come anywhere near Tripathi-ji.'

Om-ji has entangled the best of the chowk's minds in a mathematical problem these days. The question is: 'If the riots that began last October after Ramshila-pujan, the foundation stone-laying ceremony of Ram temple, led to a thousand people being killed in Bhagalpur alone, how many people across India would die during the thirty-five-day-long Rath Yatra of Advani-ji?' Rendered speechless by this, people start looking here and there. Pat comes Om-ji's answer: 56,800. Just as Plato, the Greek philosopher, had given the figure of 5,040—neither more nor less—as the ideal number of citizens in a polis. Thankfully, Om-ji is not to be seen anywhere today. Perhaps he is still nursing a hangover from last night's liquor.

Radha pandit is reciting the Satyanarayan katha. So many women crowd the front that the bride and groom are hardly visible to those on the veranda. They can only hear the sounds. Radha pandit is now relating the tale of the poor woodcutter, who performed the Satyanarayan puja so devotedly that his poverty ended. Dilip used to study in this town while living in a distant relative's home. To pay for his books and fees, he would take tuitions in affluent areas like Professor's Colony and Bharatpuri. See, today he is an IAS officer! May Lord Satyanarayan bestow such grace on everyone. Neutral observer Nirmal Jain notices that the people seated as guests are repeatedly inserting the words 'Lohar' and 'inter-caste' in their conversation in some roundabout way every ten minutes or so. The fuckers, real bastards, all of them!

Rani didi is looking unblinkingly at Puja. Rani didi, meaning the mistress of the three-storeyed house. She is recalling much that is past now. That too was a Sunday like this one. The whole house was watching Ramayan on TV. Sita-ji was imprisoned in Ashok Vatika. Listening to her heart-rending dialogue with the female demon guard Trijata, women cried buckets. Bua—Sarvdaman's sister—tried to force Puja to sit before the television, but could Puja ever be made to sit? Bua would often complain: if the girl wasn't made to watch good things, how would she acquire good values? But Rani didi would laughingly sidestep her: the children these days are not in anyone's control, what can I do?

Rani didi herself could never do anything, but her daughter had shown how things could be done. Hanuman-ji arrived in Ashok Vatika, and giving Lord Ram's ring to Sita, he bowed before her. The frame froze to the serial's sign-off tune, *'Mangal bhuvan, amangal haari'* and people glued to 'the harbinger of the auspicious who drives the inauspicious away' at last budged from the TV room. Raja sahib went towards the veranda; Rani didi went to set her room in order and relax for a while. Suddenly, the sound of rifle shots rent the air; Sarvdaman babu was particular about cleaning his double-barrel once a month.

At once Rani didi thought of Puja. She called out twice or thrice; when no reply came, she went towards Puja's room. The door, shut from inside, did not open despite repeated knocking, so Rani didi went through the kitchen to the corridor where the other door to Puja's room opens. Her room was in total disarray and there was a letter on the table.

> *Ma,*
>
> *I know I am bad news and I should not have been born in Raja sahib's clan. But was this ever in my hands? Whatever I am, just accept this was how God made me. I am an adult and can choose the way I want my life to be. Dilip and I have decided to spend our lives together. We got married in court. A photocopy of the marriage certificate is in the almirah before you. I am leaving. Do not get troubled. And don't trouble us. Take care of yourself, and if possible, forgive me. Papa will never forgive me, but still give my respects to him and Bua.'*
>
> *Yours,*
> *Puja*

Crying and breast-beating began in the triple-storeyed mansion. Sarvdaman babu at once picked up the rifle to hunt that lowlife Lohar down and finish him off. The neighbours said that if instead of doing all this, he had just sent someone to keep an eye on the bus stand and railway station, Puja could have been brought back. But Sarvdaman babu's hot Rajput blood! For no reason, he had fired in the air and landed himself in a police case.

Rani didi returns from the flashback.

Unblinkingly she stares at her daughter who is listening to the katha. Next to her sits the son-in-law, head bowed, extremely gentle- and calm-looking. After all, what crime did her daughter commit? Only married a boy she liked. None other than her own father had given her the moniker *kulachhanni*—of bad character. But if Raja sahib is hot-headed, the daughter is no less.

She was in class nine, when a letter was found in her school-bag. Written by a boy. Rani didi showed it to her husband. She couldn't have imagined what would happen next. The father picked up a belt and unleashed it on the girl. She went on screaming, but like an animal Sarvdaman babu kept thrashing her. 'This bad-charactered girl of yours will go and sit in the bazaar one day. Take her off the rolls.'

For a week, Puja wasn't allowed to go to school. After much beseeching and wheedling, Sarvdaman babu finally agreed that she could continue her studies, but with the warning that he would skin the mother's hide first if anything untoward ever happened, and deal with the girl later. Rani didi thought, would that be anything new? And whenever Puja's younger brother Ripudaman quarrelled with his sister, he would call her the bad-charactered bitch.

Puja accepted the moniker given by the father, but not the father. Both father and daughter loathed each other. Puja cleared all exams—class Xth, XIIth and graduation—in the first division but never showed the results to her father. The father, too, never gave her a pat on the back. After her twelfth grade results, Raja sahib got busy trying to arrange her marriage. But the girl's astrological chart showed a blistering defect in the planet Mars, putting her in the dreaded 'Mangalik' category. Her planets just did not align anywhere. Thanks to this hurdle, Puja sailed through graduation and was also able to enroll for a master's in Sociology.

Dilip and Puja were in the same college. Dilip was three years senior to her. They met in the college theatre group where Puja was active, and became good friends. When Puja reached university, Dilip was already enrolled in a PhD programme and was preparing for competitive exams. Most of his time was spent in the library where they would meet.

During this period, a mighty fracas erupted in Puja's house. Early one morning, Bua raised the zero-hour question that the girl was now twenty-three—parents who made a girl sit at home till such an advanced age ought to be ashamed of themselves. Bua, meaning Sarvdaman babu's unmarried elder sister, who held the rank of mother-in-law in the house. Sarvdaman babu then took a fierce pledge: whether birth-charts matched or not, that very year, Puja's wedding would be finalised.

As soon as Puja heard this fiat, she cornered her boyfriend. He was busy taking some reference books from the library. Without a preamble, Puja asked, 'Can you marry me tomorrow?' Dilip's face drained of colour. Puja offered another option. 'Okay, if not tomorrow, how about next week?'

When Puja said that she was not in a position to wait, the familiar dialogues of Hindi movies issued forth from Dilip's mouth. *If I marry you without a job, how will I feed you, where will we live? So much difference between us ... Your family will never get over my caste and class and accept me.* And in the end: *I am not worthy of you. Forget me, settle for some nice boy and set up house. But my heart will always keep beating for you.*

Thakurain, meaning the Rajput girl, heard all this, and said, 'If you don't want to marry, do one thing. Just come out.' Catching hold of his hand, Puja almost dragged him out of the library.

'What's all this, Puja?'

'Come with me to the Main Road. Hold your ears before the public, squat down 101 times and say that you were doing only *time-pass*. Admit before everyone that while you fancy romancing, you don't have an ounce of courage to stand by your word. *Arre*, had I been in your place, I would have instantly grabbed your hand and eloped. But sadly, I am not a man. And I have found out today, neither are you.'

This was how, the following week, the two got married in court. And the story of what happened after that is on the lips of every child in Aramganj. The youngsters who have come to take the prasad at the Satyanarayan katha watch this legendary couple with wistfulness. The songs from the movie *Pyar Jhukta Nahin*—love never buckles—echo in their ears.

'See, the minute he got married, he became an IAS officer. This is called Lady Luck. What do you say, Overseer sahib?'

Girish babu is not only wearing a neatly pressed suit from his almirah, but has also brought along some new English phrases. He scrunches his nose in his signature style and says, 'Something ijj better than nothing.'

Chandrika babu gets irritated. 'See? He is again trying to impress with his *bhohka-bhulari* (vocabulary). As if he is the only person in this mohalla who knows English. Something is better than nothing. *Ka matlab hua aapka ee bolne ka?* What are you implying?'

Girish babu's nose scrunches up even more. '*Arre*, you people are saying IAS-IAS, I am commenting on that. Sarvdaman babu's son-in-law is in the IRS, the Indian Revenue Service. It is an allied service, not the main.'

'You said something is better than nothing ... meaning the son-in-law became something from nothing? Is that what you want to say? *Arre*, Revenue Service-walas are the real big guns who keep Administration-walas under their thumb. Whenever he wants, Dilip will conduct a raid on DM or collector. Tell me, Gupta, am I saying anything wrong?'

The aarti is over, and prasad is being distributed. For the women of the mohalla, this is an opportunity to see the bride and groom to their heart's content. Palms shielding their eyes, the women stare at the brand-new couple with great interest.

'From his face, you can't tell he's a Lohar. He doesn't look like one.'

'A very handsome son-in-law they've got! Only prayers performed over seven births yield such results.'

'*Arre*, just look, isn't Puja's belly looking bigger?'

'Shut up!' Basanti chachi elbows Mukesh's mother.

Everyone is about to leave. Seeing Ashiq, Bua limps up to him with a leaf-plate full of prasad. 'Now even you will come only when a barber is sent with an invite?'

'*Arre nahin.* No, Bua. There was a rush in the shop, that's why I got late. Is the aarti over?'

Ashiq reverentially receives the *charnamrut* water, wiping his hands over the back of his head like a good Hindu, takes the prasad and turns towards the gate.

'*Arre* Ashiq bhaiyya, wait!'

Ashiq turns his head. Wrapped in a benarasi sari, Puja the new bride stands before him. Ashiq simply stands and stares at her for a few moments.

'So you don't even recognise me?'

'*Arre* Puja didi, I am seeing you after a long time, that's why.'

'Didi! So am I your big sister now?'

Ashiq does not reply. When Puja grew out of frocks and wore her first ever salwar-suit, it had been stitched by Ashiq. What an adorable, bubbly little girl she had been. And now a young woman! How time flies!

It was different when she was little. How can he call her by her name now! Ashiq cannot make up his mind as to what, if anything, to say.

'And is everything well in your home and family, bhaiyya?' Puja herself pushes forth the conversation.

'It is all Ram-ji's grace.'

'Please wait a minute, I'll be back.' Saying this, Puja goes inside.

'How are you, Rambhakt Hanuman? How come you are here? I see, you have come to take the *prasadi*,' Jatashankar Sharma says, stepping down from the veranda.

'Yes, kaka.'

'Okay, listen. Tomorrow there is a naming ceremony at the place where your mohalla begins. Now it will be called Shri Ram Path.'

'Shri Ram Path?'

'Yes, Shri Ram Path. You come in the morning with some mohalla boys.'

'Mohalla boys? Why them, kaka?'

'*Arre,* when even Ram-ji's bridge could not be built without the monkeys, can the naming ceremony take place without them!' Laughing out loud, Sharma-ji opens the gate and walks out.

Meanwhile, Puja comes running and extends an envelope.

'What is this, didi?'

'Settling an old account, remember?'

'*Arre*, leave it be, didi, why this settling of accounts now?'

'Bhaiyya, please keep it.'

'No, didi, if I must, let me settle accounts with the one who held this account.'

Puja looks inside. Sarvdaman babu is introducing his son-in-law to a group of VIPs. To call out to him loudly does not seem appropriate.

'After four days, his training will begin at Nagpur. But before leaving, we will definitely come to your shop. Okay, do one thing. This is not *hisaab* money. I am giving this for you to buy sweets for the children.'

Puja extends a hundred-rupee note towards Ashiq. Because Ashiq is holding the leaf-plate in his hands, Puja puts the note in his shirt pocket. If it's for the children, what can Ashiq say. He goes out without meeting Puja's eyes. 'We will definitely come before he leaves.' Puja calls out after him. Her voice travels with Ashiq.

13

ARAMGANJ TURNS ASPIRATIONAL

Look Dilip bhai's car goes pam pam pam!
To eat bhelpuri, we are off to Chowpatty,
We will yell, and we will roar!
The drums will beat dham dham dham.

The tinkling laughter of an entire gaggle of girls spills out of the blue Fiat. They are singing an old Bollywood number, fitting Dilip into its story. Every twenty or so metres, the car jumps over a speed-breaker, and a new bout of laughter erupts.

The scene seems to be straight out of a Hindi movie from the sixties or seventies—the heroine's friends accompanying the hero and heroine. The *jiju*, who has just been introduced to the lovely sisters-in-law, is taking the *saalis* out for a three-month-old superhit starring Amir Khan and Madhuri Dixit, *Dil*.

The plan for the movie caused a war of words between Puja and Dilip. Poor Dilip! Firstly, by nature, he is reticent. Second, this first visit to the in-laws' place had left him wary and extremely tense. Worn out from touching the feet of the entire Thakur clan after the Satyanarayan katha, he barely felt capable of coping with this new nuisance!

Certainly, he had written romantic letters to Puja, but it had taken him a long time to even look directly into her eyes. And then, the very idea of taking an entire flock of unknown girls for movie and dinner!

Puja told him straightaway, 'Not a flock, only five. You will *have* to go. I promised to treat them.'

After a lengthy argument, Dilip managed to get two brothers added to this list of sisters-in-law so he would feel less out of place. One of them is Puja's younger brother Ripu, and the other, his friend Sachin. Both are following the blue Fiat on a moped. The moped has been wheezing since the beginning of the five-kilometre journey. The shortcut connecting Aramganj to Navratan Talkies goes over a bridge so narrow, it's called a *puliya*, a bridgelet. The blue Fiat loaded with Dilip's sisters-in-law clatters over the puliya. Sachin's lion-hearted moped also vrooms ahead with full force, but loses steam on ascent. Now, it is unable to restart. Ripu and Sachin drag the moped over the slope to somehow cross the puliya. They will think about what to do next later.

The Main Road girls on an outing with 'the Lohar' in a blue Fiat, and two clown-like brothers-in-law following on a wheezing moped! This makes the day's trending topic in Aramganj.

Taking a break from political discussions, Aramganj has zeroed in on social issues. In the history of this chowk, there have been only two cases of love marriage. Both within the same caste. Tara babu had eloped with his elder brother's sister-in-law twenty-six years ago. And last year, his neighbour Kundan Shrivastav's son lost his heart to a girl from a family known to them. The parents' dreams of extracting a fat dowry were put to rest. The elders of the chowk have a very contemptuous outlook towards the word 'love'. They think of it as an almost vulgar thing. That is why Tara babu, now himself about to enter elderhood, is still called a *rasiya*, a loverboy, behind his back. Love is something only a dissolute pleasure-seeker would stoop to.

Aramganj Chowk's community of elders, too, has a heavy topic to broach. Whether Raja sahib, aka Sarvdaman babu, has earned dishonour by marrying into a 'Lohar' family, or gained respect through an IAS son-in-law? Consensus on this matter is not possible. One group believes that even if the son-in-law had been a prime minister, instead of an IAS officer, the damage could not have been compensated. The poor fellow has been rendered a permanent outcast. Thank God the house has no other daughter, or they would have gotten only a low-caste groom for her. At Mangal's shop, Tiwari-ji said, 'Whatever he might be, the boy's post is very powerful.' When asked if he would give his own daughter to a low-caste man at a powerful post, they almost came to blows.

Padampati Gupta has analysed the matter comprehensively. He looks upon this as a long-term investment, which might bear some loss at the moment, but in the future, will yield only profit. After five years who will care what the caste of the neighbour's son-in-law was? Such is the power of his position that seven generations after him will be well taken care of.

The younger generation, though, views this matter differently. Dilip and Puja's love story has all the elements of a blockbuster movie. Poor boy, rich girl; the girl's father ready to shoot; an idealistic hero; and a wilful heroine ready to go to any lengths to obtain her love.

Elopement from home, the tussle immediately afterwards, and then the ceremonial return of the poor suitor to the in-laws' house after clearing the UPSC examination. On the youth of Aramganj, the impact of this marriage is no less than the impact of the fall of the Berlin Wall on geopolitics. The girls of Aramganj—who had been losing hope despite the rigorous cleaning up of complexion with Fair and Lovely and the strict observance of fasts in order to appease Goddess Katyayani and obtain a coveted life-partner—can now feel their hibernating desires awaken.

Not just one, there are many versions of Puja and Dilip's love story doing the rounds. Professor bhaiyya, meaning Harendra Yadav, explains to the boys of the gali. 'Had Dilip not got into the UPSC, would the girl have married him? Not at all. The question does not arise. Puja fell in love only because Dilip had the potential to become an IAS officer. Education is paramount. The one instrument that can pull down all walls, of caste and religion, rich and poor. That is why I say, stay focused and keep your ambitions high. If you study well, then you'll get into the UPSC; if not the UPSC, then the State Public Service Commission; or if not that, the Staff Selection Commission. Meaning, somewhere or the other, you will get selected. *Arre*, if nothing else, you will be qualified enough to give four or five tuitions. You won't starve.'

Amir Khan and Madhuri Dixit have sung many romantic songs by now. The film is moving towards its climax—the junk-dealer Hazari Prasad's son finally wins over the millionaire businessman's daughter—if love is true, anything is possible. Puja's friend Sweety's eyes have filled up with tears. Choked with emotion, Chaya, too, stares at the screen. Sachin steals a look at one, and then the other. Dilip sits expressionlessly, ramrod straight, waiting for the movie to finish.

Elaborately detailed stories of this historical evening reach every household in Aramganj. *For her old friends from the chowk, only Lord Satyanarayan's prasad, and for these new girls from outside, dinner at Odeon and an Amir–Madhuri movie! Fancy people, fancy things. To each their own luck!* But there's no doubt that the younger generation in Aramganj is feeling aspirational after a long time.

Ripu, who had lost standing due to his bad-charactered sister and 'Lohar' brother-in-law, now roams the streets with a puffed-out chest. Dilip will remain busy throughout the day tomorrow: boys from the chowk will line up before their collective brother-in-law, aka *jiju*, for career counselling from morning till evening. The gali people will also get a chance. Dilip will also go with his wife to visit his uncle, the one who works as a fabricator, the one in whose home he had stayed and studied, and the one who narrowly escaped a gunshot because of him.

14

THE VULTURES RETURN

The clock ticks on. Time gallops at great speed. Without anyone realising, Holi ends. Dussehra comes and goes. Today is the third of October. It's past eleven in the morning. There is no major bustle on the street. A lone figure slowly walks towards the shop.

A lean body, fair complexion, big eyes. Ashiq looks at the poster of Ram-Sita-Lakshman pasted on the wall inside his shop. Yes, Abha didi looks exactly like Sita maiyya. Didi's full name is Abha Asthana. Her voice seems to be dipped in honey. She was doing an MA in English when she got married. She wanted to be a lecturer. But entangled as she is in household affairs, how can any profession be possible? After all, it is her responsibility to look after the needs of her old mother-in-law, husband and son.

Once every week or so, Abha invariably comes to Ashiq's shop for some work or the other. Since the Basanti chachi episode, Ashiq has minimised his interaction with women. But his equation with Abha didi is different. Passing through the four-by-two door, Ashiq at once reaches the counter of Savitri Ladies Boutique. Didi hands him an old dupatta for dyeing in a light shade of green, and starts talking about this and that. Asking him about home and family, talking of Shami and Ayesha. After some time, she comes to the real issue.

'Ashiq, have you ever seen the vultures that perch on the peepul tree in front of my house?'

The question strikes Ashiq as being a bit strange. After giving it some thought, Ashiq replies, 'I have not seen them, but if there is a tree, they can certainly come to it.'

'They can come, no? I also keep saying that the vultures have returned, but he will not accept it. Says, the vultures are gone now. Finished! But I keep seeing them sitting on the tree. The vultures are very ominous, isn't that true?'

Ashiq cannot understand what Abha is trying to say.

Abha goes on, 'My grandmother used to say that vultures feed on the dead. That is why they want more deaths to occur. I find them repulsive. I often see them in my dreams and get terrified.'

'*Arre*, no, didi, there is nothing to fear. Even Jatayu maharaj was a vulture. He gave up his life to save Sita-ji from Ravan. What's there in a dream? Anything crazy might happen in a dream.' As he says this, Ashiq tries to read Abha's face. She doesn't look very convinced.

'Okay then, do one thing. Get a Ram-raksha Stotra and keep it under your pillow. The nightmares will stop on their own.' Ashiq knows that the Sanskrit book of hymns in praise of Lord Ram can never fail in putting fears to rest.

'Is that true?' Abha asks.

'This remedy was vouched for by Pandey baba. No bad dreams will ever chase you after this. If what I say is wrong, keep a dog by my name.'

'*Dhatt!*' Abha smiles. Her face now has a tranquillity which wasn't there before. After she leaves, Ashiq starts thinking— when was the last time he had seen a vulture. He remembers his childhood days. On their way back home after playing, some friends of his would always stop to peer down the narrow old bridge. Early every morning, men would skin dead animals there. Seeing flocks of kids coming in their direction, they would warn, 'Scram from here. The work being done here is gory. You'll get such nightmares that you will wet the bed.'

But the children were curious not so much about the men as about the vultures and dogs that sat at a short distance from them, patiently waiting to grab at the cast away remains. If the dogs barked, the vultures, too, emitted a strange sound, opening their huge wings wide. The barking dogs would step back in alarm, before gathering the courage to advance again. The children enjoyed watching these scenes.

But Ashiq could never muster the courage to peer down the bridge. Some of his friends were daredevils. They would throw stones at the dogs and vultures. The dogs barked back angrily, while the men skinning the animals hurled filthy abuses at the boys.

One day, one of the boys cried out excitedly, 'Look at that. What a hit!' Thrilled, the other kids clapped. Ashiq too could not restrain himself from turning back and taking a look. It seemed that someone was writhing under a black blanket. A massive vulture's half-broken neck dangled to one side. The blood-stained murderous brick lay nearby. A few steps away, the vulture-dog banquet continued unimpeded over a dead animal's carcass. For days, Ashiq could not get that dying vulture out of his mind. If the one who eats the flesh of dead animals is abominable, what degree of abomination fits the one who takes another's life for no reason?

Startled by a loudly blowing horn, Ashiq emerges from his reverie. Akhilesh is standing right outside his shop. 'Come, *bey*, Maryada Purushottam!'

'You can call me whatever you want. But no *abey-tabey* with God's name. And ... why on earth did you toot the horn so loudly? Can't you see this is a shop?'

'I have come to fetch you for God's work only, oh great devotee. There is a road renaming function,' said Akhilesh

Jatashankar Sharma's face floats before Ashiq's eyes. He had totally forgotten. Asking Hanif to look after the shop, Ashiq hops on the pillion. The motorcycle stops at the entry point to Rayyat Toli. A total of thirty or forty people stand there. Most of them seem to be volunteers. A loudspeaker has been tied to a pole, and a diligent worker is testing the mike, chanting without a break: hullo, hullo, microphone testing, one, two, three ...

As soon as Jatashankar sets eyes on Ashiq, he says, 'Come, come, Rambhakt Vibheeshan, the coronation hasn't taken place as yet, but looks like you are already a king.'

Ashiq bows slightly, as if touching Jata's feet. Depending on his mood, Jatashankar Sharma calls Ashiq by different names. At times Hanuman, at other times Angad; sometimes Sugreev, at other times Jamwant. All the Ramayan characters who helped Lord Ram in his fight against Ravan. Today, the name Vibheeshan has caught his fancy—Ravan's treacherous brother who gave away Ravan's secrets to enable Ram to seize Lanka. Has he called him Vibheeshan today because it's fitting, or because he's simply in the mood to call him that? Who can say for sure?

'So you have come ambling by yourself? Didn't Kaka-ji tell you to bring along some boys from Rayyat Toli?' Manoj, posing as the second in command, rebukes Ashiq, while waving at the mike testing volunteer to be quiet.

'Who will be at hand at this hour, everyone must be out at work.' Ashiq gives his excuse.

'Don't you take tension, Tailor Master. No one here is relying on you. We have already made all the arrangements,' Manoj says with a flourish, pointing at Fazlu.

With Fazlu is Nazrul. And right next to him stands Imroz, sticking his yellow teeth out. The three most useless faces from Rayyat Toli. All gamblers and pot-smokers of the first order. Almost every alternate day, they get thrashed by someone or the other. Besides them, three or four more poverty-stricken adolescents hang round the corner, waiting for the function to begin. Away from them all, clinging to a pole, stands the cobbler, Gopal, his eyes brimming with a familiar fear-tinged curiosity.

Sarvdaman babu is seen arriving with a few other chowk worthies in tow. Jatashankar runs to receive him. 'See, the real chief guest has come! Let us begin quickly. I have to go for a party meeting, I don't have much time.'

When Sarvdaman babu asks after Shalabhmani Tripathi, it is reported that he has gone to Delhi for some programme. 'This Bhumihar Jatashankar is so cunning. After learning the ropes from Tripathi-ji, he has deliberately organised this rechristening when the big man is out of town. Had Tripathi-ji been here, Jata would have been obliged to get the naming ceremony of Shri Ram Path performed by him,' Chaube-ji whispers to Sarvdaman babu. Both relegate to a corner.

Jatashankar Sharma's followers and hangers-on have made the arrangements. A stone draped over with a cloth has been placed on the turn of the road, exactly in front of Ashiq's late guru Indradev Pandey's house. When Jatashankar Sharma lifts up the cloth, these words can be seen carved in the stone: 'Today, on 3 October 1990, Shri Ram Path was inaugurated by the lotus-like hands of the staunch fighter and popular leader Jatashankar Sharma.'

Chants rise from many a throat: 'Jai Shri Ram!'

But there is no real zeal in the chants. Kamlesh again shouts, 'JAI SHRI RAM!' Some young rascals chant after him. But the older folks keep standing speechlessly, as if they have come to attend a condolence meeting. Meanwhile, a face pokes through the crowd and raises a loud, shrill cry: 'Bee bill bid the tempul deyaar.'

Seeing Baiju, some break into laughter, but Jatashankar stays serious.

Today is a big day in his life. His guru Jagdhari likes to say, 'If you want to succeed in politics, learn to raise a mass movement.' But big leaders do not understand anything. 'Can one orchestrate a mass movement overnight? Is mass movement a thing that can be made to rise at once by applying a *sanda-ka-tel*-like manhood potion?' Still, Jatashankar is doing his best to create one with his 'refreshingly original' idea of renaming a road. And this is only the beginning.

Manoj starts distributing *pedas*. Kamlesh Singh slaps his forehead in frustration. The idiot does not even know that the prasad is to be distributed only towards the end. The indigent invitees start slinking off as soon as they receive the pedas. Kamlesh Singh announces in a loud voice, 'I now request our popular, most respected leader, Jatashankar Sharma-ji to grace the stage and say a few words.'

But where is the stage! Jatashankar starts speaking from where he is standing. The mike, too, turns out to be as faithless as the public slinking away after gobbling down the pedas. Had it not been a public place, Jata babu would have made the owner of Shiv Sound see the error of his ways in chaste Hindi. But with great restraint, he continues making his speech without the aid of a mike. He says that this renaming is not just a matter of pride for Aramganj, but for the people of Rayyat Toli as well. Because, instead of being called 'Mini Pakistan-walas', they will now be called 'the dwellers of Shri Ram Path'.

Looking restlessly at his watch, Kamlesh Singh says, 'The press hasn't arrived yet.' People look towards Nirmal Jain, a stringer for half a dozen newspapers headquartered in Delhi and Mumbai. But he is of no use to Jatashankar—a local man is required here. Only when the photographer of *Deshdeep Times*, Roopnath Jha, is seen arriving, does Jata babu's smile widen. The whole drill of the inauguration ceremony is repeated. All the honourable residents of the chowk stand once more on either side of Jatashankar. Fazlu and Imroz, too, are eager to squeeze into the frame, but Sarvdaman babu casts such a scorching look that they stay where they are. When the photographer tells them to look into the camera, Jatashankar Sharma shrieks, '*Arre*, where is Rambhakt Vibheeshan?'

'I am here, Kaka-ji.' Ashiq waves his hand.

In reply, Jatashankar Sharma asks him to come forward. Ashiq hesitates. Sarvdaman Singh says, 'Don't we know he's the top-most VIP at the chowk. Hey! Can't you see, you are being summoned by the leader?'

Ashiq quietly steps forward and stands in a corner of the frame.

'*Arre*, not there, come here.' Jatashankar Sharma catches him by the neck and pulls him next to himself, giving him two-three 'apparently affectionate' smacks on the back. Body language is an eloquent thing. Ashiq has a feeling that some of his chowk friends, too, have begun expressing intimacy in a similar fashion these days. He doesn't know why he senses a concealed intention to hurt or injure in these over-friendly pats and pushes.

After the photo-session, the programme is duly concluded. Showing great familiarity with the photographer, Jatashankar says, 'Why don't you come to my place? Have some tea. I am getting a press note prepared. Take that too.' But the photographer does not show any interest, saying he is busy and must go, and that the press note will be sent from *his* end to Jata's office by evening. The crowd disperses and everyone walks off to their homes. Ashiq also makes for the shop.

The next day, the chowk is abuzz with a new piece of news. 'If not today, then tomorrow, Ashiqwa will definitely fight the municipal elections.' This news creates a frisson in Mangal's paan-shop and, in the blink of an eye, spreads to the farthest corners of the chowk. A photograph printed on page-three of *Deshdeep Times* is the basis of this news. In it, the local neta-ji is performing the naming ceremony of Shri Ram Path, and the unflappable Rambhakt, aka Ashiqwa, is standing next to him, his chest puffed out.

Even more significant and baffling than the picture is the text printed below, praising the popular people's leader Jatashankar Sharma. It also states that Sheikh Nizamuddin Wali Ashiq, a social activist from the Muslim community, said, that with this renaming his long-cherished dream has come true.

For the chowk shopkeepers, this photograph of Ashiq with Jatashankar Sharma in the paper is the biggest news of all. However, the chowk intellectuals read something else into this. That Jatashankar has cleverly sidelined Shalabhmani Tripathi. Tripathi-ji may be a scholarly man, but politics is a different ballgame altogether. Jatashankar has a strong rapport with Jagdhari Singh, whose connections go all the way to Delhi. Meaning, Jatashankar is swiftly climbing up the ladder of politics.

'Instead of Jata, this man should be called "Jhanta" or "Crotch Hair" Shankar—he is like a flea that burrows in the crotch hair of important men, initially inducing only a pleasantly addictive itch. But sensing an opportunity, he suddenly bites so viciously, as to cause the poor man to leap up in the middle of the bazaar, holding on to his dhoti!' It is Tripathi-ji's turn to jump now. A trunk call informed him that his follower conspired and dealt an ace in his absence. But Tripathi-ji is one of those people who eat only after the meal has cooled off. Possibly, he never did jump. But even so, he must surely have uttered 'Hey Hari!', rubbing himself tenderly.

The moniker 'Crotch Hair Shankar' is Om-ji's coinage. Hence the most authentic analysis of this news should be given by him. If the rest at the chowk try to discreetly slink away on seeing Om-ji, Jatashankar takes swift, long strides. Several stories shine a light on the background to this antipathy. The most recounted incident is from Rajnarain Singh's younger son's marriage entourage. Three buses carrying the wedding party were going to Sherghati. Jatashankar babu lay sprawled on a double seat of one of these buses. Three or four young men who had imbibed whiskey and rum occupied the back seats. On the very last seat, Om-ji reclined, having smoked pot. Truth be told, as per the custom of a wedding party, even Jatashankar had had a few. The lights had been switched off and people were dozing. Suddenly, the staunch leader shrieked in a terrified voice, '*Hai ge mai!*'

People sitting in the front seats asked, '*Arre*, what happened?'

'It felt like someone slapped my head.'

'Really?'

'There is no one here.'

'Are you sure you weren't dreaming?'

'*Arre*, no bhai. Someone is here. Some *sasura* rascal!'

'The bus must have jumped over a speed-breaker. Go back to sleep.'

No one paid much attention to Jatashankar's mysterious experience. Fifteen minutes later, the same terrified sound issued from Jatashankar's mouth. This time it was followed by two-three choice abuses as well. In fact, he got up from his seat, checked both in the front and behind, waking up half-asleep young men. But nothing came out of this search. The bus kept going.

The incident was about to recur a third time, but Jata caught hold of the attacker's wrist in a tight grip, simultaneously flipping on a torch. But the unknown criminal was a step ahead. In one-tenth of a second, he lifted his lungi to cover his face. Jatashankar clearly and closely saw everything except the face. In sheer disgust, the torch fell from his hand.

The bus was made to stop. The buses behind them were also made to stop. Jatashankar Sharma was so enraged that for ten minutes he couldn't coherently tell what had happened. With great difficulty, he brought Om-ji's name to his lips. But Om-ji wasn't on that bus. He was found asleep on some other bus. Despite a thousand efforts, not one witness could be found to say that Om-ji had been on that bus and was behind the sordid nuisance.

Jatashankar threatened to go back. But how could one go back at night from the middle of a jungle? With great effort, he was persuaded by the groom's father, Rajnarain Singh, and was seated next to Rajnarain himself on another bus. The whole mohalla knows that the unknown criminal was none other than Om-ji. But nothing was proved and no one brought to justice.

Sarvdaman Singh also knows that this *haramipana,* this entire misbegotten enterprise is Jhantwa's handiwork. Snaring him, Jata picked the costliest tiles from his construction site, but had only his own name engraved on the foundation stone. Even that could have been overlooked. If he wants to raise his political profile, let him do so. But what about the thing printed in the newspaper?

Thakur Sarvdaman Singh stood in the hot sun for over an hour, along with Madhukar Chaube, Vibhuti Mishra and Lakshmikant Sahay, but there wasn't even a passing mention of them in the report! When asked, Jata simply said, 'I wrote down all the names in the press note, how is it my fault if the newspaper decided not to publish them?'

'If names were to be dropped, wouldn't the newspaper-walas have dropped Ashiqwa's name? If Jata wants to be the leader of the Hindus, why did he give the name of that *katua*, Ashiq? If this isn't Muslim appeasement, what is?'

When Kamlesh hears this allegation as he noisily sips tea at Bajrangi's dhaba, he carelessly shrugs it off. 'It's not appeasement, it is something else. Just wait and see how everything pans out.'

Ashiq, too, has been hearing the phrase 'Muslim appeasement' since morning. People are saying that now there are two VIPs at this chowk: Jatashankar Sharma and the Two-in-One tailor, Ashiq Rangbaz. He is so exhausted by all the clarifications, taunts and congratulatory wishes from the chowk people that he hasn't really paid attention to what exactly has been printed in the newspaper.

Ashiq recalls that when he was returning home after shutting shop last night, he sensed a strange restlessness in Rayyat Toli. Someone called out, 'Will you be at peace only after destroying us, Misir?' Ashiq does not remember exactly who it was. Ashiq never pays attention to random voices like these. Today his name has featured in the newspaper. What must the people there be thinking? But how would they find out? After all, who reads the news in Rayyat Toli! Had they known how to read and write, would their lives have been like this?

Ashiq reaches home, washes his face, and sits down on a low stool in front of the kitchen. Zulekha silently places roti-tarkari before him. Ashiq starts swallowing the morsels wordlessly. Ayesha is already asleep beside her grandmother. Shami is rubbing his eyes, as if warding off sleep. As soon as Ashiq swallows the last morsel, Shami asks, 'Abbu, are we Muslims or Hindus?'

These innocent questions are not new for Ashiq. But today's question stirs up a strange annoyance in Ashiq. Even so, he affectionately asks, 'You tell me, son—what do *you* feel we are?'

'Today Rahim was saying, your abba is a Hindu.'

Ashiq gets up laughing. But Zulekha, who has been standing before him, flares up. She says, 'Don't ever play with that lowlife, luckless boy again. Let them find the guts to say this to my face. Who goes to whose house, who comes from where—I will tell all!'

'*Arre*, why are you getting so angry?'

'What else should I do, if not get angry? Should I sit in the bazaar and invite people to come and humiliate me? Someone makes things up about someone's spouse, and her husband says, don't get angry. What can be said for such a man! Allah has given brains to the entire universe except my husband.'

'Don't talk nonsense. How does your character figure in all this?'

'*Hai Allah!* You brain is so full of shit. Will this also have to be explained to you as to who is being abused when someone calls your child the son of a Hindu? You go and live at your Aramganj Chowk and leave us to our fate.'

Zulekha Bano drags Shami by the hand to her room, bolting the door from the inside. Only two or three times since their marriage has Ashiq seen her so enraged. The bolting of the door means Ashiq will have to sleep on the cot in the courtyard. Now even if she calls, he will not go inside. The whole world's stubbornness pales before Ashiq's. Should he make up his mind, he could put even his neck on the block. And yet, he refuses to bow before anyone.

He has never seen Zulekha flare up like this at the very mention of the word 'Hindu'. When people tease Ashiq, calling him Misir-ji, he experiences a strange pleasure. The idea that this teasing could connote something vulgar hasn't occured to him before. But after Zulekha's outburst, strange thoughts begin to haunt him. What if the people calling him Misir-ji are deriving the same pleasure one feels after calling the enemy a 'motherfucker'?

'Will you be at peace only after destroying us, Misir.' The voice he heard last night was perhaps that of Rakibul's son, Mohsin.

If the rest in Rayyat Toli are 'us', who is Ashiq? He comes to Rayyat Toli only to sleep, just as he goes to Aramganj only to work. And it's not just the shop—his whole life is in Aramganj. But do the people living there think the same way? Vibheeshan, Sugreev, Jamwant, Nishad-raj—the various names he is addressed by ring in his ears, enveloped in Jatashankar's evil laughter.

15

CHINTU'S DISQUIET AND A MARCH FOR PEACE

Chintu is in deep trauma since morning. As soon as he had stepped out for 'research' at daybreak, binoculars around the neck, he was struck by a fiasco. To move forward in life, some calculated risks need to be taken. For how long, after all, could Chintu have kept riding the stallions of fantasy by merely ogling at the ladies' undergarments set out to dry on Verma-ji's terrace? The 'geography', meaning the structure, of Verma-ji's house was unlikely to change. No matter how long Chintua lay in wait—draped like a commando over the water tank—the bathroom window would stay where it was. All he ever saw were hands—adjusting the shower knob, or taking off a hair-band. Nothing beyond that.

So, changing his 'Look East Policy', Chintu began looking west. There is a public stepwell in the low-caste Bhuiyan Toli, where their women bathe early every morning. This was revealed to Chintua through his binoculars. The scene was potentially magnificent, but such was the distance, that the finer details weren't really visible. So, like a committed student of Biology, with binoculars around his neck, out went Chintua.

After a careful application of mind, he singled out a point on a large hillock, at a certain angle from which he could get a clear view of the bathing beauties without them ever sensing that a naughty Lord Krishna was soothing his eyes close by. Clutching his binoculars, Chintu had just started climbing the hillock, when a clod flew by his ear, hitting him on the shoulder. When he ran his eyes around, he saw a boy standing below, catapult in hand, and with a friend by his side.

'Who are you, *bey*? What are you doing here at such an early hour?'

'I am an ishtudent, doing research,' Chintu answered, rubbing his shoulder.

The boy waved at him to come down.

'Right, so if you are an ishtudent, let us give you tuition.' And the boy with the catapult caught Radhey babu's sixth offspring by the collar.

'Hey you! Be civil. Don't you know who I am? If Kamlesh bhaiyya finds out—'

Hearing this, the second boy gave Chintu a tight slap. Subsequently, the proud owner of the tallest building on the chowk, Sandeep Shrivastav, aka Chintu, was made to hold his ears and squat up and down ten times. The twenty rupees he had in his pocket were also confiscated by the investigating officers. But the worst—was the confiscation of his Calcutta-bought binoculars.

The looted and beaten Chintu went straight to Kamlesh Singh's house and, in a single breath, related how the scoundrels of Bhuiyan Toli had wreaked havoc on him—all because he lived on the chowk, belonged to a forward caste, and was Kamlesh Singh's wingman.

On hearing this tale, Kamlesh Singh laughed for a while, and then said, 'Lala-ji, when even pulling a radish out of soil is beyond you, what made you go on patrol in an area full of criminals!'

Chintu beseeched: 'Bhaiyya, never again will I go there, but please get me my binoculars back, they were an expensive purchase.'

Kamlesh turned serious. 'Go and talk to Alokwa. The Bhuiyan Toli boys are his sidekicks. If you still don't get it back, tell me. I will see what can be done. Right now is not the time for fomenting spats in any Hindu area. There's too much tension in the town.'

Truly, there is too much tension. The Ram Rath is far away, but the direction of the wind is visible. A curfew has been imposed in many neighbouring towns. The administration in Aramganj, too, is on high alert. The district administrator has been directed to brief the home secretary twice a day.

In this tension-laden atmosphere, some people are slowly gathering at the Kutchery Chowk. They stand in groups under trees, talking. The rickshaw-pullers and hawkers cannot make out what is up.

Many people are holding banners in their hands, on which a variety of slogans and couplets are written in a beautiful hand.

> *'Insaan se insaan ka ho bhaichaara, yeh paigam hamara'*
> *'Na main Hindu na main Musalman, main toh bas ek insaan'*
> *'Jiyo aur jeene do'*

> 'Universal brotherhood for universal good'
> 'Neither Hindu nor Muslim, I am just a human being'
> 'Live and let live'

In no time, a crowd big enough to form a small procession has gathered. This procession of writers, journalists, students and cultural activists will commence from Kutchery Chowk, and pass through the mohallas spread on both sides of the Main Road. An appeal will be made to people that they step out of their houses and join the peace march.

On the right side of the Main Road are rich Hindu settlements where Punjabis, Marwaris and Bengalis live. To the left are mixed pockets; tucked between old Hindu houses lie Muslim pockets like Karbala Chowk. It is decided that after winding through the lanes on both sides, the procession will assemble on the ground in front of the station, where the participants will peacefully conclude the programme after a small public gathering before the Gandhi statue.

A tempo mounted with a sound system and decorated with banners calling for unity leads from the front. The people walk behind it. The town's famous theatre personality and poet, Ashok Anchal stands atop the tempo.

Mike in hand, the slender-bodied Anchal sings a song for peace with great intensity.

> *'Insaniyat ka jazba har dil mein jagana hai*
> *Har qaum se nafrat ko mil-jul ke mitana hai'*

Following after the poet, a chorus of voices repeats:

> *'Har qaum se nafrat ko mil-jul ke mitana hai ...'*

The procession first enters Prem Ratan Street. People watch this spectacle from their terraces in amazement. Many processions often pass by this street—the Ramnavami tableaus, Shivaji's baraat—but this somehow looks different. In the two-hundred-strong crowd, there perhaps are twenty-five to thirty women too, who, going by their dress and deportment, look like activists. There are some college girls too. Vibha and Shambhavi are holding a big banner with lines from one of young activist Rajesh's poems:

> *'Aap jiska ugaya gehun khaate hain*
> *Kya uska mazhab jaante hain?'*

'The one who grows the wheat you eat,
Do you know which god's name he repeats?'

The peace march proceeds slowly. In between, people keep joining in ones and twos. Over the mike, Ashok Anchal, in his deep voice, exhorts people to come forward. 'This town needs peace. We will not let riots and strife occur here. Please step out of your homes and send the message of peace to every single person.'

When the march arrives at Loha Mandi, it is heard that Saanwarmal Maroo, the leader of businessmen, will himself felicitate the procession at his door. But the minute someone tells him that the tempo has a banner calling for declaring the Ramjanmabhoomi-Babri Masjid complex a national monument, he backtracks.

'It's okay to talk of peace, et cetera. We need it too. But how can we compromise on ideology?' he tells Trideb Ghosh, one of the coordinators of the peace march.

Parag, the town's upcoming writer and Aramganj resident, has toiled for almost a week to mobilise the students. Turning his neck around, he tries to count them. Sudhir, Praveen, Kamal have come; but there is no sign of many others who had seemed enthusiastic. When the procession enters the lanes to the left of Main Road, he sees the count go down by almost forty to fifty.

The painter Himanshu Bose says, 'What's new about this? Even when a dead body is carried from Marwari Tola to Poorna Ghat, one finds that half the people have vanished by the time the procession reaches the cremation ground.'

When the procession passes through Meena Bazaar, Ashok the poet hails his old friend and advocate Rouf Siddiqui to come and join. Rouf comes out, bows and says his salaams, but refuses to join the march.

'The times are very bad. When people like you come out into the streets, you get the tag of being progressive. But if we come out, we will be tagged as rioters. This is what's written in the fate of Hindustani Muslims.'

Rouf's words pierce Ashok's heart. He says, 'Peace is essential for all. If educated people don't raise their voices for peace, who will?'

Rouf's brother Rifat is standing beside him, looking angry. He says, 'Sahib, please save this lecture on peace for those who bang drums every day, screaming into our ears, "we will build the temple there itself". When what is to be done has already been decided, why come here to mislead the Muslims, so that we are forced to silently bear whatever injustice is done to us.'

While saying this, Rifat's gaze is fixed on the banner pinned to the tempo's flanks, on which is written—'Declare the Ramjanmabhoomi-Babri Masjid complex a national monument.'

Rouf gestures at his brother to be quiet and says, 'Ashok-ji, I've known you for the last thirty years. I have great regard for you. That's why, with folded hands, I beg you to excuse us. Our well-being lies in staying away from such muddles.'

Khalid, the first to take part in any cultural activity in town, who participated in the organisation of this rally right from the very beginning, looks on shamefacedly, as if trying to say, what can I say about them? I am with you people.

> *'Insaniyat ka jazba har dil mein jagana hai*
> *Har qaum se nafrat ko mil-jul ke mitana hai'*

Ashok Anchal continues to sing on the mike.

> 'From every group let's rub hatred out
> Kindle brotherly love in every heart'

His voice still carries the same sweet timbre and confidence as on Kutchery Chowk; but the energy levels of those singing the chorus have gone down. Peace marches have been taken out many times in this town before. And every time, the same fifty or hundred familiar faces participate. Apart from a few new faces, the story this time, too, is the same.

'The biggest trouble with educated people is that they believe that they know everything. Perhaps none of us has a true understanding of this society. Peace is the biggest imperative of this hour. The purpose of this programme is to tell that if there is a fire in the town, all houses will get burnt. At a time like this, raising the slogan, *declare the disputed site a national monument* is misguided. You can see for yourself how it's making both Hindus and Muslims balk.' Peace-walker and senior writer Vidyabhushan says to writer Samaresh Samar.

In reply, Samaresh Samar delivers a mini-lecture on the rise of Fascism in the twentieth century, and comes to the role of the US in the Cold War. Taking a pause at the Soviet's disintegration, he summarises: 'To talk only of immediate peace is to take a revisionist approach. We need revolutionary ideas. Through this peace march, we had the option of demanding that properties of all religious organisations be confiscated and nationalised. But we've missed it. Religion is opium. And till the country comes out of its intoxication, nothing can be done.'

Now the procession arrives at the mouth of Karbala Chowk. The very mohalla where an incident of knifing occurred a week back. The railway station is quite close from here. The peace marchers in the front can see a huge police picket here. Three or four Jeeps are parked across the road to deliberately block the march.

On seeing the police, suddenly, the chorus revives, and everyone's voice soars.

'From every group let's rub hatred out
Kindle brotherly love in every heart'

'You must turn back. You don't have the permission to go further,' says a police officer, who is probably an inspector.

'Why should we turn back? Is calling for peace in the town now a crime?' Comrade Ghosh walks to the front and says. On seeing him, many realise that this is not a procession by cultural outfits, but of one of the Communist parties in town.

'Establishing peace is the police's job. Leave it to us.'

'You mean, the citizen of this country has no responsibility? If the police is so capable of establishing peace, then why is there so much rioting and strife everywhere? You have no problem with religious processions, but you get troubled by an appeal for peace,' Ghosh babu says in a single breath.

The inspector and Ghosh babu keep arguing. After sometime, the city SP gets down from a vehicle. Taking the leaders of the procession to a corner, he explains that the situation in town has turned volatile all of a sudden. Section 144 has been imposed, and quite possibly, by tonight, a curfew will be declared. Hence the peace march will have to conclude right here.

16

CURFEW, MY FOOT!

On their way back from the failed peace march, the handful of Aramganj-walas—Parag, Rajesh, Satyaprakash and Vivek—observe shutters of shops all along the way being yanked down with a clatter. The evening edition of *Deshdeep Times* is out, and people gathered at crossings are reading the news anxiously.

The headline reads, 'Riot in Jaipur Claims Two Brothers from Town'.

From the headline it appears that both have died in communal riots. But on reading the whole news, it is found that while one brother is somewhat critical, the other has been discharged from the hospital after treatment. On getting this news, the boys' father left for Jaipur.

A shop has been set on fire in Chandpur, the part of the town these boys hail from. Despite the imposition of Section 144 in town, people are huddled together in groups at many spots, reading the newspaper aloud. The four youths—Parag, Rajesh, Satyaprakash and Vivek—are headed towards Aramganj. As soon as they reach the Rayyat Toli patch, Rajesh hesitates. 'Is it okay to venture through?' This question crosses the minds of others as well. Parag and Rajesh both live on the chowk. Vivek and Satyaprakash stay a little further from there, in Vidyanagar. They decide that as it takes hardly more than five minutes to cross Rayyat Toli, they will simply gallop through. What else! But upon entering Rayyat Toli, they find that there is no need to gallop. They can pace through leisurely, like on any other day. Goats and defecating kids are nowhere to be seen on the street today, but yes, the chickens can still be spotted.

A little later, the group of four arrives at the ground called Imli Maidan by the Rayyat Toli residents. It's hardly a ground, merely an empty area of around a thousand square metres, with the remains of an old stepwell now chock-full with rubbish, and two tamarind trees from which it derives its name. The Rayyat Toli residents use this ground for community purposes, for weddings, feasts, et cetera. The rest of the time, the empty space is used either by goats to graze or by children to play.

A few anxious-looking people can be seen on the *chabootra* under the tamarind tree. Before them is a radio. Newspaper in hand, an old man is telling the people something. The new generation of Aramganj does not know him. But old-timers are well-acquainted with Hakim Ismail.

Hakim Ismail had fairly good social relations with the chowk's previous generation. He would visit people like Mukut babu, who had a deep interest in Homeopathy and Unani medicine systems. Hakim Ismail has the successful treatment of Basant babu's daughter's epilepsy to his credit, and Prabhat Dayal's 'inflammation', a shorthand for venereal disease.

But Hakim sahib is more renowned as a Maulavi. He reads out holy verses—the *kalma*—for the sick, and gives them 'miracle-water'. He knows how to exorcise victims of snake and scorpion bites.

With the passing away of the old-timers, Hakim sahib's link with the chowk has become a thing of the past. Even otherwise, he is nearing eighty now. Among the four Aramganj youth, none except Satyaprakash recognises Hakim sahib; but they all recognise Fazlu. Standing against one of the tamarind trees, Fazlu casts a scorching gaze at them. Who would believe that the same fellow was playing the role of a simpering representative of Rayyat Toli at Jatashankar's Shri Ram Path function!

The moment the four of them arrive at the mouth of the lane leading out of Rayyat Toli, near Inderdev Pandey's house, Vivek shouts, 'Look behind you. The house there has Pakistan's flag fluttering atop it.'

Parag says, 'It isn't Pakistan's flag, it's their religious flag. They must have hung it to mark the Chehlum festival that just went by.'

'No, it is the Pakistani flag. It has a star and a sickle moon on it.'

'*Arre*, bhai, Pakistan's flag has a white band on it. And the position of the star and sickle moon is different than that in the Islamic flag.'

'*Saala!* Why must these people have such a confusing flag? Everyone is bound to think, no, that it is Pakistan's flag, aren't they?'

Marching, the group arrives in Aramganj's heartland, that is, at the chowk. The evening's atmosphere is as unlike the morning's as the earth is unlike the sky. Every fifteen to twenty metres, a different group is gathered. The maximum crowds are at Mangal's paan-shop and at Ojha-ji's kiosk. People are quickly lining up in queues outside grocery shops to stock up. The stationery, radio–TV repair and electricals shops have already been shuttered. The remaining shopkeepers are awaiting confirmation of the news.

Not one, but there are many bits of news. First: the town is under curfew. Second: an incident of knifing has occurred in Gudadi Bazaar. Besides these, everyone already knows about the shop set on fire in Chandpur.

'Musalman businessman Jalil Shah, from Kaanta Toli, has ordered two hundred drums of kerosene. If there is a fire, just think how many Hindu houses would get incinerated.' This is Satya bhaiyya, whose full name is Satyanand Tiwari. He is Nityanand Tiwari's double MA son, who has no interest in any 'work'. That's why he never took up any job, and remains unmarried despite crossing forty. He can latch on to a line of any information floating in the air, and cook up an elaborate story to entertain the listeners.

'Two hundred drums! There won't be that much kerosene in the whole town! Satya bhaiyya, at least think before you say such things,' says Vivek.

'*Arre*, reduce the number a bit, what else! But it is verified news that Jalil Shah has ordered the kerosene oil. A bomb went off at Karbala Chowk. At least fifteen have been injured, who knows how many will survive!'

'A bomb blast at Karbala Chowk? When? At what time?'

'Around two o'clock. Akhilesh saw it with his own eyes.'

'Such stories you cook up, bhaiyya! We were there till four o'clock. Nothing happened.' Satyaprakash casts the light of truth on Satya bhaiyya's lie. He wonders whether all his other stories too were plain rumours.

'Ccc ... urrr ... fu. Oh my Faaa ... ther ... Curr ... fu.'

Fussu from Valmiki Nagar suddenly appears at the chowk, running from God knows where. His screaming is of the same style as that of the Copa América commentators shouting GOOAAAL.

CUU ... RR ... FUU ...!

Once a week, a bottle of acid in hand, Fussu makes a back-door entry into the chowk houses. He cleans their toilets and goes back. At the end of the month drops a twenty-rupee note from a foot's height. No need to even meet the eyes!

But today, he has come equipped with news that has not made its way even to the evening edition of *Deshdeep Times*. So it is fitting to talk to him.

'How did you come to know of this, Fussua?'

'CUUU ... RRR ... FU ... is coming. They are announcing from a vehicle, CUU ... RR ... FU ...'

And, making the announcement in the same vein, Fussu enters the Valmiki Nagar lane.

Soon, the echoing sound of the loudspeaker reaches the chowk. The same Aramganj shopkeepers who normally take a full five minutes just to scoop out and weigh one kilo of sugar and half a kilo of flour, now pull down their shutters at lightning speed. Groups standing about here and there start disbanding rapidly. People who had come to have paan, or to gossip, head to their houses. Before leaving, Murli babu bestows this piece of wisdom at Mangal's paan-shop: 'Provided that there is no loss of one's own life or property, one can get more entertainment from a riot than from going to any fair or bar. A curfew is no less than a tamasha being held at your doorstep for free. Enjoy the show as long as it's on.'

Lakshmikant Sahay's whole life has been spent in courts and administration. He intercepts those rushing home: '*Arre* wait, maharaj. Only the announcement is being made. Is anyone firing rounds at you? Why so fearful?'

The Jeep making the announcement comes to a stop. An official is sitting in the back, holding a mike. Sahay-ji recognises him at once. 'This is Singhesar. He used to be my assistant.' From the front seat, a police constable waves his rifle at people, telling them to clear the road.

'What's up, Singhesar? *Arre o!* Singhesar Singh-ji, how do you do?' Sahay-ji asks in an emphatic voice, in order to impress those bravely standing with him. But Singhesar is in full sarkari swagger today. He does not even turn his neck to look at them.

'Don't you know the situation, chacha? Don't crowd the street, or you will be thrown into a lockup. The patrolling party is coming,' the armed constable replies with utter discourtesy.

'Yes ... yes, we are going.' Lakshmikant Sahay starts for his house, mumbling.

Bhola babu says, 'The minute they get power, it goes to their head. He is just a constable ... that Inspector Phoolan—'

'Who? Shukal-ji's son-in-law?' Lakshmikant babu enquires.

'Yes, who else? Inspector Phoolan had once told me, "During the '81 riots, chacha, I felt no less than an army officer fighting on the front. The moment the stone-pelting began in Islam Nagar, picking up the carbine, I fired non-stop."' Bhola babu reminds Lakshmikant babu of the forgotten story.

'And rightly so. But showing such hot-headedness in a Hindu area is not right. Whatever they have to do, they should do in the Musalman basti. Who is indulging in rioting here?' Sahay-ji opens his gate and goes inside. But as he goes, he gives Bhola babu a small sample of his administrative acumen. 'But did policemen even have carbines in 1981? Whosoever you see talks tall these days.'

All shops on the chowk have pulled down shutters. Two-in-One was the first to lower its shutter, but Ashiq is inside the shop. When the tension began, Ashiq instructed Hanif, 'Lock the shutter from the outside. I will lift the shutter of Savitri Boutique to step out when I have to. Go home, and tell your sister-in-law that there's lots of work to do. I will return only by seven or seven-thirty.'

'No, bhaiyya. If I go and say this, she will get angry at me. Please shut everything up, no? When the tension subsides in a day or two, then finish the work. Even otherwise, who will come to collect clothes during this curfew?'

'You see this mountain before me? Eight salwar-suits from Jaiswal-ji of road no. 6. The wedding will hardly stop for this reason.' Who can equal Ashiq's obstinacy? Hanif pulled the shutter down and left.

There's a simple rule for negotiating the streets during a curfew: count to ten every time a police or army vehicle passes through. If it's a cavalcade, the next vehicle will come before you've finished counting. If it doesn't, infer that a vehicle won't come for the next fifteen minutes. This fool-proof formula had been given by Ashiq to chowk-walas in 1984.

The new generation is enthused because since they came of age, they haven't seen a curfew. But those older and more experienced are subdued. 'Fuckers, is this even a curfew? If this lasts longer than a couple of days, change my name.'

'The real riot occurred in 1967, when the counting of dead bodies went on for more than a week. Even the '73 riots were solid. Just to give you a rough idea, half the population of this chowk would have been wiped out but for the strong fight put up by Nanka and Bajrangiya; their resistance changed the game. Before '73, there used to be a Muslim Jolaha basti where the Gwala basti is now. Within fifteen days, the area was cleansed. For a full month, chopped hands and feet kept floating up to the surface of the ghostly pond there. Finally, they had to fill up the whole pond with mud.'

Murli babu sits in his house, recounting macabre events like these to the younger generation, in the same way as one talks about an exciting turning point in a cricket match—like when, after losing wicket after wicket, the home team clinches the game unexpectedly.

'Papa, will the army come?' His youngest asks, full of fervent hope.

'Like hell they will come! The thing is not going to last for more than a couple of days. Tomorrow the BMP will go to the Miyan basti, bash everyone up with lathis, and the whole story will end.'

The youngest son's face falls. There isn't any scope for excitement for the younger generation! They must make do with the stories told by the older generations. In the same vein as in, 'You wouldn't dare to even touch the amount of ghee we ate,' they hear, 'What sort of lame riot is this now—not a patch on the ones we had in our times.'

The elders of Aramganj know that the first twenty-four hours of a curfew are as boring as the first day of a Test cricket match. Radhey babu is chatting on the phone with his fast friend Misir-ji. One disadvantage of a curfew is that even to chat with one's neighbour one must spend money. But the call has been made by Misir-ji who works in the telephone exchange, so there is no worry.

'What a hoax to foist a curfew here! What's the need for all this frippery when Miyans are not even living here!'

'Why? Aren't they living in Rayyat Toli? Must easily be forty-fifty houses.'

'*Bhakk!* Can they even be called Musalmans? They are bangle sellers, washermen, tailors, barbers—who earn daily to eat. If their chulhas are not lit for a day, they will die crying for their fathers. To arrange a real riot, you need someone like Bannu Miyan, the barrister. If from this side, funds were arranged by the rich Sindhi and Marwari brothers of the Business Association, from that side, it was Barrister Bannu. Despite being alone, he was weightier than all of them.'

'Babuji says that during the '47 riots, Barrister Bannu held a rifle and kept firing from his terrace, all by himself. The riots went on for three days, but could anyone dare enter Bannu's mohalla? No. One, he was very wealthy; two, his network was so strong, he supped and dined with Jinnah himself! Had so much property that he couldn't leave it all behind and go, hence he stayed on with his clan. The riots ended, but no one managed to even touch him. Men of his kind are not found anywhere these days!'

Misir-ji's voice is tinged with pain, as if lamenting that an India versus Pakistan cricket match without Imran Khan on the field could hardly be fun. One glance at the envelope, and the elderly can divine the contents of a letter. Till now the curfew hasn't even been properly imposed—but most, along with Misir-ji, are of the same opinion. That this bloody tamasha is not a curfew but a disgrace in the name of a curfew.

The first night of the curfew has fallen. For many at the chowk, it is a night of thrill tinged with fear. But nowhere near what it had been in 1984, when the flames leaping up in different areas of the town could be seen from afar. Tonight, the only thrill falling to people's share comes from stories cobbled together from feverish imagination blended into the screech of patrol sirens.

Ashiq looks carefully at the pile of clothes cut for stitching eight salwar-suits and one lehanga-choli, all 'designer' cuts as per Aramganj's fashion trends. Colours of many festivities twinkle in his eyes. Obsessed with finishing the work, he didn't think even once of what was going on outside. In the dim light of the shop, he casts an eye on the clock now. It is a quarter to eight. But given the stillness outside, it seems as if it is two a.m.

For a long time, ears to the door, Ashiq listens to the sounds outside. There is no major patrolling today. He quickly opens the door to Savitri Ladies Boutique, lifts up the shutter, then locks it from the outside, and after checking to his right and left, swiftly heads home. He has a small torch in his pocket, and a long tailor's scale, which, if required, can be used as a baton.

He is well-acquainted with the dogs at the chowk. And the Rayyat Toli dogs wag their tails when they see him. But the rascals in between Rayyat Toli and Aramganj Chowk cannot be trusted. *The Hindu dogs are my own and so are the Musalman dogs, but the ones who are only dogs, can, at times, chase and bite.* This strange thought makes Ashiq laugh as he walks alone.

Which one is scarier—a riotous mob, or the pin-drop silence of a deserted street? This is the second thought that crosses Ashiq's mind. Right now, only his shadow walks with him, changing pace as he hastens or slows down, and sometimes, even disappearing into darkness like some spirit. He is now at the border of Mini Pakistan, where the signage of 'Shri Ram Path' stands erect, as if welcoming him. The rubbish strewn on the ground during the inauguration function has not been cleared till now. Tonight, the moon competes with the dim lights of the municipality. The peepul tree's trunk, wrapped with countless wish-threads, is just a faint outline.

In such stillness, when someone comes near the peepul, their breath gets stifled, for Inderdev Pandey's haunted house looms close to it. This house arouses fear in everyone except Ashiq. As Ashiq nears it, he hears a strange noise coming from Baba's house. It's like the sound of a wet cloth being flapped.

He switches the torch on and scans the area, but he cannot see anything. He is about to turn away when his eyes fall on a lime bush. Ensnared in a thick spider web, a small bird flutters desperately. Ashiq realises that due to its constant fluttering, the bird's wings are so caught that it can scarcely come out of the web. Ashiq goes to the wall and extends his long scale, but there is still a foot and a half's distance between him and the bird. He picks up a stone then. If he throws it with full force at the top half, maybe the web will collapse and the bird will be freed. But what if by mistake, the stone hits the bird? This is not the solution. The only other way is for him to jump over the gate and go in.

The gate is entirely coated with a thick layer of rust. Ashiq rubs his palms and, holding the edge of the gate, jumps over. It is so dark that one hand cannot see the other. But suddenly comes a stream of light so strong that every leaf of the peepul begins to glitter. Followed by the sound of motorcycles. Unmindful of nettles, Ashiq attaches himself to the inner wall of the compound, like a lizard, so that even if someone were to look inside, they wouldn't see a thing. Ashiq realises that the light-throwing motorcycles are patrol vehicles. Not a single patrol on the chowk—but here, there is a cavalcade of motorcycles! Ashiq is reminded then that this is a Musalman basti.

The sound and light of the motorcycles disappear soon. After remaining stuck to the wall like something lifeless for some time, Ashiq breathes in and, flipping the torch on, moves towards the lime bush where the bird is trapped. The height of the bush isn't much. Coiling the spider web around his scale, he tugs at it, and extends a hand when the bird comes closer. Wrapped in the spider web is this tiny bird, whose heartbeat Ashiq can feel in his palms. But suddenly, an agonising pain racks him. In his childhood, he had seen a *gehuan*, the Indian cobra, emerging from this very place! But thank the lord, there is no snake. It's a thorn from the lime bush. Now blood is dripping from the three-inch gash it has left in his right arm. The bird is in Ashiq's hands. Holding the torch between his teeth, he quickly starts clearing strands of the spider web off its wings. From the bird's round eyes, he makes out that it is a tiny owl.

So, for this foolish baby owl, this *ullu ka pattha*—son-of-an-owl—Ashiq Miyan got himself splattered with blood! Laughter bubbles up inside him, and the torch nearly falls from his mouth.

But regaining his grip on it, he removes the remaining strands of the web from the owl's wings, and opens his fist. Without wasting a moment, the bird disappears into the dark.

Walking on cat's feet, Ashiq opens the gate and enters the courtyard of his house. Quietly, he plucks and crushes a few marigold leaves, and applies the juice to his wound. The blood-flow has staunched now, but if they notice the wound, his family will make his life hell, interrogating him as to how he hurt himself. And telling the truth would mean listening to Zulekha Bano's taunts and advice for half an hour.

So what can Ashiq say? He racks his brain, and gets an idea. He will, like Yudhishthir in the Mahabharat, tell a half-lie. 'This happened because of some *ullu ka pattha*. Who knows why people throw broken bottles on the road! Thank goodness, when I fell, the glass scraped only my elbow and nothing else.'

17

THE CURFEW VIPS

On the first night of the curfew, the chowk elders slept like always—without a care. But the youngsters, in their excitement, slept fitfully. As soon as they woke up, they ran to their terraces. By nine a.m. all the terraces were full, but there was nothing to see except an empty road. It's 11 o'clock now, and a curfew-like atmosphere is finally building up.

When a Matador van with a rifle-barrel jutting out of the front window stops at Aramganj Chowk, the people peering down the terraces immediately retract their heads like turtles. When his son extends his neck again, Durga pandit pulls him back by his shirt collar. An announcement issues from the vehicle.

'People involved in providing essential services will get a curfew pass. Government employees, doctors, journalists may show their identity cards to obtain the passes. Arrangements have been made to drop them to their respective workplaces.'

After five minutes of quiet, people observe Kishor Sahu and Triveni Yadav coming out of one of the inner lanes. Kishor Sahu works in the deputy commissioner's office, and Triveni Yadav is posted in the fire-control department. A little later,

Prem Chaurasia emerges from a different lane and inches his way to the Matador. Then a boy—twenty-three or twenty-four years old—also walks towards the vehicle in rapid strides.

'Who's this, bhai?'

'Bhaiyya, this is Rajendar Paswan's son, Ranvijay. Got employed by the state information department last year.'

The people on the terraces are counting. Pasi, Teli, Gwala, Tamboli—folks from all such low castes are government employees. All of them are curfew VIPs, getting passes. Not a single person from the chowk's upper castes! Truly times have changed.

Suddenly, Girish babu, nose scrunched up, arrives near the Matador van. Thank God! The chowk's honour has been restored! Nirmal Jain also arrives. He has great connections in administrative circles. Now Govind Jha of All India Radio is also seen walking towards the Matador. Uday Verma and Vachaspati Pathak can be seen too. Still, only five upper-castes in all. The rest are 'those people'.

'*Hey bhagwan!* Only this was left to be seen,' Tiwari-ji says with a sigh, when Sugna Ram of Valmiki Nagar walks in, his chest puffed out. Sugna is a sanitation worker, a part of the cleanliness crew at the airport, and also its union leader.

'Keep your mouth shut or you will be put behind bars under the SC-ST Act.' Vibhuti Mishra pulls Nityanand Tiwari's leg from the adjoining terrace.

The counting of the curfew VIPs fills the elderly with a peculiar vexation. While going to the latrine downstairs, Verma-ji is accosted by his grandson, who lovingly enquires, 'Baba, why can't we have curfew all the time?'

'If there is a curfew all the time, what will you eat? How will the groceries come?'

'Why, Mithilesh Grocery Store downstairs is ours only.'

'Wonderful, my son! Your father eats off my pension and rent, and you plan to eat the shop itself.' Verma-ji slams the latrine door in his grandson's face.

His daughter-in-law's eyes tear up at these harsh words. If advocate sahib had heard his father's taunts, he would have gone to the chowk in a huff, and not come back till he calmed down. Thank God, he is on the terrace now. Where could he have gone, had he sulked today?'

For the women, whether it be the Dussehra fair or a curfew, in their destiny, the kitchen and the stove are a constant.

Because the men are at home, this 'curfew mela' means double the usual workload for women. Demands for tea, pakoras and halwa keep spouting from the terrace to the kitchen. After that, lunch. Then dinner. Tiwari-ji's only daughter-in-law, Gauri, has already slapped both her kids twice. But will venting anger reduce her workload?

Just now, the government vehicle has declared curfew relaxation from three to six p.m. The dejection of the first-time curfew-watchers at the chowk is akin to the dejection felt by a cinema-goer when barely twenty minutes into the movie, comes the intermission. The curfew's relaxation means that all essential work can be dealt with. For chowk-walas, the most essential work is to step into the streets and move their limbs. When has there been any dearth of grocery in their households? The moment the hands of the clock touch three, people start gathering on the streets.

Away from the chowk, Alok smokes, leaning against a pillar outside his house in gali no. five. His eyes fall on Chintu who has come to him for the third time in two days.

'What *re?* Don't you have any work-shirk?'

'Bhaiyya, were you able to find out anything?' Chintu's soul is still tangled in his binoculars. Would Sanjay be such a significant character in the Mahabharat if not for his divine vision?

Chintu—otherwise held to be a top twerp—is considered worthy of company these days solely because of the miraculous binoculars and the stories connected to it.

'*Saala*, you will make Radhey chacha lose face again. How many marks did you get in Intermediate?'

'Bhaiyya, my answer sheet got ruined.'

'Splendid!'

'Bhaiyya, those binoculars cost me eight-hundred rupees. Please help.'

He first came yesterday evening, with the request to 'please help'. Then today morning, uncaring of the curfew; and now again, as soon as the curfew relaxation was announced.

'Banwari!' Alok calls from where he is standing.

A skinny twenty-year-old comes strutting from somewhere, and stands before Alok.

'See to it that his stuff is returned.'

Chintu continues standing, petrified.

'*Abey*, go now!' Alok says, almost rebuking him.

Chintu timidly follows after the boy. The boy takes him beyond the mud-hill, via a narrow path he has never seen before. There, he knocks on the door of a hut. A boy comes out—the same boy who had made Chintu hold his ears and do squats. Banwari and the boy talk for a while among themselves, and then the binoculars are returned to Chintu.

'What about the twenty rupees?'

The two boys look at each other and laugh. 'Your father too came to do research here. The money has been given to him. Go ask him.'

Ashiq Miyan's son Shami is playing Ludo with him. The ringing of a cycle bell announces Hanif's arrival. It is 3.15 p.m. now,

Ashiq will have to leave for the shop. Referring to last night's drama, Ashiq's mother reminds him that he promised Zulekha he wouldn't go anywhere during the curfew. Ashiq tells her that there is no curfew right now. There is a relaxation till six p.m., and in any case, he will be back no later than 5.30. Amma and Zulekha exchange glances, as if saying, 'Only Allah can save us.'

On reaching the shop, Hanif sweeps and dusts with electric speed and then fetches the cloth pieces cut for salwar-suits. The maestro is ready to stitch. Ashiq notes that four-five people are standing on the plinth of the shop. Had it been any other day, he would have told them to get lost, but today there is no need. After all, which woman will come to the shop on the day of a curfew?

'All this ruckus has been created by the miyans. Can't a Hindu even make one temple for his god in his own country? If this is not slavery, what is?' A man standing on the veranda says.

'Yes, as long as we keep yielding before them, everything is fine. But the moment we start talking a little bit about our own rights, these people start rioting. *Arre*, will calamity strike if the Ram Rath passes through?'

'Sometimes, I get the feeling that this Beepiya (V.P. Singh) is some low-caste person. He certainly cannot be a Rajput. Had he been a true Rajput, he would have launched tanks and cannons on them and then stood aside to check which Khuda-Allah rushed to their rescue.'

Every sentence uttered by those on the veranda makes Hanif throw a look full of misgivings at Ashiq. But like some spiritual-seeker, Ashiq is focused on his work. Once or twice, when his eyes meet Hanif's, he has a detached expression on his face, as if to say, 'All this is mere talk, what can be done about empty talk!'

'So Aramganj's first group of religious volunteers, the karsevaks, will pass through the lane of the famous 'Mohmeddan Hindu',

Ashiq Miyan Rangbaz. Preparations are on … *waah*!' This is Om-ji's voice.

Neutral observer Nirmal Jain says, just as the arrival of a langur sends the monkeys running, the sound of Om-ji's voice makes the blathering old codgers of Aramganj bolt.

'*Arre* Gupta-ji, where are you going, sir?'

From his strangled voice, it seems that poor Gupta-ji has fallen into Om-ji's clutches. 'A very bad habit, this. Let go off my hand and talk.'

'First tell me, why have you abandoned your faith?'

'When did I abandon my faith?'

'How much donation did you give that day in Jagdhari Singh's procession? Tell us …'

'Who remembers that?'

'I remember. I was standing right there. Lakshmikant Sahay had given twenty-one, Vibhuti Mishra had given fifty-one, and you gave nothing.'

Gupta-ji sniggers.

'The largest donation was made by "Mohammadiya Hindu" Ashiq, and you stand right outside his shop and talk of training tanks on Muslims, that too during a curfew! What if the government comes to know that you are provoking a riot?'

Poor Gupta-ji starts stammering. Om-ji lets go of the man's hand, but continues pulling his leg.

'All of you are idle braggarts. Your Advani is a worshipper of Jhulelal. What does he have to do with any temple. It's all just a political game for him. Just as you don't have anything to do with any religion or ritual. You are all Hindus only in name.'

'Listen, that's enough. I held your father in high regard, hence I kept listening for courtesy sake. You have had your fill of insolence—don't go on and on about my faith.'

'Bollocks to your religiosity! Beating your chest, you scream temple-temple on one hand, while raking in cash by selling kerosene on the black market on the other. If asked, you won't even have a hundred rupees to give in the name of Ram.'

'When it's time, I will show you how religious I am.'

'The time has come. A *Sapt-chandi* yagya is being held at Nathuni pandit's place. Give donation.'

Hesitating a little, Gupta-ji puts a hand in his kurta-pocket. His fingers keep rummaging as if trying to locate the smallest currency note. But such is his luck that a fifty-rupee note comes out. He starts stuffing it back in.

'*Arre*, stop, were you about to donate a hundred? No matter. God values the sentiment. Whatever is given with true devotion is enough.' Om-ji stuffs the fifty-rupee note into his pocket, and starts walking off.

'But when is the yagya?'

'As soon as the date is set, you will be properly intimated. You call yourself a Rambhakt, no? Do you know how the word Ram came about? It comes from "rum", which in Hindi means "to be immersed in". You keep immersing yourself in God's welfare. Where there is rum, there is Ram.'

Tiwari-ji barely manages to stop snorting. He says to himself, 'This Omwa is a top-level bastard. He has duped Gupta-ji and extracted fifty rupees to get drunk.'

Hanif comes to inform that a boy is standing at the Mr India counter, asking for Ashiq Miyan. Ashiq goes to Mr India's door. Abha Asthana's son, Guddu is standing there.

'Ma sent this. She has asked you to take this home.' There are fifteen-twenty pooris packed in a big polythene bag, and two more bags with sabzi, tied at the mouth with rubber-bands.

Ashiq is astonished. '*Arre*, what's the need for all this? Why did didi take so much trouble?'

Without giving a reply, Guddu turns to go. Ashiq cannot figure out what to say. He calls after him, 'Tell didi that I will have the dyed dupatta delivered to your house.'

At a time like this, when mistrust between communities is rising, there is someone in the Hindu mohalla, who is thinking about his family! Kareeman, who came to Ashiq's house to borrow rice this morning, taunted as she went out, 'You people get stuff from Hindu mohallas. Who will give to us?' Ashiq now thinks that Kareeman had spoken the truth. Till the chowk people are around, he need not worry much.

The clock ticks on. Ashiq glances at its hands. It is thirty-five minutes past five. When you finish work on time, you experience a different kind of peace. Ashiq hunts for a polythene bag and tells Hanif to take out as many pooris as he wants to eat, and a whole packet of sabzi. The curfew resumption announcements have begun. Ashiq picks up the poori-sabzi, and leaves for home. Today he will not give Zulekha any cause for complaint.

The first night of the curfew was dull due to the sheer inexperience of the younger generation. But tonight will be different. From the chowk to the lanes, the youth are now fully ready. Despite parental prohibitions, many from the 'ishtudent comoonity' have already done the rounds of the town during the relaxation. Everywhere, the atmosphere is like that in Aramganj. No major tension. There are rumours, which always fly at times like these. But nothing thrilling. The Aramganj youth have now realised that there is no need to stay indoors, fearful of the curfew. And so, by evening, all kinds of activities start.

Some nameless youths loudly chant funeral chants of '*Ram Naam Satya Hai*' outside Nathuni pandit's door. When poor Pandi-ji comes out, they chant in his ears, 'Ram's name is the only truth'. One of them asks him, 'Baba, will you read this chart and tell when the thirteenth day of mourning is due?'

Riled up, Nathuni pandit's younger son Girdhari lays a trap. The rest manage to get away, but Lallan gets caught. The stench from his mouth reveals he is properly drunk. When questioned, he retorts, 'If Ram's name is not the only truth, then is it a lie? And is it now a crime to take God's name outside a temple?'

When the complaint reaches Lallan's father Jagdish babu, he strongly condemns the son's antics. 'Had he done all this outside the mohalla, it could have been ignored. But antics like this in one's own mohalla! Very bad. *Shiv Shiv!*

At seven p.m. in the evening, Lakshmikant Sahay is holding a pakora party. Why be scared even if a curfew is on? Every group at the chowk is denouncing the lacklustre curfew. But there are some others, who stay serious through all this jocularity.

Kamlesh Singh calls young volunteers to a meeting and tells them that it is possible that the curfew will be lifted tomorrow, and then the real game will begin. They have to be smart, stay in touch, and help one another. The most important thing being, if needed, they must be ready to fight, to protect and save their religion. They have all been rendered impotent due to the lies of charlatans like Gandhi, who touted non-violence as the best policy. But now, times have changed.

18

THE RIOTOUS GOAT

Sukh ke sab saathi, dukh mein na koi ...

In good times, all are friends, in rough, none.
Your name is the sole Truth, beyond it, none.
Mey ... re ... yyy Raam ...

In the dead stillness of night, the voice rising from somewhere in Valmiki Nagar echoes all across Aramganj without the aid of a mike. From the way the vowels stretch while intoning, *'Meyy ... reyyyy ... Raaaam',* anyone can guess that this is none other than Bhagtu Ram.

Bhagtua can sing in several voices. When his father tried to get him established in the ancestral line of sanitation work, the artist son had rebelled. Thrown out of the house, he wandered around for many days. Then, he became a disciple of a sadhu living in the Bhoothnath Temple on the cremation ground. There, not only did Bhagtua learn some *nirgun* bhajans in praise of the formless, infinite God, but also how to smoke pot. After reconciling with his father, Bhagtua is now back in his home, but not in the sanitation line. He is Pawan Hatwal's man Friday of sorts. This helps him meet his personal expenses too.

There's hardly any platform for a talent like Bhagtu in this town. But whenever he gets the opportunity, he lets the world know that the artist within him is alive and kicking. When Prabhat Dayal's younger brother passed away unexpectedly on a night as still as this one, Bhagtu had crooned, *'Man reyy … tu kaahe na dheer dharey'*—O heart … why can't you carry on, making God knows how many people break down in their homes.

But right now, Anilwa is laughing. With nominal effort on his part, the lock on Akram the butcher's shop—located on the road going towards Poorna river, at the other end of Aramganj—has been broken. The 'shop' meaning—a thick wooden plank on which mutton is chopped, one cot, a wooden stool to sit on, and three hooks on the wall to hang up skinned goats. But there is another ten-by-twelve enclosure inside. The treasure must be there.

'Isshhh … look *bey* Haria, what a strapping treasure!'

Hari too steps inside. The room stinks of rotten leaves. It appears that two zero-watt bulbs are glowing at the other end of the tiny room. Hari lights a match. Before them stands a sturdy, muscular he-goat, the size of a calf. 'Just one, but so solid!'

'Don't make any noise. Untie the rope.'

'But first, we must take the bell off, or everyone will come to know.'

The bell tied to the goat's neck is tiny. Utterly stuck to the neck. The minute Anil touches the goat's neck, it rears up on two hindlegs like a horse and eyes them challengingly.

'This daughter-fucker is a complete bastard … will we be able to take him?'

'Not just him, we will make even his daddy go! If the bell doesn't come off, let it stay. We will take him like this only. Just check—there isn't any patrol vehicle on the road, is there?'

Haria peeks outside and gives Anilwa a signal. Anil steps out, hands the goat's tether to Hari, and takes the iron-rod he had used to break the lock in his own hand.

Anil taps the goat's backside with the rod, and Hari trots, rope in hand. Crossing the road and dashing through inner lanes, they arrive at their destination in five minutes. The destination being, the Yuva Shakti Sangh cum Saraswati Puja Committee, a Hindu youth club. This place in gali no. 6 is away from Aramganj Chowk. That is why many youths have gathered here after hoodwinking their parents to indulge in some fun on a curfew night.

Since the Mandal agitation, the distance between the residents of the chowk and those of the galis has increased. But all that has had no impact on this club's bonhomie because political rant is totally prohibited here. *Saala*, whatever else a man may do, he must not go anywhere near politics and caste, because both are terrible. The members of the Yuva Shakti Sangh have been warned, 'If our religion and community are in peril, rise up and fight; but for the rest of the time, just eat, drink and be merry.'

Many boys come to the club to beef up their bodies, to do social service, and for general entertainment. Hence, they have gym-like arrangements here. Along with a carrom-board, card decks and chess sets, there is also a passable volley-ball court. But no library.

There are young men from every caste—the upper castes like Pandit, Lala, Bhumihar and Rajput, and the lower castes like Teli, Kahar, Nonia and Koiri. Only a few 'studious low-castes' from gali nos. 3 and 6 boycott this club, possessed as they are with the idea of becoming an SP or collector. The likes of Ranjit roam about, inciting low-caste youths that the Yuva Shakti Sangh is a hotbed of communal politics, and will lure the low and backward castes away from studies and betterment. *Let them incite*! It hardly makes any difference to Kamlesh bhai. The majority of the youth from the galis are on his side anyway.

Under Kamlesh Singh's leadership, the Yuva Shakti Sangh has been continuously expanding. Often, non-Aramganj residents can also be seen here. The club also has the protection of the staunch leader, and future MLA, Jatashankar Sharma. When tensions mounted in town recently, the club had deliberated in an emergency meeting, whether the time had come for stockpiling weapons to make the area secure. Some members opined that they should start collecting donations right away.

'But when there is no Muslim settlement in the vicinity that poses any danger, who will make a donation?' As no answer could be found to this counter-question, the motion got dismissed.

But the consensus is definite, that whatever happens, these Musalmans must be kept within bounds. Right now, no major action is needed, hence only a cultural festival has been scheduled. A VCR has been hired. Mothers and sisters not being around, no point in wasting time on movies with social messages. Straightaway, they will come to the 'main programme'. The plus point of the curfew-like ambience is that one can openly have a drinks party. Right now, one such party is on.

Glass in hand, Akhilesh stands in the droll manner of Bachchan's character Vicky babu in *Sharaabi*. Suddenly someone comes up and whispers in his ear. Still holding the glass, Akhilesh goes straight to the club's backyard. Seeing the dappled goat tied to the handpump, his eyes widen in amazement.

This goat symbolises a major triumph of Hindu unity over Muslim appeasement. The plan masterminded by a Rajput was fructified by the warriors of Nonia-Kahar caste, and now, the cooking will be done by a Kayasth. Following Kamlesh Singh's example, Akhilesh, too, has learnt how to lead the lower castes. He is very pleased with his progress.

'*Jiyo mere laal!* This will yield at least two full buckets.'

'*Arre* no, bhaiyya, no less than two-and-a-half buckets,' Haria asserts with complete conviction.

From Bada Talaab to gali no. 6, in every Aramganj club, buckets are the measure for mutton. In the Saraswati Puja after-parties, or on similar major occasions, cooked meat is kept in buckets for ladling out to members seated for a meal. Last time, half a bucket of meat had been pilfered. Till date, no clue to the scam has been found.

Akhilesh feels a surge of affection for his two sidekicks. Stuff worth at least two thousand rupees has been purloined by them. Almond coloured, with white spots. Very healthy too. But the question is, if butchered at this late hour, when will the mutton be cooked, and for how long will the dining go on? Half the members must already have eaten. This valid issue is raised by Ramesh.

'If not now, when else can he be butchered? The stuff is stolen. Cook, eat and finish it off. *Saala*, if the news spreads, within the hour, there will be another drama! There's no bastard bigger than the administration. Besides, in this mohalla too, there are enemies who keep an eye on everything.' Akhilesh hints at Alok and company.

'All that is fine, but who will cut him up?'

'*Arre*, I will cut him up. One only has to wield an axe, bring it down on the neck, what else?'

Dropping in from nowhere, Manojwa says, 'All right, you will cut him, but who will skin him? There isn't a single Hindu butcher in this area, all are Muslims, and there's a curfew outside.'

'How hard can that be—I will skin the goat! And Munna bhaiyya will cook. Who cooks better mutton than him in Aramganj!' says Haria.

Munna, Chintua's elder brother, is impatiently waiting for the film festival to begin. Seeing an interruption in his programme, he starts making excuses. 'Skinning is a tough job. Intestines, gall-bladder ... who will clean all that?'

'That's no big deal, bhaiyya. There's no need to take off the skin even. If only we can obtain a packet of blades, it will be sufficient. Shaved goat meat is as soft as a rasgulla.'

'*Saala* low-born, you have shown us your standards. No one here will eat mutton with the skin on. This is a goat, not your pubes that you will just shave it,' Manojwa says, seething.

Both Manoj and Hari are from 'Other Backward Castes' according to the new list issued by the Mandal commission. But Manoj does not think of himself as any less than a Rajput. His insulting words hit Haria at the very core.

'*Arre*, you son of a high-caste, if you try to boss me around like this, I will fling you on the ground here itself and skin you from head to toe! As if I don't know which clan you really come from! *Saala*, your father used to queue up for free condoms outside the Kutchery ... And should I tell where he went after that?'

And the two begin to wrestle. Viewing this as a threat to Hindu unity, Kamlesh Singh intervenes, pushing the two men away from each other.

After listening to the whole story, Kamlesh asks, 'This goat-theft, whose idea was it?'

The two warriors point a finger at Akhilesh. Kamlesh tells them to go and tie the goat at Akhilesh's house.

Akhilesh looks non-plussed.

'*Saala*, Akalesh, you have a fitting name. You are totally 'akal-less'. Brainless! This is not a *khassi* mutton goat, but a full-blown un-neutered male goat, weighing no less than sixty kilos. See how he stinks. No one will buy him even for the Bakrid Qurbani. Akramwa breeds these goats as well, and he must have kept this one aside for that. And you idiots kidnapped and brought him here. Do you know that if you put this meat to cook now, it won't soften even till tomorrow afternoon? The flesh will be so tough that you will have to tear it apart like dogs.'

Hearing their leader say this, the whole team's dicks droop. Pat comes the next order: 'Go with Akal-less and tie the goat back where you got him from.'

'*Arre* bhaiyya, if we go back, the police might catch us. Police patrolling is on. Last night, Om-ji had stepped out to buy liquor. The cops made him hold his ears and do squats. And they dumped Das babu, the compounder, on Bano Manzil road. Hiding and slinking, he had to walk back all the way somehow. Not possible to go back, bhaiyya,' Haria revolts.

'Then do one thing. Go via the inner lanes, and leave the goat somewhere beyond Nonia Toli ... And you, Akal-less, you go with them. Understand?'

Akhilesh swallows the insult. Had it been anyone else, he would have taught them a lesson at once. But Kamlesh is from his own community, and is also three-four years elder to him. Their families, too, are related. These days, the idea of Hindu unity and of being a leader has so possessed him that he thinks nothing of putting Akhilesh down in front of these low-castes. Such humiliation! And this is when he hasn't even drunk enough to feel tipsy!

Unwilling but helpless, Akhilesh joins Hari and Anil to drive the goat outside Aramganj's boundary. While leaving, he wheedles that they hold off the movie screening until he returns. The three take hardly twenty steps out of the club, when the goat gives an enormous tug, frees himself from the rope, and takes off full-speed towards the chowk. Rod in hand, Haria runs after the goat.

Tan ... tan ... tan ... tan ...

'Damn! A fire engine!! Fire ... Fire ... There must be a fire ...' Durga pandit almost falls off his bed.

'Where ... where's the fire?'

Tan ... tan ... tan ... tan ...

Half the chowk residents climb up to their terraces and start looking around anxiously. They don't see a fire anywhere.

But Durga pandit is quite sure he heard the fire engine. And the rest heard *of* it from their neighbours. Within minutes, the sound can be heard echoing across the entire chowk with stereophonic effect.

Tan ... tan ... tan ... tan ...

'There ijj sometheeng phissy.' Girish babu pulls out a new English sentence from careful concealment and lobs it at Durga pandit's terrace.

'What did you say, Girish babu?'

'There is some conspiracy to attack the neighbourhood. I will immediately intimate Sinha sahib to send cops.'

Sinha sahib, meaning, Girish babu's brother-in-law, who is an IAS officer. Within ten minutes, a police vehicle halts on the chowk and then goes into a lane in pursuit of the *tan tan* sound.

And after that is heard—'Run, Manojwa!'

'Run, Anilwa ... *arre maiyya re!*'

Half-an-hour later, the police come out of the lane. A constable from among them addresses Girish babu's terrace and says, 'No cause for worry. Some young rascals were making mischief. All of them have been dealt a couple of blows with the lathi. You can all go back to sleep.'

'Where did the fire brigade go?'

'Despite being educated, you all rear goats, and leave them to graze on roads at midnight ... You may go to sleep. No need to be afraid.' The policemen get into their vehicle and leave.

Rubbing their heads, the members of the Yuva Shakti Sangh discuss among themselves whether the bigger dunce—*ullu ka pattha*—is the Akal-less Akhileshwa, or the chowk elders who cried 'fire'.

Along with the club workers, the budding leader Kamlesh too got thrashed. The transfer of the erring police inspector will, of course, be orchestrated, but only once the curfew is lifted. The disgrace, however, cannot be undone. The film festival, too, got scrapped. When Munna reached home after the thrashing, at a quarter to twelve in the night, his father, Radhey babu, welcomed him with slippers—that too in front of the other sons and daughters-in-law, filling Chintua's heart with glee.

But thank the Lord, the police did not pick up any of the boys. Had they been thrown into a lockup for three-four days, it would have been a real headache. Ashiqwa is right, when he says, Ram-ji's grace protects this mohalla.

Anyhow, the next morning, the administration lifts the curfew.

Even a current of four-hundred-and-forty volts becomes a minor tremor by the time it reaches Aramganj. But what if the tremor is minor to begin with? Then, the denizens of Aramganj deploy all their creativity and diligence in blowing it up to such a scale that the next ten days are spent discussing it at great length. At best, the town's riot was nothing but a mole rat's squeak. A shop set on fire, stone-pelting at three-four places, some lathi-charge. Nothing more! But the minute the curfew lifts, a thousand stories slither out like snakes—God only knows from where—and collectively cavort on the chowk.

Every group has a different tale to tell. The group of elders believes that had Girish babu not taken swift action and summoned the police, the mohalla would have burnt down. Who knows, from where all—Kasai Tola, Karbala Chowk,

Kunjda Mohalla—goons had come to raze Aramganj to the ground. Girish babu accepts adulation for his role in saving the mohalla, and lobs another English sentence: 'Prevention ijj better than cure.'

On the other hand, having drunk turmeric milk, to heal from the thrashing, the members of the Yuva Shakti Sangh emerge on the chowk once more, airing the regret that the Muslims could not be 'properly tightened' and 'straightened out' anywhere during the two-day curfew because the administration had openly sided with them. The police even seized and took away the conch shell that Nathuni pandit's grandson Bhutkun was blowing. The minute the government changes, all these bastard inspectors will be singled out and taught a lesson. Kamlesh bhaiyya has already delivered one such lesson—by giving a policeman a slap so tight that the rascal will remember it for life. Had so many armed policemen not been around, Kamlesh Singh would have surely broken his legs and deposited them in his hands.

Akhilesh is depressed. The lathi hit him so hard, his back is still blue. A straight-forward chap, he does not know how to cook up stories like the rest. He lies groaning in bed. His scared mother has intimated sundry relatives, who keep asking all sorts of questions, making his life hell. His paternal uncle—who looks like Mikhail Gorbachev's Bihari edition—is doing a Perestroika on him. In the spirit of complete transparency, poor Akhilesh has been made to take off his pants before everyone. 'See these marks? The butt will need to be fomented morning and evening with a hot water bag. Or else, the clotted blood will not melt, and a wound will form.'

Among the under-nineteens, Chintua has emerged as a hero once again. One, he entered the lair of goondas and got his 'thing' back; and, even better, he saw the 'live telecast' of a 'doubles game' through his prized binoculars! The second-floor tenants—a doctor and his wife—had been making good use of the free time afforded by the curfew. Chintua stood on a stool and peeked in through the ventilator ... The game was going on—*ekdum dhaka-dhak*—back and forth, back and forth!

Things worth gossiping about must have transpired in Valmiki Nagar as well. But the minute the curfew lifted, all its residents rushed to work. Some said, Akram's goat had reached Valmiki Nagar early that morning, and a feast was planned for the night. But Fussu, who comes to clean Verma-ji's toilet, denied this. He said that Pawan Hatwal saw to it that the goat was sent back to Akram. Politics is everywhere.

Because the Rayyat Toli residents are not employed like the Valmiki Nagar people, they can be seen sauntering about in the daytime. Amidst rumours, fear, doubts and discussions of all kinds, the peon at Anjuman Islamia, Mohammad Kamruddin, aka Mufti sahib, makes public information that makes young men pay attention: 'A big conspiracy is afoot to destroy Muslims. But until the time there is Ummah, no such conspiracy can ever succeed. The Ummah respects Pakistan, and everyone knows that in the Asian continent, Pakistan is America's most faithful partner. So Pakistan must get America to tell India that atrocities against Muslims in Hindustan must stop, or else the Indian government won't be allowed to run. Let us see what happens now.'

Let us see what happens now. This sentence is being used in different parts of the country in different ways. In some places, as a question; in others, as a warning. In some places, the phrase is a threat; in others, a symbol of fear.

19

THE MOSQUE FIRST, OR THE HOUSES?

MLA Jagdhari Singh is extremely stressed. It's the 8th of October today. Less than two weeks to go before the Ram Rath's arrival. The ceremonial welcome gateways are yet to be readied and erected. Unless flower-bedecked welcome arches become visible at least ten days prior to a programme, the buzz can hardly build up. Jagdhari babu's standing among townsfolk and in the party is at stake.

During the daytime, the entry of trucks into Main Road is barred; and the night curfew is still on. So how can the bamboo poles be brought in? First, Jagdhari babu tries to browbeat the district magistrate. Then he tries to wheedle him into agreeing, but gets the same reply both times: 'No relaxation of rules is possible. At the most, the night curfew will last for two more days. You will have sufficient time to ferry the bamboo poles and erect welcome arches after that.'

Aramganj does not fall under any 'No-Entry Zone' for trucks. As soon as the truck loaded with the bamboo poles crosses into the mohalla, unkempt urchins who are spinning tops on the street, break into a dance. *Jai Kali, Kalkatte-wali!*' After crossing Aramganj Chowk, the truck splutters towards the Poorna river, and comes to a halt at the empty ground to the right side of the road, a little ahead of the butcher Akram's shop. Right now, dogs and pigs are rooting in the rubbish piles here. But over the next four days, the 'geography' of this ground will transform. Today, the preparations for the grand Kali Puja function will commence. Unlike the Durga Puja function, of which upper-caste strongmen are custodians, the organisation of the Kali Puja is the prerogative of Dalits and Backwards.

Corporator Balchandra Saha is the custodian of the Kali Puja Committee. Prem Rajbhar, the famous history-sheeter—who these days is seen as a part of the inner circle of the former central minister Radhemohan Sahay—is the president. The secretary of this Kali Puja Committee is Valmiki Nagar's emerging leader, Pawan Hatwal. This Hatwal is quite the player. At a time when every other corner of this town is resounding with cries of 'Jai Shri Ram', the Lotus-party-walas haven't managed to hoist a single saffron flag on his turf, Valmiki Nagar. Jatashankar Sharma tried his best to incite Sugna Ram from the sanitation workers' union there—Sugna had even been willing, smacking his lips in anticipation of his coronation as Valmiki Nagar's leader—but in no time, he came to realise that the enterprise was bound to fail. Not even a leaf stirs in the basti without Pawan's will. Young or old, one signal from him turns them all into slaves! He keeps all parties—the Wheel, the Hand, and even the relatively newer Elephant party—in his pocket, waiting till just before the day of elections to cut deals. For the time-being, he is siding with Balchandra Saha of the Wheel-party.

Even though the Kali Puja organising committee is dominated by the low-castes, everyone is welcome to the function itself. Though in minority, the upper-castes come as well to enjoy the disco-dancing behind the pandal, and to drink and gamble.

Alok is very active here. From ensuring that donations are coughed out, to getting the pandal erected, he does it all. Like the Yuva Shakti Sangh, Kali Puja Committee, too, has liberated itself from the shackles of casteism. The only bone of contention between them is their political ideology. While the Kali Puja Committee is secular, the Yuva Shakti Sangh members believe in Hindutva.

For shopkeepers like Ashiq, both pujas imply the same things. That donations be made, shops be kept shut on the day of the immersion, and that they join the revelry in the actual procession. Most other shopkeepers have little to do with the procession. But because of his dancing skills, Ashiq is a superstar on that day. Whether it is Dussehra or Kali Puja, such is the spell cast by Ashiq's dance, that people cannot but remember the event throughout the year.

The events of the past few days have filled Ashiq's heart with a strange emptiness. To keep bad thoughts from taking over his mind, he wants to plunge headlong into work. But is there enough work to keep him occupied thus? Dussehra, the festival of new clothes, is already over. The wedding order from Jaiswalji's house has also been met.

The remaining new orders can be fulfilled in three-four days at his normal pace. What will he do after that, if there are no new orders? How will he pass the time? He looks out. Afternoon onwards, whenever business is slow, carrom-games begin on Mithilesh's veranda. But not today. Head lowered, Mithilesh sits quietly in his shop. Apprehensions about the days to come are making everyone uneasy. The hands of the clock are at four now.

'Ashiq chacha ... Ashiq chacha ...' A scream assails his ears suddenly. For a moment he imagines he's in his Rayyat Toli house. Within seconds, the owner of the scream—Sajid, the younger son of Ashiq's cousin Idris—is standing before him, his face strangely colourless, his eyes filled with infinite terror. Ashiq cannot recall Sajid having ever come to the shop before this.

'Chacha, come home at once! Dadi is asking for you. Right now!'

It crosses Ashiq's mind that even this morning Ayesha had a slight fever. His heart fills with a strange dread.

'What is it? Is everything okay?'

'The house ... no ...'

'What happened to the house?'

'They are getting it vacated ...' Sajid tells Ashiq in a strangled voice.

'Whose house?'

'Everyone's ...'

Ashiq grabs the cycle keys from Hanif, and, with Sajid on the carrier, pumps the pedals. Within minutes, they are at the mouth of the gali leading to Rayyat Toli. People are assembled outside their houses, as if a death has occurred. Handing Sajid the cycle, he says, 'Park inside the house, and tell Dadi, I have arrived.'

Outside Masood's house, people are standing in a circle. They are peering at the notice pasted on the wall. The scene outside Jumerati's house is similar, but with fewer people. He hurries to Jumerati's door, on which a government notice has been pasted.

He begins to read.

All are informed that the district administration has, under the Honourable High Court's directive, initiated a drive for the removal of encroachments. Any illegal construction made on government land may be removed and the land vacated before 30 October 1990, or strict legal action will be initiated.

By orders,
Regional Officer, Circle 2

'What's this? When was this notice pasted?'

'Two hours ago.'

'Where all?'

Jumerati seems to have been struck by paralysis. Not a word escapes his mouth. He indicates with his hand—everywhere.

Ashiq glances up. Everyone is standing at their doors. Bewildered, he too goes towards his house. Affixed to the wall, with the seal of the government, the notice seems no less than a death warrant.

His mother has been crying her heart out. Zulekha stands beside her with a glass of water in hand. The children are sitting quietly in the next room. Amma can't read, but she has heard from the neighbours what the whole matter is.

'When Allah sends trouble, he sends it from all sides. To this day, we have not wronged anyone ... Allah Miyan, have pity on us!'

Amma had last cried like this when Ashiq's Abbu passed away.

'Don't be scared. Nothing will happen. This house has been here since Dadajaan's time—how can it become illegal now? Let me find out.'

Opening the gate, Ashiq goes next door to Barkat Miyan's house. Barkat Miyan is Ashiq's father's elder brother. The house was in the name of Ramzan Miyan, Gani and Barkat's father. After his death, it was divided among the two sons. Not a legal division, they had simply erected a wall separating the two households. Idris is Barkat Miyan's son. Sajid is his grandson.

'Bade Abbu, how did this happen all of a sudden?'

'What can I say, son? For years we have lived in this very place, and suddenly we are being told today that our house is illegal! They won't even let a Musalman *live* now.' Barkat Miyan's voice breaks as he speaks.

Ashiq recalls his Abbu's tales. He would recount how once jackals prowled the area at night and big wild rabbits roamed about freely. 'I, along with Barkat bhai, would jump into the waters from the walls of Kashinath School, and swim from one end of Bada Talaab to the other in five minutes flat.' Abbu would talk as if Rayyat Toli hadn't been established some fifty-sixty years ago but had existed since the universe came into being.

'How won't they let us live, Bade Abbu? Is this some joke? You would have all the house papers, wouldn't you?'

'Not a single thing can I recall, son. All court-kutchery work was handled by Gani. Now he is no more. I have no idea whether the papers were in our father's custody or with Gani. And you know how your brother Idris is, no? He's hardly left with any time after running his shop and wrestling, to get a hang of these house-related matters. Allah only knows what will happen ...' Barkat Miyan breaks into loud howls.

What transpired overnight to turn those living here for more than half a century into intruders? This question haunts everyone, but no one has an answer. After hearing about the notice, most have abandoned their trade and work, and returned home. The whole mohalla is out on the street. Many things are being heard now that no one ever paid attention to earlier.

'Two months back, a man came from the circle office and began measuring something in my lane. I asked him what was being done, and he said it was a regular government survey. I didn't realise at the time that this was all part of a plan to render us homeless,' Majid Miyan says.

'Yes, even my gali was measured. I thought they were planning to dig some drain or the other,' says Mumtaz.

'*Gajab budbak ho ji!* How amazingly stupid you are! Ever seen a drain being dug in a Musalman mohalla? *Saala*, this definitely has been planned to uproot us all, and such big donkeys are we, that we never got a whiff. Allah only knows what will happen now.'

'There has been some misunderstanding with the administration. Our houses are totally legal. Gather all papers related to your houses. There's no point in crowding the street,' Ishtiaq Miyan says to the people gathered in front of his house.

Ishtiaq Miyan is the sole man in Rayyat Toli who has a government job. He is an employee of the District Leprosy Eradication Centre. There is no work in that office, so he is at home half the time. Being a government employee, people listen to him attentively, whatever the issue.

After Ishtiaq Miyan's counsel, the streets of Rayyat Toli empty out. Only one or two people remain standing. The rest are busy turning their houses upside down. Jumerati had kept all the property papers carefully, but five years ago, rainwater got into the houses of this basti, and the wooden trunk ended up being steeped in water for half a day. Those papers are nothing but pulp now. So how can Jumerati fetch them? Allarakha and Najeeban are hearing for the first time in their lives that papers are required for their house. The electricity bill is the only paper they know.

Masuriyadin finds a very old document in his late father's trunk. He does not know how to read, but he carefully wraps it in a piece of cloth. By its looks, it seems to be an important document. Majid Miyan, too, finds one stamp-paper and half a piece of paper inscribed in Kaithi script. He cannot make out what it is.

In Ashiq's house, eight trunks stand with their lids open. One by one, everything is taken out. Amma, Zulekha and Ashiq are drenched in sweat. Little Shami tries to help in his own way. But till now, the results have been nil. A wedding album, some old clothes, books like *Musalman Aurat* and *Bahishti Zevar*, old durries, and all manner of old, forgotten stuff comes out, one after the other. But not a trace of any house-related papers. Haplessly, Ashiq's eyes jump from one trunk to the other, as if trying to X-ray the littlest of things with naked eyes. His mind is crowded with all kinds of thoughts.

What is the meaning of this sudden notice? People have been living here for three to four generations. If the mohalla wasn't illegal earlier, how did it suddenly become so? This is not just a notice; this is a ploy to snatch their houses and to leave them out on the street. That, too, in just twenty days. The mohalla people are right to call this a punishment for being Muslim. Nothing else. Never before did Ashiq think much about his name and identity. But whether he thinks about it or not, the reality won't change. The truth is, Ashiq's position is no different from that of the other Rayyat Toli residents. His happiness might not have always been in common with the other residents of the basti, but his sorrows are. If the basti dwellers are being punished for their Muslimness, then Ashiq, too, must bear this punishment with the rest of them.

'That big box, Amma, where are the keys to it?' Ashiq asks, pointing at an iron trunk.

'Leave that alone, son, that's Dadajaan's trunk. Nothing there, except old brass and bell-metal vessels.'

There's a knock on the door, and they learn that a mohalla meeting has been called at Imli Maidan. Everyone must come at once. Ashiq goes out after telling his mother and wife to search all the trunks once again. The maidan is full. Even women who normally stay indoors have gathered. This is no ordinary panchayat meeting.

People like Shamsuddin, Tabrez and Ishtiaq Miyan, who always take the lead in social activities, have been relegated to the back rows. The stage at the other end is being managed by

Kamruddin Miyan, i.e., Mufti sahib, and Mohammad Shamim. Shamim Miyan is a labour contractor who also dabbles in local politics. He has good connections, not only in Rayyat Toli but also with the residents of other Muslim mohallas of the town. At the moment, the lofty voice of Shamim Miyan is holding forth on things that earlier he would whisper only to those close to him. 'Rayyat Toli is a victim of a big conspiracy. Using some High Court directive as excuse, an old basti like ours has been sent this notice; even though all these houses are registered in your names. On the other hand, many areas in town openly encroach on government land but have never received any such decree. This is a dirty trick, but you must not be afraid. This notice will get shredded to bits in court. As soon as possible, we must head for the court. How many of you have the original registry of your house?'

This question stuns everyone into complete silence. After some investigation it is found that, except Ishtiaq Miyan, not one person has the requisite papers or registration documents. Some people do have old, torn bits of paper, but it's hard to say if anything can be proved with them. Obtaining copies of documents from a government office is no child's play. It requires pursuing the matter day and night, paying bribes to petty officials, and even having someone put in a good word for you with the higher-ups. By the time all this gets done, the date of demolition will arrive.

Because Ishtiaq Miyan is a government employee, he does not want to be openly embroiled in anything to do with courts. So it is decided to make Hakim chacha the defendant on behalf of the whole mohalla. Hakim chacha has papers to prove that this land was willingly conferred by Raja Prithvinath Shahdev upon the residents. Showing those papers will render the allegation of encroachment meaningless. But this being a legal matter, some expense will be involved. Every household must deposit a thousand rupees at Mufti sahib's house by evening.

The sum involved makes most people feel dizzy. 'A thousand rupees is too much. Who has so much money in their house? There's a whole month to get through,' someone says. After giving the matter some thought, Shamim sahib says, if this seems too much, they may deposit five-hundred rupees each. 'Even to get hearing dates, the court needs to be bribed. It is a question of ancestral property. You might lose the house by being tight-fisted.'

'Who will be our advocate? In matters of land and property, the two senior lawyers Bishwambar babu and Banshi Prasad are known to be good,' Hakim sahib avers.

'Which world do you live in, chacha? All this ruckus has been created by these very upper-caste Hindus. If a lawyer is hired, he must be from the *qaum*, from our community. Ali Imam sahib has already been approached. He is a top-class lawyer. His fees are a little high, but when requested, he said that if this is for the *qaum*, I will accommodate you as much as I can. This case needs a lawyer who is a Musalman, and that too, a Sunni. What do you say, Mufti sahib?' Concluding his speech, Shamim turns to Kamruddin Miyan, aka Mufti sahib.

Eyes shut philosophically, Kamruddin Miyan sits as if in conversation with the One above. After staying silent for a few minutes, he speaks: 'Allah is punishing the mohalla for our bad deeds. Since forever I have been asking that a small mosque be consecrated on this ground. Allah makes a house for those who make a house for Allah. Had there been a mosque here, people would have learnt pious ways and not fallen into bad company, or turned into tag-alongs of Hindus. But no one ever pays any attention to what I say. There, they are planning Babri Masjid's martyrdom, and here, the homes of Allah's people are in danger. Now we can only wait and wonder whether our houses will get demolished first, or the mosque. Lord, have pity on us! *Ya Allah!*'

A voice rises from the crowd: 'We will give up our lives, but not the houses. If need be, we will show them that we, too, are the sons of Mughals.'

'Yes, this is a fight for rights, a fight against lies. For our collective rights, we must go into battle with a shroud tied around our heads. We must be ready for *qurbani*, for whatever sacrifice it calls for. Allah never helps those who live in fear. Inshallah, we will fight.' Chants praising the greatness of Allah resound in the air. So loud are the voices rising from Imli Maidan, that they must surely be reaching inside every house in Rayyat Toli.

Nara-e-taqbeer, Allah-hu-Akbar!
Nara-e-taqbeer, Allah-hu-Akbar!

Such is the magic generated by Mufti sahib's little speech, that every fist tightens and every voice soars.

Nara-e-taqbeer, Allah-hu-Akbar.

'Hold on, chacha, let us go easy on the chants. The times are bad,' Ashiq says, cutting through the crowd and walking towards the stage.

'Look! Here comes the advocate of Hindus. Now we will have to take his permission even to chant Allah's name!' taunts Kamruddin Miyan.

'*Aey* Misir, don't give lectures here. All of this is happening because of traitors like you.'

'*Abey*, who are you calling a traitor? With whom have I committed treachery?'

'You, who else? I will call you a traitor a thousand times. You are nothing but a scrounger. *Saala*, Jatashankar's hanger-on! Just to get his photo printed in the newspaper, he turned us all homeless! You son of a bastard!' Salim roars.

Ashiq catches Salim by the collar. The hands that stitch and embroider are still quite strong. But within minutes, the scene shifts. Who knows from where, people emerge to stand with Salim, the notorious loafer of Rayyat Toli. Ashiq gets pushed aside and dragged away.

The boy who slaps Ashiq across the face is hardly eighteen. Ashiq recognises him. He is Farzan's grandson—the luckless electrician Farzan, who was handicapped after a fall from an electricity pole. Ashiq's Abbu would often go asking after him. Every Eid, till the day the electrician was alive, Gani Miyan would stitch a kurta at his own expense and gift it to Farzan. 'To cover some hapless man's body is an act of piety,' he would say.

Ashiq feels as if Farzan's grandson has disrobed him before the crowd. The slap has struck not just his cheek, but his very being. Until today, nobody dared touch Ashiq. It seems as if nothing is left now. Salim's abuses fall all over his uncovered body like drops of acid. A blister pops up with every drop.

'This could not have happened without any treachery from within. If you all want to save this mohalla, then this lowlife who lives off the leftovers of Hindus must be told not to get in our way.'

Though silence reigns over the mob, everyone is getting affected by Salim's words. Suddenly, Fazlu pulls out a comb-like object from his pocket and starts baying like a madman. 'The one who is a traitor to the *qaum* will get killed like a dog.'

People see Fazlu brandish a half-open straight-razor—an *ustara*—in his hand.

A whizzing slap rises from nowhere and hits Fazlu below the ear. He falls face down on the ground. This is Ashiq's cousin,

Idris. Even at forty-five, he has a wrestler's body. Every Moharram season, he teaches the Rayyat Toli boys how to wield the lathi and the spear on this very ground. Idris Miyan aims two-three kicks at Fazlu's prone body. Farzan's grandson leaves Ashiq's collar and runs away. The crowd, too, distances itself from all this.

Seeing things turn the other way, Kamruddin Miyan tries to salvage the situation. 'It is wrong to exchange blows with those of your own *qaum*. This strength must be saved for more fitting occasions, janaab.'

Idris confiscates Fazlu's razor and somehow drags Ashiq away. The meeting continues on Imli Maidan, with elders warning Salim to tamp down his hot-headedness. After much discussion, a consensus is arrived at. Whatever happens, all of them should stick together and file an appeal the very next day in the High Court to get the notice cancelled. Also, Ashiq Miyan must be kept away from it all, because by no account can he be considered trustworthy.

Evening falls, and then the night. In the last fifty years, Rayyat Toli has seen half a dozen riots and hundreds of curfews; but never before have they witnessed such an ominous night. Dogs often howl at night, but tonight, their howls seem to portend some major disaster. Weighed down by grief, Majid and Jumerati have stopped eating. And Ashiq? He does not know which is worse: the fear of homelessness, or the persistent pain of public disgrace.

After coming back, Ashiq falls on the cot without meeting anyone's eyes. Zulekha dares not ask anything, but she has heard it all from Idris's wife. She was already troubled by Ayesha's fever, and now this! Lost in herself, Amma sits in a corner. Shami is running around cluelessly. In the afternoon, he had asked, 'Ammi, when will we go to Pakistan?'

'May the tongue that speaks so burn to cinders. Why will we go anywhere? Who teaches you such things?'

Looking scared, Shami had slunk away, without giving any answer.

'*Ya Allah*, have pity on us!' After putting the kids to sleep, a wet-eyed Zulekha looks at her husband. How innocent and helpless her man looks when asleep!

She dare not wake him up. She quietly keeps the covered plate near his head. Dead to the world, Ashiq sleeps on. Somewhere in the middle of the night, his eyes open, and he sees the plate. He is not hungry at all, but how can he reject this loving offering? After eating, he falls asleep again.

It isn't easy to open one's eyes after a deep slumber. They hurt, taking time to adjust to light. But keeping them shut is hardly a solution. For the past few days, opening his eyes has become an ordeal for Ashiq. Had mornings not been there, it would have been great. Today, he is forced to open his eyes due to his mother's mutterings. He sits up, disorientated.

'Fetch another half a bucket.'

Why is Amma's voice coming from outside? From the veranda, Ashiq moves towards the gate. Bucket in hand, Zulekha is coming inside. In gestures, he asks, what happened? Zulekha shakes her head to say: nothing. Amma is trying to scrape off something written in black letters on the wall with a reed broom. Most of it has been erased, but from the unerased letters, Ashiq can make out the phrase. The letters on the wall are: '*Hi ... Au ... d.*' 'Son of a Hindu'. That would only be three letters, so what's this second line? '*Gaddar kahin ka.*' 'He, the Traitor'.

Before Ashiq can react, Zulekha Bano takes his hand, drags him inside, and pulls him tightly to herself in the way a mother hugs her son. Amma comes inside after a minute. She stands quietly and then says, 'Let it go, bachwa. It is just a turn of the Time. Just as other days have passed, these too shall pass.'

'Gani Miyan was a simple man, but his wife is not the sort to get intimidated by anyone.' Ashiq grew up hearing this in the neighbourhood. And it is true. His mother has always been a lioness when angry. Even Zulekha never flinches when enraged, no matter who is standing before her. What's happened to them today? Never before has Ashiq witnessed such restraint.

It seems that these two women are now a shield protecting Ashiq. Do Zulekha and Amma also feel that this mohalla, where their family had such standing, sees them as the enemy now? Amma keeps saying that the way other days passed, this, too, shall pass. Ashiq can't decide whether this thought is consoling or frightening.

Like every day, Ashiq gets ready for the shop at nine-thirty. Zulekha feels that Ashiq must not go to work, but she does not stop him. If staying in the house makes him unhappy, he should go to the chowk. It is better for a man to be caught up in work. It is true that the ancestral house must be saved, but it is even more important that the livelihood is guarded and kept safe. Zulekha makes Ashiq swear on the children's heads that he will forget what happened yesterday, and at no cost will he get into a fight with the neighbours. Ashiq does not reply. But while going out, he tells her, 'Go to Idris bhai, and tell bhabhi to hunt for the papers, and remind her to send five-hundred rupees to Kamruddin chacha's house.'

The Mister India shutter is up. Ashiq is sitting inside the shop, and his eyes fall on the Ajanta clock. This clock is from Abbu's time, and Ashiq has not replaced it till now. The broken seconds hand keeps twitching, like a lizard's tail. God knows for how many years that hand has been twitching this way. It seems as if it will stop in a minute or two. But that never happens. Sometimes, looking at the clock depresses Ashiq. At other times, he feels as if this twitching embodies some deep philosophy of life. Even if you cannot move on, continue holding your ground.

The minute he picks up the scissors, Ashiq becomes the embodiment of detached wisdom. Foot pressing down on the pedal of the sewing machine, eyes focused on the needle going up and down at electric speed, Ashiq enters a meditative state. Good-bad, respect-insult, all that has gone by, all that is yet to come—he goes far, far away from it all. He does not even hear the traffic's din. All he hears is the clatter of the sewing machine, which for him, holds the sweetness of a musical note.

After readying two salwar-suit orders that came from Valmiki Nagar, Ashiq hangs them carefully in the mirrored display wardrobe. This is the same wardrobe that had so incensed Basanti chachi the other day—for Ashiq had dared to hang in it clothes from Valmiki Nagar. Life seems to be divided into so many boxes. Religion-caste, rich-poor. But what do these things even mean? Basanti chachi had threatened that day that she would never step inside his shop again. But within a week, she came back, with lots of old clothes for alteration. Men may draw as many lines of division as they please, but can mutual relations, built upon meeting one another's daily requirements, ever get ripped apart so easily?

20

ORDER, ORDER, ORDER

Ashiq is busy working when he senses someone's presence at Mister India's counter. Hanif is not in. Ashiq quickly crosses the four-by-two door to go from Savitri Boutique to the other side of Two-in-One tailoring shop. He finds a grim-faced Mithilesh standing there. After a moment's silence, they start talking. Mithilesh inquires if what he has been hearing is true.

'What have you been hearing?' Ashiq asks him.

Mithilesh says that since last evening, news has been circulating on the chowk that the government will evict the Rayyat Toli residents as they have been illegally encroaching on the land belonging to Kashinath Middle School. The government plans to put half the vacated land inside the school boundary, and use the remaining for widening Shri Ram Path.

The name Shri Ram Path startles Ashiq. Mithilesh confirms his suspicion. 'Jatashankar's hangers-on are going around telling everyone that Mini Pakistan is being removed solely due to Neta-ji's efforts. Action is being taken only because his lobbying with the top-most levels of the government put pressure on officials. The minute the road gets built, land prices in Aramganj will start rivalling the land prices of Main Road and Kutchery Chowk. Such daydreams are being shown to people by Jatashankar's followers.

'That Jhantwa has turned me into a washerman's dog that gets shooed away from every door. How I respected him! Calling him kaka—as if he was my own father's brother. That's why I went to the road-naming circus without reading too much into it. Now, my own mohalla people think that I am a part of his dirty game. As for the chowk people, for them I have always been just a Musalman. In my own caste community, I never had a standing. Now my house too will go. And who knows, tomorrow this shop might also be snatched away!'

Putting a hand on his shoulder, Mithilesh says, '*Arre*, nothing will be snatched away. All these antics will last only till the Rath Yatra. Jatashankar wants to grab the limelight by showcasing his leadership skills. That is why he is striking combative poses, saying, he will see to it that Mini Pakistan is removed before Babri. What are the Rayyat Toli people saying?'

'The case is in High Court. We have a hearing tomorrow morning. Only Ram-ji can help us cross this—'

As he says this, Ashiq suddenly stops.

Why did his tongue falter saying Ram-ji's name for his own work? The same Ram-ji with the help of whose name he has consoled and reassured the chowk people for years. Is he conceding that in this changed atmosphere, even the right to take Ram-ji's name has been snatched away from him?

No, it's not that. He is a true follower of Inderdev Pandey. He would constantly remind Ashiq that the path to Ram is riddled with hardships. And only the man who knows how to overcome ordeals can find happiness. Something he would often say now echoes in his mind.

Hoihe soi jo Ram rachi rakha
Ko kari tark badhave shakha

Everything happens by Ram's design
What's the point then of polemics fine?

Right from his childhood, Ashiq has faced many hardships. No matter how big the trouble, he never falters. But life now seems divided—into two different, wholly separate parts—and he has grown fearful of bringing Ram's name to his lips. The chowk considers him a representative of Rayyat Toli. But Rayyat Toli sees him as an agent of the Hindus. In order to continue living in Rayyat Toli, he must save his house. That's why he will have to prove that he is a 'true Musalman', like the rest of them.

Yesterday, while explaining to his Bade Abbu, Ram-ji's name had popped out of his mouth. 'Our house is *halal*—every brick has been put together using the money earned with our sweat and blood. By Ram-ji's grace, nothing bad will happen.'

Idris at once cautioned him, 'There's no problem in saying this before us, Miyan. But don't talk like this in front of the neighbours.'

Ashiq won't—he will not even show his face in the courtroom for tomorrow's hearing. This decision had been taken by consensus among the Rayyat Toli residents, and the message conveyed to him through Hakim chacha.

On the day of the hearing, the Fajr namaz is read out with extra fervour by everyone in Rayyat Toli. Before stepping out, people beseech Allah that their prayers be answered, and—as per their station—make promises to offer a *chador* at Ajmer Sharif or Maner Sharif, or to visit the shrine of Hazrat Nizamuddin

Auliya. Kamruddin Miyan, a strict Deobandi, considers all these things a sham. He believes only in Allah's justice.

People come out in droves, the way they do when going for namaz. In this locality of daily-wage earners, how many can afford the rickshaw fare from here to the court? By foot, they will reach in an hour or so. At his age, Hakim Ismail cannot walk. He takes a rickshaw with Barkat Miyan. Mufti sahib, i.e., Kamruddin Miyan is respectfully given a bike-lift by Mohammad Shamim, who is in charge of pursuing the court case.

The court is packed with Rayyat Toli folks. Theirs is the first hearing. The court clerks have arrived. Everyone is waiting for the judge. Mohammad Shamim keeps going in and out of the courtroom restlessly. Salim and Bashir, too, follow after him. People watch the movement of these leaders with eager eyes. Elders like Barkat Miyan quietly recite prayers, sitting on the back benches.

'Order ... Order!' With the strike of the gavel, all eyes come to rest on the front of the courtroom. The Sikh judge sitting in the high chair seems no less than an emperor. Not just an emperor, he is no less than God himself. He can make or mar anyone's life and luck. Justice B.S. Kang is renowned for his integrity. The application by Hakim Ismail was made on 9 October. Within three days, the judge summoned both parties for a hearing.

When the man who is to make the plea on behalf of Hakim Ismail stands up, whispers are heard buzzing this way and that in the courtroom.

'Who is he?'

'Must be the government advocate.'

'But he is appearing on our behalf, and he is not Ali Imam.'

'He is just a boy!'

'Sit quietly! This is Ali Imam's son, Fazal Imam. He has just finished his law degree from Delhi. Imam sahib is busy today with some big case.'

Advocate Fazal Imam begins his plea. He says that the case has been filed by the senior-most citizen of Rayyat Toli, Mohammad Ismail, and that he be considered a representative of all the forty households. These families have been living in this mohalla for more than fifty years. Some families have been living from even before that. All the houses have electricity connections and papers of registration of property. As a proof, the petitioner Mohammad Ismail has submitted a photocopy of his documents. These houseowners have never been served a notice like this before. It is clear that a politically motivated step has been taken by the administration with an intent to trouble these innocent citizens. Hence a request is being made to the honourable court to order the government to halt its proceedings with immediate effect.

The government counsel stands up. Around fifty-five years of age, the man looks not only more experienced, but also devious.

At once he says, 'Huzoor, the step taken by the district administration is in pursuance of honourable High Court's orders. Hence calling it wrong or motivated, is to question the intent and motives of the honourable court. And this is exactly what the advocate for the petitioners is doing.'

Fazal Imam stands up and says something in English. But the judge orders him to sit down. The government counsel proceeds with his argument.

'The plea, as to why a notice was never given earlier, is not legitimate on any count. It could be that the government was negligent earlier. But it cannot be taken to mean that this makes an illegal encroachment legal. Now, I will present the map that is in government records. You can see that the map shows an eight-acre plot in Raja Prithvinath Shahdev's name. On this land,

Raja Prithvinath got a school constructed in his father's name. The school was run by a trust. Raja sahib himself was the chairman of the trust. After Raja sahib's death, the trust donated the entire chunk of land to the government. So after 1957, this land came under the ownership of the government. And these people, who are occupying a portion of this land, are occupying it illegally.'

A shiver of dismay runs through the courtroom. Hakim Ismail gets up on unsteady feet and utters a cry. Judge sahib strikes the gavel: 'Order. Order. Be quiet. Put the case before the court only through your advocate.'

Hakim Ismail's message is conveyed to the advocate through a chain of people sitting in the rows in front of him. Fazal Imam gets up. 'Your honour, the government counsel says that the land was donated by the trust to the government in 1957. But our document proves that the piece of land on which Mohammad Ismail's family has a house had been given by Raja sahib to Mohammad Ismail's father, Gafoor Miyan, in 1931 itself.'

The government counsel asks tauntingly, 'In 1931? Milord, as per government records, this land was transferred in Raja sahib's name in 1937, on his father's death. Is the petitioner's advocate saying that Raja sahib gave Gafoor Miyan a piece of land that was not even in his name at that time?'

Hakim Ismail again gets up shakily. When his word travels from the back to the front, advocate Fazal Imam says, 'Sorry, not 1931, your honour. I think, no ... I mean, 1941 ...'

The government counsel says, 'The petitioner's lawyer himself does not know when the registration was done because all their documents are fake. This land has belonged to the government since 1957. Hence it is the lawful duty of the government to get all illegal occupation removed.'

The judge addresses the litigant's lawyer in a serious tone, 'Do you have anything to say to this?'

'Your honour, we have all the evidence. We have mutation papers and even house tax receipts. Please give us a little time to put it all before you.'

'If you have the papers, why were they not presented in court today? You are a novice it seems, young man. You have appeared in court without due preparation. I give you three days. If you are not able to present evidence by then, this court will not be able to help you.'

Everyone is stupefied. Head in hand, Hakim Ismail sits hunched over. What has this foolish advocate said? That they have mutation papers and receipts of deposited taxes! Without thinking or bothering to find out, he has declared that they have what they don't have. And on the other side is the judge, ready with a pen to write a judgment against them.

What will happen ... *Ya Allah! Khwaja Gareeb Nawaz!* The saviour of the poor, help us!

21

MULLAS, GO TO PAKISTAN!

Bhola Chowdhary lifts the shutter of his grocery shop, cursing, and then goes on muttering for another five minutes. When Chowdhary-ji arrived in the morning to open his shop, he found a pamphlet pasted on his shutter.

Hindu, Hindi, Hindustan
Mullas go to Pakistan.

'Daughter-fuckers, why not go and paste this where Mullas live!'

Mangal from the paan-shop kept sprinkling water from his *lota* till the black letters printed on the pamphlet became all but pulp.

A new current cat-footed to the chowk yesterday, and is now coursing through the veins of the youngsters like breaking news.

Mini Pakistan is going to be cleared! Land prices on the chowk will quadruple.

'So take your trousers off, tie them around the head and dance. Not an iota of work, but just look at his dreams!' In less than a minute, Radhey babu had snuffed the euphoria out of the bearer of this good news—his fourth offspring, Munna. Seeing the elder brother get a scolding, Chintua grinned from the other corner.

Somehow, the older generation of Aramganj is not too enthused by this breaking news.

'If Advani-ji is coming, they should put up temple-building posters. What does this "Mullas go to Pakistan" mean, ji?'

'This Jatashankar is such a twisted man. If made to eat nails, he would shit out screws. It's impossible to read his mind.'

'Whatever you say, Rayyat Toli is indeed filthy.'

'Yes, of course, Lala-ji. As for you, you live next to the Dal Lake, isn't it? Where pigs come to root early every morning? If a place is unsanitary, does it mean that you will uproot the mohalla? And what is the meaning of pasting posters all over the chowk and creating this tamasha?'

'Okay, okay. It's all right. Now let it go.'

'How is it all right? If such lunacy is not cut short, one day all of us will have to hold our heads and cry.'

'It ij *pathetic*.' Girish babu arrives with a new English word.

'Come, Girish babu, come and tell us—why are you getting all this done?' This is Aramganj's staple manner of speaking. If it gets too cold, people question one another: 'What makes you inflict this icy weather on us?'

'*Hum kahliyo* ... I mean to say, it ijj a very bad thing, to engage the mohalla boys in such unproductive stuff. This country haj no future. This country, we must accept, haj already sinked.' 'Country already sinked' is Girish babu's favourite phrase, his familiar way of expressing worry over the state of affairs. And along with this, he always repeats that his son Harish is going to settle in America.

Despite annoyance among fathers, the repressed excitement in young men due to the news of Mini Pakistan's demolition is impossible to contain. Om-ji has explained to Prakash Kumar—another honorary advocate of the chowk—that real benefits can accrue to the chowk-walas only if Valmiki Nagar is cleared out as well, and in its place, a swish and shiny market is built. Jatashankar-ji alone can get this done.

In no time, Advocate Prakash ensures the constitution of a representative body headed by Prabhat Dayal. They are already on their way to meet Jatashankar Sharma. Om-ji has accomplished the second stage of this project as well. Via Phussu and Bhagtu, he has cautioned the whole of Valmiki Nagar. 'This Jhantwa will not rest till he has uprooted your mohalla. Save it if you can!'

As for Rayyat Toli, its residents are struggling to force even a morsel down their throats. The chowk youth have no enmity with Rayyat Toli—why then are they so thrilled? Bigger than any intrinsic feeling of contempt, it's the sheer thrill of watching the drama unfold before their eyes. The subject of discussion in all the nooks and corners of the chowk is: *What does a bulldozer look like?* Till now, the boys here have seen a bulldozer only on screen. Now they will have the opportunity to see it live.

But the chowk youth also have a soft spot for Ashiq.

'Whatever may happen, *yaar*, his house should not get bulldozed. He is such a *"my dear"* guy!'

'When demolitions happen, every house will get demolished. Mites get crushed along with the millet—that's the rule.'

'But where will Ashiq go if his house is pulled down? Who knows he might even have to fold the shop up?'

'*Arre*, he won't go anywhere. He will just carry on with his shop as before. One, he is a Rambhakt; and two, he is very smart, a true *rangbaz*. He will rent a house in one of the other lanes, what else?'

But Rambhakt Rangbaz, aka Ashiq Miyan, is far from these chowk discussions. Face drained of colour, of all humour and wit, his will seems to have dissipated. Right now, he is sitting with his begum at Dr Ram Nagina Prasad's clinic. Ayesha's fever hasn't gone down, though six days have passed.

'She has typhoid. Buy a thermometer, ask the compounder to show you how to read it. Take her temperature every four hours. If the temperature is over 102 degrees, immediately apply a wet wash-cloth on her forehead to bring it down. Take care that the fever doesn't persist too long, or it might affect the child's brain. It may take three or four more days for the fever to abate. If it doesn't, we will have to run a blood test.'

On their way back from the doctor's clinic, Ashiq stays quiet the whole time. Zulekha, too, does not speak. After all, what can be said? After yesterday's court proceedings, half of Rayyat Toli has accepted that even if the year 1947 did not do any major harm to their ancestors, the year 1990 will uproot them for sure. When Ashiq heard what transpired in the court, he told Zulekha: If anything happens, take the children and Amma to your brother's place. On hearing this, his mother got incensed. 'I am a daughter of Sasaram town. Not one to get terrified of things. I won't go anywhere. I was brought here by marriage. I will live here, and die here.'

After dropping Ayesha and Zulekha at the house, Ashiq steps out immediately. Today as well, Imli Maidan is crowded. But is there anything for Ashiq to do? He stays on his path. Today the atmosphere is like that of a political rally. There are seven-eight chairs on which notable people from outside Rayyat Toli are seated. The chief guest is the leader of the backward Muslims, Faheem Ansari. But the mohalla is now split down the middle, and tensions are running high between the two sides.

Hakim Ismail is enraged. The advocate hired by Shamim, the labour contractor, did not come to court and his novice son bungled the case. Without doing his homework, he declared before the court that not only did the Rayyat Toli inhabitants possess registration documents, but also mutation papers. If at the next hearing, the judge dismisses the case after giving them all a dressing down, who will be responsible? Shamim and his hangers-on took the lead, not bothering to consult the elders of the mohalla. Hakim sahib tells them straight-up that as the case has been filed in his name, the advocate for the next hearing should be selected only with his approval.

Barkat Miyan, Ishtiaq, Shamsuddin and Tabrez are with Hakim sahib. The group on the other side, comprising Shamim, Kamruddin and Salim, insists that this matter is not just legal, but political. It is a conspiracy to destroy the Muslims, hence they will have to take the whole *qaum* along. Faheem Ansari is related to the famous Ansari family of the region that owns thousands of acres of land. Someone or the other from his family is always a minister in the government. Ansari sahib has already announced that if the case gets dropped, he will constitute a cooperative and offer habitable land at discounted rates to every family of Rayyat Toli.

Salim prompts everyone to clap loudly at this announcement. But many questions remain. The leaders don't offer any concrete answers, only reassurances. 'If the matter is not resolved in court, Ansari sahib can also use political pressure to save the houses of our oppressed brothers from demolition. After all, he is in the party which heads the government in this state. In this fight for justice, against falsehood, we must heed the leaders of the *qaum*. If the need arises, be ready to take to the streets to express our distress and anger.'

Izhar Miyan notices that the house next door has a new sign-board: *Mohammad Salim, social activist, Islam Nagar*. Rayyat Toli has now become Islam Nagar! Just as the other street was named Shri Ram Path a week ago. Similar boards announcing the new name of the mohalla have been hung outside two or three other houses as well.

Rayyat Toli—like most small mohallas of this town—lacks resources, but is an independent unit, where people are not in the habit of looking beyond the mohalla to meet any of their needs. Despite small tiffs and disagreements, people stand together through ups and downs. But this crisis has changed the character of Rayyat Toli. Half the people have lost the right to speak. The problem facing the mohalla has now turned into a *qaumi*—the entire Muslim community's—issue. And people who have never been seen here before are counselling and taking decisions about everyone's future. Faheem Ansari's speech continues in Imli Maidan.

Sajid's elder brother, Wahab, is among the few youth in Rayyat Toli who go to college. Wahab has brought in a troubling piece of news. 'Many big Muslim leaders were present in the meeting held in Taufiq Masjid. When the Rayyat Toli issue was brought up, Janaab Fayyaz Malik said that the Rayyat Toli case is a lesson for the entire Muslim *qaum*. This *qaum* never unites while casting its vote, the way Hindus are doing these days. If the eviction of Rayyat Toli can rouse the Muslims, then this eviction will eventually prove beneficial for all.'

Tahir tells his father, Haji Shamsuddin sahib, Rayyat Toli's only Mecca-returned Haji, 'Salim was saying, a cowardly *qaum* will get wiped out from the map of this world, while a brave *qaum* will rule. No *qaum* is braver than the Muslims' in this world. We must help each other and gather weapons for the fight. We have spoken to the Kasai Toli residents too. The Qureshi brothers are fearless. Should the need arise, they will not hesitate to lay down their lives.'

Haji sahib slaps his forehead. Since when did the uneducated Salim begin using such weighty words? Not only will they lose their houses, many blameless Rayyat Toli people might even lose their lives! *Ya Khuda*, give some brains to these stupid people.

The night curfew has been lifted; even so, the stillness prevailing at eight p.m. is unnerving. Shoulders slumped, Ashiq is passing by Inderdev Pandey's house, and walking towards his lane, when a feeling—that he is not entering his own mohalla, but a place full of strangers—overtakes him. What happened that day in Imli Maidan has changed Ashiq's life in an irrevocable way. While leaving his house for the shop every morning, his eyes cannot help but fall on the wall. The words have been erased, but they continue to stain his entire being. 'Traitor ...' 'Son of a Hindu ...' These voices chase him night and day. He does not care about the house, shop, property, or wealth. Nothing. If only somehow this stain could be wiped off, he would happily kick all else away. As Ashiq opens the gate to his house, a question pops into his mind: How many days do we have left here?

'How is Ayesha's fever?' Ashiq asks, as soon as he enters.

'She was okay during the day, but since evening, the fever has returned. It is 101 now. If the temperature goes higher, I will apply a cold compress ... Allah is testing us.'

'Everything will be fine,' Ashiq says in a low voice.

Like every day, Shami comes and stands before his father and tries to read his expression. Even on the worst of days, the sight of his children brings a smile to Ashiq's face. But today he keeps sitting quietly. Then all at once, he pulls Shami to his chest. Kissing him on the forehead, he tells him, 'Son, go sleep beside your Dadi, it's very late.'

After pushing the dinner down his throat with some effort, Ashiq sits down on the cot. Putting a hand on his shoulder, Zulekha says, 'Listen, I have something to say.'

'Don't think too much about the house. We will face whatever comes our way.'

'I am not talking about the house, but about Ayesha. Hakim chacha gave her holy water and read out *duas* for her, but the fever did not subside. Why don't you try your methods ...'

'What do you mean?'

'The chowk people always say that with your methods, they find relief. That Ram-ji's *upay* ...' Zulekha speaks haltingly.

Zulekha keeps all thirty Rozas during Ramzan. No matter how much housework there is to be done, she takes the time out to read the namaz. She has fought with her husband countless times about his not going to the mosque. But Ashiq gives her the same answer every time: 'Work is worship. When Allah Miyan himself comes to meet me, why should I go to a mosque?' This reply always irritates Zulekha.

And the same Zulekha is asking him today to try Ram-ji's mantras to cure Ayesha!

'Ram Nagina Prasad is a renowned doctor. A doctor, too, is a form of God in a way. He has said, hasn't he, that she will be fine in two-three days?'

'Along with medicine, prayers, too, are needed ... Please, why don't you get the same things done for her that you do for the chowk-walas?'

'But they are Hindus, and you are a Muslim ... I mean ... we are Muslims.'

'For a little girl, what does it matter whether she's Hindu or a Muslim? Even the chowk people come to Hakim chacha for medicines. The old timers would even ask him to read the water. When your hands have the power to heal, is there any harm in curing your own child? They are right who say, there is darkness beneath the lamp. See how you go around doing good to the world, but ignore the pain of your own loved ones.'

'Shut up! There is no healing power in my hands. Had I been a saint, mahatma or pir-auliya, would I have spent my time tailoring? You are making life impossible for me,' Ashiq explodes without warning.

Zulekha Bano is silenced. She looks at her husband quietly and then says, 'So you make fools out of the chowk-walas in the name of religion? You have left your own faith, and you cheat people of the other religion as well. Maybe that's why Allah is punishing us.' So saying, she walks off to the room where Ayesha is asleep. Trembling with rage, Ashiq too stomps out of the house. He does not know where he is going and why.

A terrible spectacle dances in his eyes, a scene which often haunts his dreams: a large-eyed deer being pursued by a pack of wild dogs ... its body punctured in places by their teeth ... Within minutes, the dogs tear through and start eating the deer alive ... the eyes of the deer, still open, hold a mute acceptance of its destiny.

Ashiq does not get to watch TV much. One night, he had unthinkingly switched it on. A wildlife programme was running on the channel. For the first time in his life, he learnt that on this earth, there existed creatures that did not wait for the prey to die before devouring it. Cats and lions strangled their prey before consuming it; even the prey got a modicum of respect. But these wild dogs—they respected nothing.

Ashiq gets up, as if waking from a deep slumber, with a shooting pain. His hand goes to his left leg and feels the ants crawling up his ankle. It is not a dream, but the breaking of it. After stepping out of the house, his feet had moved on their own. He has no memory of arriving at the *chabootra* in front of the Bada Talaab in that semi-conscious state. The flood-lights are bright here. Removing two-three ants still sticking to his leg, he holds them in his palm. Despite being crushed, a little life is left in the red ants.

'The tiny black ant is a Hindu. If it crawls up on you, all you feel is a slight tickle. The red ant is a Musalman. It only bites Hindus, not Muslims.' Pawan Hatwal had revealed this nugget of wisdom to Ashiq in Inderdev Pandey's school.

'This is a black ant. It will bite you, for you are a Musalman. It's biting you, no?' Pawan had asked, after letting an ant loose on Ashiq's body.

'No, I only feel a tickle.'

'*Bhakk saala!* Then you are a Hindu, not a Musalman!'

And now after years, the red ants, by biting him, have once again reminded him that he is a Hindu, not a Musalman. Contrary to this, Basanti chachi had, without mincing words, said that a Miyan like him had no right to sermonise on the Vedas and Puranas. Even if Ashiq concurs with her views, what should he do about the Rayyat Toli people, who say night and day that he is a Misir and not a Musalman. The limit, of course, is his own wife telling him that he is neither a true Muslim, nor a true Hindu—only a trickster who deceives people.

Who, after all, is this Ashiq? His identity, akin to a deer caught in the jaws of contentious wild dogs, is being pulled in opposite directions, while he watches—helplessly, mutely—as his own body is split asunder.

His heart is still heavy at Zulekha's words. 'You have left your own faith, and you cheat people of the other religion as well.' Which faith has he left behind? As prescribed by Islam, he is circumcised, and he ensured that Shami, too, was circumcised. On Eid, Bakrid, and other such occasions, he goes with his clan to the mosque. His mother and wife impart to the children whatever religious teachings they want to. Has Ashiq ever stopped them?

How has he deceived those from the other faith? He is constantly asking himself this question, but is unable to find an answer. Inderdev Pandey used to say, 'Children are like water. They take the shape of whichever vessel they are poured into. But if the vessel itself is misshapen, is it the child's fault? If the potter did not mould the wet earth properly, what is the point of blaming the clay?' Inderdev Pandey never cursed his own son Markandeya for going astray. Always accepted that he himself must have erred in raising him.

Ashiq is thinking, thanks to the time I spent time in Inderdev baba's company, I imbibed some *doha-chaupais*, rituals and mantras. If Abbu had put me in the madrasa with Kamruddin chacha, I too would have spoken of *haram-halal*, *sunnat*, *ummah*, *jihad* all the time. But is there anything wrong in that? People say Ashiqwa is a *kafir*, a non-believer. Teaches his children stories of Ram and Hanuman and who knows which Hindu deities. But are stories ever learnt in our mother's womb? Whether the story is of Lanka or Karbala, they are always taught to us. Whatever a person is, he does not become that on his own. He becomes only what his circumstances ordain.

Zulekha has unwittingly hurt him with her words. How has Ashiq been deceiving the chowk people? He remembers how Inderdev Pandey would prescribe remedies to anyone who came to him in distress. Ashiq merely repeats whatever he used to prescribe. When he offers the remedies, he feels as if Inderdev baba himself is speaking through him. It is all natural and impromptu. Leave alone taking money, or seeking any other benefit, Ashiq never even mentions it. So how can it be called deception? But the more crucial question before him is—why did he not prescribe a remedy to his own daughter? Zulekha's accusation stemmed from his reluctance. Sitting alone in the darkness, Ashiq has still not found an answer to this question.

Maybe the reason lies in the helplessness in Zulekha's eyes. She takes a lot of pride in her faith. From her childhood, she learnt that if there is a religion worth following in this world, it is Islam; and solutions to all the problems in life lie therein. Maybe Ashiq doesn't want his wife to compromise on her beliefs out of sheer helplessness. But an even bigger reason lies hidden in his subconscious mind. After a lot of contemplation, Ashiq has been able to pin it down.

For the last three-four days, he has been desperately trying to leave behind Ram-ji in the shop. This is very difficult for him, because Ram-ji's name lives on his lips, like some aphorism that pops out readily whether one is awake or asleep. But for the sake of keeping the peace, he has been trying his best to stop Ram-ji's entry into Rayyat Toli. And when Ram-ji cannot enter Rayyat Toli, how can He enter Ashiq's home? This is the real reason that prevented Ashiq from prescribing one of Inderdev Pandey's remedies despite repeated requests from Zulekha.

Truly, religious issues are very complicated. Ashiq's father Gani Miyan used to say that believing in the One above lessens a man's troubles. Another thing he heard in his childhood from Gani Miyan, which he came to understand much later, was: 'Following a *mazhab*—religion—is a good way to lead one's life, provided the brokers of religion let you.' But the men of religion are hardly letting him live these days, whether on the chowk, or in Rayyat Toli.

Fragile as a flower, Ayesha is very sick. The ancestral house is about to be snatched away. Even neighbours have turned into sworn enemies. The chowk, where he roamed all his life without a care, is saying, 'You have no one here.' Yesterday evening, when he was returning to his house from the shop, even Baiju jeered from behind, 'Mulla, go to Pakistan!' The same Baiju who always gets a rupee or two to buy something to eat from Ashiq. How did hate suddenly enter his weak, vacant head?

In the last ten-fifteen days, Ashiq's well-ordered life seems to be unravelling. Even if he wants to remember, he will not be able to recall as to how this unravelling began. Every day, a new trouble rears its head before him. Today, Triveni Mishra, that is, Pandi-ji, sent word through his nephew: 'Need to speak about an important matter. Meet me tomorrow morning, no later than seven.'

Ashiq thinks that Pandi-ji is planning to have the shop vacated on the pretext of renovation. This is the easiest way of getting rid of a tenant. Ashiq has already decided that he will immediately say, 'Chacha, no need to be so roundabout. The shop is yours, whenever you say, it will be vacated.' When Ram-ji has given so many tribulations already, what difference will one more ordeal make! His life has suddenly entered some blind cave, the way out of which isn't visible.

Ashiq peers into the Bada Talaab pond. The water must be ten feet deep. Every year some drunkard or the other falls into it and dies. The thought flashes in his mind: What if I jump in? Then he feels like laughing at himself. The one who knows how to swim cannot commit suicide by drowning, no matter how hard he tries. He remembers Zulekha Bano's face, then Shami's, Ayesha's and Ammi's.

Amma is right to say, 'The way other days passed, these too shall pass.'

His feet then turn towards the house. On the way, he remembers his favourite star Anil Kapoor crooning a song full of hope against all odds, in the movie *Meri Jung*.

> *Zindagi har kadam ik nayi jang hai*
> *Jeet jayenge hum, tu agar sang hai*
>
> *Every step here brings new strife*
> *We will triumph if we are together for life*

'I have started overthinking things these days. If I simply get a Ram Raksha Srotra from Bada Bazaar, and keep it under Ayesha's head, will it do any harm? I will do this tomorrow itself,' Ashiq says to himself as he opens the gate and steps inside.

The children are asleep inside. The veranda light is on and a quiet Zulekha is sitting on a folding chair. Ashiq is about to say, 'It was my mistake, forgive me', but Zulekha speaks first, 'I was anxious for Ayesha, so I said whatever nonsense came to my head. Please don't take it to heart.'

'I will prescribe the *upay* tomorrow. Ram-ji will set everything right.'

This promise of hope is reciprocated by Zulekha with good news. 'Ayesha's fever is slowly coming down.'

Ashiq takes Zulekha's hands in his own. They speak no words, but the meaning is felt deeply by both. Even if the whole world is engulfed by a deluge, these two will stand by each other.

22

CHANCE AND DESTINY

The thuggish Valmiki Nagar rooster strolling on Verma-ji's terrace lands on the railing, and crows vociferously, *Kookroo koo.*

Taboos on social relations apply to humans. Interaction is plentiful as far as canines, felines and fowl are concerned. Some upper-caste and backward caste houses in the inner lanes keep hens. Only hens, not cockerels. The *swayam-sevak* cockerels of Valmiki Nagar voluntarily undertake the moral obligation of ensuring an uninterrupted egg supply.

After taking in a drag or two of ganja, Bhagtu Ram suddenly starts singing in the middle of the night. Mimicking playback singer Sudesh Bhonsle's style, he belts out a song from Amitabh Bachchan's *Jadugar*, whose lyrics go—'*Padosan, apni murgi ko rakhna sambhaal ...*'

Look after your hen, O lady next door!
What if my cock goes out of control.

His voice carries over to many houses in Aramganj, and the girls living in them giggle, covering their mouths. 'Is this a song, or a true story?'

In the manner of legendary fictional lovers—Majnu, Mahiwal, Farhad—the passion of these Valmiki Nagar roosters is completely genuine. However, the houses where the love-interests of these roosters reside, have occupants whose interests include a 'love' for roosters. That is why, keeping a count of the exact number of Valmiki Nagar roosters attaining martyrdom in Aramganj is almost impossible. Om-ji once pronounced: 'A pious soul stays loyal to their faith even beyond life. The rooster that crows on the terrace continues whistling even from inside the pressure cooker.'

The bodily sacrifices of these roosters are worthy of reverence from every angle for those from the poultry-lane. But for the chowk residents, a rooster alive has little utility. The proprietor of Bajrangi Dhaba, Bajrangi, gets up before any cock can crow, and takes out last night's hooch by sticking a finger into his throat. Then, to make the helper boys get on with their jobs, he starts hurling filthy abuses. Bajrangi's voice echoes inside every house, automatically terminating the slumber of chowk residents.

Pandi-ji, that is Triveni Mishra, is bathed and ready. When the call-bell rings, he does not waste a moment in opening the door. Before him, stands Ashiq.

'Parnam, chacha,' he greets.

'Come inside,' Pandi-ji says, without looking at him.

Their relationship is old. Ashiq has known Pandi-ji since he came of age. But never before has an occasion cropped up for him to step inside his house. Even the monthly rent is collected by Pandi-ji while out strolling.

'Is everything all right?' Pandi-ji asks, after shutting the door.

'Chacha, what can be said, after all. You know everything.'

'Times have changed. Now things are not like before. When your father had come to ask for the shop, I barely knew him. Even so, I gave him the shop. Today no one will do that ...'

'No one,' Ashiq agrees.

Pandi-ji stops. Every moment of this silence is weighing on Ashiq. He is preparing himself for the calamity that's about to strike him.

'I wasn't aware of the goings-on in Rayyat Toli. It's only yesterday that Girish babu apprised me of the developments. All this is very wrong. What do all of you plan to do?'

'What can I say, chacha? *Hoihe soi jo Ram* ... whatever Ram-ji wills—'

He breaks down before he can finish the sentence. When Pandi-ji gets up and puts a hand on his shoulder, he starts to shudder convulsively. Ashiq is an emotional man, and his eyes often moisten; but does he ever let a single tear drop? Crying and wailing are things women indulge in. When Zulekha cries, instead of consoling, he teases her. But today, the same Ashiq ...

'All the chowk boys say that Ashiq is a top-class rangbaz, he will surely find a way. Is a single government notice enough to blow away all your rangbazi? *Budbak*! Stop crying like a blockhead, or your brain will stop working. Things that can be set right will be ruined.' Pandi-ji chides him gently and pats him on the shoulder. Ashiq immediately wipes off his tears.

'Be brave, son. A way out of this will open. Aggarwal sahib was my senior in the AG office. His full name is Balram Aggarwal. He lives in the Marwari Tola and practises law after retirement only to help the poor and the helpless. Tell him that Triveni Mishra from Aramganj Chowk has sent you. He will certainly advise you. If there is some elder from Rayyat Toli who is willing, take him along as well.'

How can Ashiq tell him that no elder of the mohalla will come with him because the community has cast him out? He gets up quietly, touches Pandi-ji's feet and turns to go. 'Don't be afraid, son. Ram-ji will watch over you.'

Ashiq laughs a wan laugh. 'What will be gained from fear now, chacha? Hasn't Goswami Tulsidas-ji said, *Hani-laabh, jeevan-maran, jas-apjas ...*' Loss-gain, life-death, fame or shame/ All is destiny.

Seeing Ashiq return to form, Pandi-ji smiles. As he shuts the door, he says, 'Keep this discussion confidential. These are unfavourable times.'

Ashiq feels somewhat better after many days. Pandi-ji's words have acted like a magic potion. The minute he comes out, he looks at himself in the mirror of a parked bike and keeps staring for a few moments. He feels like giving himself two tight slaps. How did it even occur to him that Pandi-ji had summoned him to get the shop vacated? Constantly expecting the worst, his face has acquired a permanently dejected look. Cursing himself, Ashiq decides that whatever may happen, he will never, ever, cry like a *budbak* again. He will fight like a man.

There are only ten to twelve Maruti gypsies in the whole town. Among them Jagdhari Singh's vehicle can be recognised from afar. His name, along with his designation, 'local MLA', is printed in bold, black letters on the rear windshield. From morning to evening, this vehicle can be seen running across the town, so that the diligence and dedication with which the MLA is ensuring the Rath Yatra's success is known to everyone.

As soon as the night-curfew lifts, contractor Dheeraj Gupta unloads bamboo poles on every crossing from Station Road to Tara Pol Maidan. The frameworks of decorative gateways can be seen coming up. But the putting up of welcome gateways is not the only preoccupation Jagdhari babu has. How will a crowd of one lakh be made to gather on Tara Pol grounds on the day people will be busy celebrating the Bhai Dooj festival?

Jagdhari Singh is not one to surrender so easily. In mohalla-level street-corner meetings, he has been telling people that the mere sight of Advani-ji is akin to the *darshan* of Ram Lalla himself. Time is short; the work to be done, enormous. The clock is ticking away.

Ashiq glances at his wrist watch. It is past six-thirty in the evening. It's been a full one-and-a-half hours since he has been waiting outside advocate Aggarwal's chamber. Ashiq did not go to the shop today. His entire day was spent running from pillar to post. After coming back from Pandi-ji's house, he again searched all the trunks in his house—with the same result. The key to the eighth trunk still hasn't been located. His Amma again said that it contained only utensils. Ashiq told them to find the key or he would break the lock. After much bickering with his mother and wife, he went out to meet Advocate Aggarwal. Aggarwal sahib sent him back to bring the case papers. But who would give the papers to Ashiq?

Hakim chacha doesn't want to complicate mohalla politics any further. So he refused to even talk to Ashiq. His cousin Idris also advised him not to get involved in the convoluted court case. If it led to further enmity with the mohalla, they would all suffer.

Ashiq learnt from Ishtiaq Miyan that the court clerk could be of help, in getting a copy of the case papers. Ashiq reached the court, and after befriending the peon, sent in one-hundred-and-fifty rupees for the clerk. To the peon, whose job was simply to make photocopies and send documents inside the court, he handed some money for sweets. Case papers in hand, he then ran to the advocate's house, and now finally it is his turn to see him.

Aggarwal sahib reads the papers word by word, and asks Ashiq several questions. At last, he says, 'The case is strong. The government is finding fault with all of you on one technical ground. But there are too many drafting mistakes. Looks like your advocate did not argue this properly.'

Ashiq quietly tries to read Aggarwal sahib's face. When he stops speaking, Ashiq says, 'Sir, pull us out of this disaster somehow. This will earn you a lot of merit and fame. No one in Rayyat Toli has slept properly since the demolition notice arrived. Even putting a morsel down our throats has been impossible.'

After thinking for a while, Aggarwal sahib says, 'If you want a guaranteed solution to your problem, seek out advocate A.K. Rai straightaway. He is the only one who can get you a definite solution.'

Ashiq stares at him. Aggarwal sahib explains, 'He was a towering, influential lawyer of his time. A lawyer from Raja sahib's times—the same king who gifted the land to the people of Rayyat Toli. He would have all the old papers with him. Even today Raja sahib's relatives treat A.K. Rai as a family elder. He is a little short-tempered, but his heart is in the right place. I don't know what his fees are, you will have to talk to him about that. But I can write a referral letter addressed to him.'

Ashiq watches the curlicues of English appear on paper. Inderdev Pandey had given him a working knowledge of English, but not to an extent that would enable him to understand everything. After filling the page, Advocate Aggarwal writes five to six lines on the other side as well. Ashiq feels as if this is not just a letter, he has got the Sanjeevani booti—the mythical cure-all.

Due to extreme stress, Ashiq hasn't slept well for the past many days. Tonight, he is unable to sleep because he can finally see a glimmer of hope. Ayesha's fever, too, has subsided. 'With Ram-ji's grace—' Ashiq stops and hesitates. Then smiles to himself. Taking Ram's name is prohibited in Rayyat Toli. But what stops him from taking Ram's name in his heart? Thinking thus, he falls asleep.

Advocate A.K. Rai lives five kilometres ahead of Kutchery Chowk in a luxurious farm-house like mansion. The road is uphill, and Ashiq pumps the pedals of his cycle with all his might. Ashiq has gathered all the necessities of life for his home, but all he has by way of transportation is this ancient bicycle that once belonged to his Abbu. It is not as if Ashiq cannot buy a scooter or a motorcycle; but when life involves going only from the chowk to the house and vice versa, what's the point of blocking so much money?

Upon reaching the mansion gates, Ashiq feels a pang. A board is hung on the gate, saying, 'Do not contact for any legal cases.' Ashiq is staring at the board, when a man comes up to him and indifferently asks what he wants.

'Is Rai sahib at home?'

'Can't you see this board?'

'Ji, I haven't come for a case. I have been sent by Rai sahib's friend Balram Aggarwal with a letter.'

'Okay, give it,' the man says.

'The thing is, this letter is very personal. He has said it must be delivered only in Rai sahib's hands.'

The man opens the gates. A little fearful of the sound of a dog's barking, Ashiq follows after the man. Crossing the long yard, they reach the veranda; and opening the door of a room to the left, the man ushers him in. Ashiq sits there quietly. After a ten-minute wait, an old man with a thick grey moustache, walks in and asks, 'Who are you?'

'Sir, I am from Aramganj. Balram Aggarwal asked me to meet you. I have this letter from him.'

'If you have come for some legal matter, forget it. These days I don't concern myself with court cases,' Rai sahib says flatly, holding the letter in his hands.

'*Huzoor*, please read the letter. Just once.' Saying this, Ashiq falls at his feet, and opens his fists. In his palms are two thousand rupees and two gold bangles.

'*Arre!* What is this tamasha? Get up and sit down like a decent man.'

Sitting on the floor, Ashiq keeps crying. After reading the letter, Rai sahib takes a deep breath and says, 'Stop this filmy drama, pick up all this money and gold, and put it back in your pocket. Have you brought the case papers?'

Ashiq always sticks to his word. But the promise to never cry that he had made to himself has been broken again in less than twenty-four hours. For the first time, he realises that sobbing and crying are not foolish female pastimes. They have their own benefits.

'Do you know the biggest defect of the Hindu *comoonity*? They look for personal gains in everything. They don't know how to take 'rikks' and fight. That's why, despite being six hundred million in population, they keep getting beaten with shoes in their own nation.' Manojwa is giving this fiery speech to the young men in Bhuiyan Toli. The job of getting as many youth as possible to attend Advani's rally has been delegated by Kamlesh Singh to eager young workers like Manojwa. But the prospects don't look good.

'Even a trip from the chowk to Bada Bazaar makes these rascals start moaning for their grandmas. Imagine, trying to make them walk all the way to Tara Pol! These good-for-nothing sons of Kayasths are the biggest nincompoops on the chowk. They will stand around talking nonsense on the streets for as long as they please. They will come to the club, play carrom and drink. But the minute any work for society and the *comoonity* is to be done, they start slinking away.' Kamalesh sighs as he makes this sociological observation.

'Even the gali-walas are no longer what they used to be, bhaiyya. The bastard Kali Puja volunteers have fragmented the society. All *bhetnar* (veteran) criminals, from Bhuiyan Toli to Nonia Toli, are with them. To rise in politics, that Balchandra Shah from across the river is spending money indiscriminately. And our leaders? Without a single paisa in the pocket, what would rushing to the bazaar achieve?'

Manojwa may be a rascal, but he has identified the real problem immediately. The Yuva Shakti Sangh members taking part in the discussion approve of his sentiments. The leaders of Hindutva politics in the entire district have money in their pockets, that's why their workers are so full of fervour. What does Aramganj have, except empty talk?

'*Arre*, don't say that. Politics is played not just with money, but with brains. And no one has more brains that Jata kaka. No one would have dared to send an eviction notice to an old mohalla like Rayyat Toli. But look at the way the man's mind works. God knows what strings he pulled to make the *saala* circle officer come and put up that notice at once.'

'Will Rayyat Toli really get demolished? The government always takes the side of the Muslims. Will the government not put a stop to any such action?'

'It is a complex game. If Mini Pakistan is removed from Aramganj, there will be massive development in this whole area. Jatashankar Sharma will get all the credit. And if the government tries to save these people, then every son of Aramganj will get to know about their politics of appeasement. Just think—who stands to gain from this?'

'*O teri!* I never thought of all this. And if Valmiki Nagar also gets demolished alongside Rayyat Toli, it will be even better. Advocate sahib had gone with Prabhat bhaiyya to talk to Neta-ji Jatashankar the other day. The Valmiki Nagar residents should be sent packing from here.' Akhilesh speaks up for the first time. Only now, after a prolonged three-times-a-day hot-water bottle fomentation, has he begun to move normally. Kamlesh Singh is about to say, *Akal-less, you will forever be an asshole.*' But exercising restraint, all he says is, 'Don't ever talk like that, even by mistake. The Valmiki Nagar people are not 'others'. Hindu unity is under threat, and we must take everyone along.'

Unity is in great peril in Rayyat Toli as well. Displaying excessive enthusiasm, Salim and his friends had gone to explain to Hakim Ismail in their customary manner: 'Listen, stop this constant croaking for a 'new' advocate. Decision has already been made by our committee and the advocate will not be changed now.' The only two people in that house were Hakim sahib and his bed ridden wife. The minute Salim raised his voice, the old man lost it and raised his walking-stick. Salim tried to catch the stick to save himself. But Hakim sahib began screaming at the top of his voice, 'Help! Help! He is hitting me ...'

Within minutes, scores of people came running, and Salim and his friends got soundly thrashed.

'The whole mohalla is indebted to Hakim sahib. Hakim sahib is this bastard's grandfather's age, and this is the way he treats him!'

'This is enough. Such hooliganism cannot be allowed to continue.'

Even Shabberati's brother Masuriyaddin, who never opens his mouth, said, 'Do you talk to your own father and grandfather like this? Scoundrel! Bastard!'

Salim and his friends took off. But the matter did not end there. The news reached Ashiq's cousin Idris Miyan, who runs a wholesale vegetable business from Kunjada mohalla. Within an hour, he arrived with three well-built men.

Don't ask what happened then. A sturdy cane in hand, Idris Miyan knocked on every door, looking for the accused. After much effort, they caught hold of Imrozwa. Idris Miyan tied Imrozwa's hands to a tamarind tree, and gave him such a thrashing that his screams echoed in every house. 'I will save land and property later. First, I must shove back the hooliganism up your ass. Who else here wants to be a leader, *re*? If you have any guts, come out!' Like a crazed elephant, Idris Miyan bellowed.

Idris Miyan is not seen much. He runs his business, reads namaz five times a day, and trains youngsters in how to wield the stick during Muharram. People know only this much about him. The other day, too, he got quite angry. But today? By God, what rage!

The criminal-in-chief, Salim is still nowhere to be seen. Idris Miyan finally released Imrozwa after ten canes on the backside, and after making him squat up and down fifty times before everyone, holding his ears. Amidst this, contractor Shamim vroomed in on his motorcycle, and the two exchanged words. Suddenly Idris Miyan gave three tight slaps to him as well.

Rayyat Toli seems to be under curfew. People are now hiding inside their houses and speculating. Who knows what will happen next? Salimwa *saala* is a criminal. And Shamim sahib's network is far-reaching.

By that evening, when tempers cooled down, a perplexed character arrived at Mufti sahib's house. Impressed by Mufti sahib's arguments earlier, the man posed a simple question: 'Just as Pakistan can stop the persecution of Muslims in India with America's help, can't America also help in the matter of Rayyat Toli?'

Kamruddin Miyan was in a bad mood. So instead of Mufti sahib, the peon within him answered, 'Get out of here, you cunt-fucker! Do I look like Zia-ul-Haq to you? Who knows what will happen now?'

As the perplexed character escaped, he reminded Mufti sahib that Zia-ul-Haq was now *jannat-makani*, an inhabitant of Paradise. That, it would have been more apt if he had said Benazir Bhutto. But in his heart of hearts, he agreed with Mufti sahib. No one knew what was going to happen now. After the ruckus created by Idris Miyan, nothing much has happened in Rayyat Toli. Two days have passed, and the day of the hearing of their case in court has arrived.

The scene is different this time. Hakim Ismail sits on the front bench. This morning he stepped onto the court's campus surrounded by seven or eight people, like some VIP. Barkat Miyan hasn't come, but Idris has come in his stead. And around him, his strapping Kunjda Mohalla followers. Government employee Ishtiaq Miyan, who usually shies away from court matters, can also be seen sitting in the front row, next to Gafoor and Jumerati.

Though not in the front, the other faction of Rayyat Toli is also present in court. After all, their houses are at stake too. Kamruddin sahib is sitting by himself. Salim is nowhere to be seen. But his brother can be seen sitting in a corner. People had been whispering about contractor Shamim. But putting the 'incident' aside, he has also arrived in court. Right now, he is probably out for a paan.

'Mohammad Ismail and Sheikh Nizamuddin Wali Ashiq versus the State of Bihar,' the court messenger announces.

This announcement reveals that overnight a sea change has occurred in the political landscape of Rayyat Toli. The very person who did not have permission to open his mouth earlier, has now become a co-appellant in the case. Advocates of both sides stand up. This also comes as a big surprise to everyone.

Despite his wrinkles, A.K. Rai looks very sharp. On seeing him, Judge Kang's face momentarily registers surprise. He smiles at Hakim Ismail and says, 'So you all have come with a new lawyer this time. Hope you have brought the relevant evidence as well.'

A.K. Rai gets up, and in his old-fashioned British accent declares that much has changed since the last hearing. A new name has now been added to the list of complainants and the appellants have also changed their legal counsel. Hence it is necessary to start the argument afresh.

The government advocate, Purushottam Sinha, opposes this, saying that the arguments were done with in the previous hearing. Now the appellants only have to produce evidence. But the judge orders the government lawyer to sit down, saying that he will be given an opportunity to present his counter-argument.

A.K. Rai starts speaking. 'Your Honour, this is not an ordinary case, but a proof of the fact that in the last four decades, our system of governance has not changed one bit. With time, this system has become even more corrupt, insensitive and ineffectual. The poor and the helpless of this nation are alive, not because the government does its job, but despite the government. And this, Your Honour, is nothing less than a miracle.

'And ... excuse me, Your Honour, as far as the legal system is concerned, the judicial process in this country is nothing but a rope that can be tugged only by the hands of the powerful. A rope that turns into a noose for the weak. Today, the poor people of Rayyat Toli look towards you. Not only for a decision, but for justice.'

The judge perhaps did not expect a seventy-eight-year-old to speak in such a powerful voice, in so melodramatic a style. Rai sahib proceeds with his argument. 'For thirty-two years, my father S.P. Rai was the lawyer of the Shahdev royal family. This is where the history of this case begins. After my father's death in 1949, this responsibility passed on to me. And as long as Raja Prithvinath Shahdev lived, I discharged this duty. Owing to this,

I would like to assert that no one on this earth knows more about the facts of this case than I do.'

The government lawyer gets up and registers his objection. 'Your Honour, the appellant's lawyer is much senior to me, and I respect him for that reason. But nothing can be gained just by making statements. The last time, too, the appellant's advocate did not present any evidence, and this time as well, advocate sahib is only making circuitous statements.'

Before the judge can say anything, Advocate Rai gestures at his assistant who is holding eight or ten files. 'Your Honour, with your permission, I would like to present the evidence one by one. Firstly, the registered will of Raja Prithvinath Shahdev that my father had prepared on his request in 1940. You can see in the will that Raja sahib specified how his properties in Ranchi, Palamu, Jashpur, Cuttack and Calcutta were to be divided up among his relatives after his death. Alongside that, he talked about giving six-and-a-half acres of land to a trust which would build a school named after his father, Kashinath Singh. Your Honour, I repeat, six-point-five acres and not eight acres, as is being claimed by the government. Now my second evidence: this is a certified copy of the map of Kashinath School. You can see that the plot here has the same measurements, that is, six-and-a-half acres. Not eight acres. Meaning, the one-point-five acres where Rayyat Toli has been settled is a completely different piece of land.'

Rai sahib says in a jocular tone, 'Your Honour, the hands of the law are long, but the legs of a seventy-eight-year-old man are weak and wobbly. If you permit, I will sit down and rest for a while.'

The judge smiles and permits him to sit down, and starts turning over the pages of the documents presented. After some time, he asks the government lawyer, Purushottam Sinha, 'In the will as well as in the certified map of the school, the area mentioned is six-point-five acres. But your entire counter-argument is based on the claim that the school is on eight acres of land.'

'Your Honour, in any case, government documents take precedence over any other document. And the government documents show that the school is built on the entire eight acres of land. They make no mention of Rayyat Toli or the houses built on that land,' says the government's counsel.

A.K. Rai gets up again. 'The defence is being most helpful, Your Honour. Does he mean to say that one set of government maps is legal, and the other illegal? This is really amazing.'

Rai sahib uses a lot of English to make his points. The audience cannot understand half of the things he is saying, but they can guess that the arguments are working. Tabrez whispers to Shamim the contractor, who has been going out and in, 'Wait and listen, very strong points are being made by "our" lawyer.' Shamim cannot decide how to react to his usage of the possessive pronoun 'our' for the lawyer.

Shamim spots Kamlesh, who is standing in another corner of the court. Kamlesh gets flustered when their eyes meet. As if his eyes are saying, he was only passing by, so he thought why not watch what's going on.

'Order order ...' Irritated by the rising tide of whispers in the courtroom, the judge strikes the gavel.

'Your Honour, there is a big game hidden in the story of this map. This game involves taking shelter behind the screen of government rules and regulations and inflicting them on poor, innocent citizens so that they keep running around, until they are forced to accept that they are no better than insects who can be crushed at will by some official.'

'Objection, Your Honour. The appellant's counsel cannot rely on film-style dialogues alone. He has no answer as to why the government map does not show any presence of the Rayyat Toli houses,' the government counsel, Purushottam Sinha, corners A.K. Rai.

Rai sahib smiles at this question. 'I will certainly answer this question. But first, I will present other important evidence. This is the list of mohallas in the city, dating back to the British Raj. Rayyat Toli is listed here as one of the mohallas. And this is the letter sent by the electricity department in 1952, in response to Raja sahib's recommendation letter for the installation of an electricity pole in Rayyat Toli.

'These proofs are sufficient to prove that the residents of Rayyat Toli never illegally squatted on Raja sahib's land. Due to the division of properties among the progeny of the later generations, the number of houses has certainly gone up to forty, while initially, there had been only sixteen houses. Raja sahib had willingly given the land to those sixteen people. Photocopies of their registration papers are with me. Had the district administration wanted, they could have easily checked which people had the registration in their names and who did not. But without any investigation or enquiry, they simply sent everyone a notice on the basis of a map.

'The whole argument made by the defence rests on only one thing—the map. Your Honour, names get inscribed on the map only when mutation takes place. That is, the name of the new owner is admitted and the old or deceased owner's name is removed. It may be that due to ignorance, laziness or to avoid paying taxes, the Rayyat Toli residents did not get their mutation papers made. But that cannot be taken to mean that they have no right over their properties. I would like to present the house papers of the co-applicant in this case, Sheikh Nizamuddin Wali Ashiq.'

When Ashiq, who has been sitting quietly in a corner with his nephews Sajid and Wahab. gets up, many people realise for the first time that he too is present in the courtroom. Ashiq comes forward and hands A.K. Rai the papers.

'This house is in Ashiq's late grandfather Sheikh Ramzan Miyan's name, and has duly undergone mutation. Had the government counsel looked carefully at the map he refers to again and again, he would have seen a small portion of land marked with chalk, which was Sheikh Ramzan's, and now, my client Ashiq sahib's house.'

A shiver of excitement spreads through the courtroom. This document had emerged after breaking the lock on the eighth trunk. Amma had been saying that the trunk contained no papers, but both the registration and mutation papers were found in that trunk.

A.K. Rai makes his closing statement: 'Your Honour, as per state government rules, if anyone has been living on a piece of land for thirty or more years, he has ownership rights to that land. From this angle alone, this is an open and shut case. I could have given this argument right at the beginning. But I want the hearing to be prolonged. Do you know why? So that people come to know how the governance system functions in this country. So that people come to know the extent of corruption in the country. From Dam Road to Chandan Bagh, there are so many illegal constructions on government land. Despite legal prohibitions on the sale of tribal lands, the poor tribals are misled and their lands taken over by the powers that be every day. Have you ever seen any action being taken against that? But for following High Court orders, a soft target is found—this unlucky mohalla.

'Most Rayyat Toli residents are daily wage earners. Because they are doing the rounds of court-kutchery, even chulhas are not being lit in many houses these days. The fundamental principle of justice is that the one who is alleging must prove the charge.

But the government has torn this principle to shreds and turned innocent people living in their own houses into the accused.

'I recently underwent a cancer surgery, and have returned to this courtroom after a full eight years. The sole reason being one hapless man, Ashiq, who surrendered his wife's jewellery and all his savings at my feet, crying for help. What if I hadn't been sympathetic? Who would have fought on behalf of these unlucky people? A huge proportion of our population can only helplessly ask for pity, instead of demanding justice. But, Your Honour, my request is only this: Don't take pity. Decide the case on the basis of facts. That's all I have to say.'

The judge then asks the public prosecutor Purushottam Sinha if he has anything to say. Advocate Sinha says, 'The notice only says that those who have encroached illegally should move. If someone has not encroached, the notice does not apply to them.'

The judge gets irritated with this reply. 'Your whole argument was that Rayyat Toli itself is illegal, but now you are saying that if it is not illegal, it may not be removed. Do you take this court to be a joke?'

And then Judge B.S. Kang grants a stay, and starts dictating his orders. 'It seems that the district administration lacks information on ordinary rules of procedure. Sending a notice for demolition of houses without examining the facts is a terrible crime. The court orders a stay with immediate effect on this one-sided action of the district administration. The district officials must present themselves in court and explain as to what led to this deficiency and what is being done to remove encroachments in other areas of the town.'

Wahab, who studies in college, can follow English. When the judge gets up after dictating the order, Wahab tells everyone what the judgement says.

'So the house has been saved?'

'Yes, yes ... saved.'

'Whose houses?'

'*Arre baba*, the mohalla has been saved, so everyone's house is safe.'

'*Allah-karam*. God is merciful.'

'*Mubarak bhaijaan*. Congratulations, brother.'

'*Meharbani Garib-nawaz ki*. It's all by the grace of the One who saves the poor.'

'*Ya Allah*.'

'*Arre o* Miyan-ji, go out and say whatever you want to say. This is a courtroom, not your house,' the court clerk issues a strict warning to the rejoicing Rayyat Toli residents. But no one minds his admonition.

23

TRUTH ALONE TRIUMPHS

Deewaron se mil kar rona achcha lagta hai
Hum bhi paagal ho jayenge aisa lagta hai

It feels so good crying, face to wall
Looks like I too will lose my mind, after all

Pankaj Udhas's silky voice echoes from a tape-recorder in Shankar's Radio Repair Centre. But the chowk shopkeepers have no tears to shed when they face a wall. They cry only when they don't get a wall to face. Hand on zip, a hapless shopkeeper weaves his way through a melee of rickshaws, scooters, pushcarts and cows. Only towards the south—behind the transformer next to the rubbish dump—between Sakaldeep Sahay's house and Valmiki Nagar, does he find barely sufficient place to stand. Towards the north, another such place is near Inderdev Pandey's house. The long wall between his house and Gopal the cobbler's belongs to an old ceramic factory, no longer in operation. This wall is the dream destination of all chowk shopkeepers. College students like to scribble lines from one of Shaharyar's ghazals on this wall:

Is anjuman mein aapko aana hai baar-baar ...

You will grace this gathering time and again
In your memory, let these doors and walls remain

Despite countless attacks of forceful saline jets, this ceramic factory wall stands guard, the way our democratic system stays upright. With a wry laugh, the chowk shopkeepers often say, 'Even dogs are luckier than us. There are a dozen trees for them to lift their legs and piss on. For us, there is only one wall.'

But today, even this wall has been snatched away. Early this morning, someone duly whitewashed it, and inscribed in capital letters:

SAUGANDH RAM KI KHATE HAIN
MANDIR WAHIN BANAYENGE

We swear on Ram's name
There itself we will build the temple

Below it, is the invite. 'To welcome the Ram Rath, come to Tara Pol Maidan on 20 October. Seize the opportunity to listen in person to the fiery speech of the emperor of Hindu hearts, the *'Hindu Hriday Samrat'*, Lal Krishna Advani.'

Whether to inscribe a revolutionary message or simply pass water, everyone needs a wall. No party worker would think it ideal to inscribe the greatness of his leader next to advertisements promising to 'cure piles'. But what's anyone to do if this is the only wall available? Everyone—from Prabhu Ram to Hakim Usman—must adjust on this one wall.

Those who squat with the sacred thread wrapped behind their ears, have no problem with what's written on the ceramic factory wall. But the young men of Aramganj have an objection to it. Like the unstoppable flow of Time, their 'flow', too, is beyond stopping. Had nature granted more than one hue to this water, the young men of Aramganj would have achieved worldwide recognition for their innovative school of painting—'Urinism'. These young men get a sense of release only when they wet the factory wall; but how can anyone do so today with all this written on it?

Early on the same morning, when Ashiq's Amma stepped out, she saw that their boundary wall was being painted over. Seeing Imroz, she started abusing him. He tried to say something in his defence, further enraging the old woman. Meanwhile, Idris Miyan came out of his house. 'Chachi, I told him to whitewash the wall.'

Then turning towards Imroz, he said, 'Babua, if the wall is not shined properly, I will shine your bum.'

Idris Miyan is short-tempered. Everyone in Rayyat Toli knows that. But no one really expected that in merely four days he would turn the whole game on its head. Rayyat Toli has now unanimously accepted him as its leader. He has issued the order, 'The scoundrels who wrote abuses on Ashiq's wall must wipe them out, and also apply two coats of whitewash.' Imroz and Fazlu have been at work since then.

Yesterday evening, he had called a meeting in Imli Maidan, where hot jalebis were distributed and a motion publicly proclaiming thanks to Ashiq Miyan was passed. Afraid of his cousin since childhood, Ashiq has always obeyed him. But when he proposed this meeting, folding his hands, Ashiq asked to be excused. 'Bhaijaan, I will do whatever you say, but I will not stand there and get garlanded. I will be mortified.'

In the meeting, the rising hooliganism and ingratitude in the mohalla was roundly cursed. And the people in the habit of calling Ashiq 'Misir' and 'Hindu ki Aulad' were also criticised. Those welcoming this criticism included Taufiq and Badaruddin, who had, only a short while ago, openly supported the proposal to boycott Ashiq. Kamruddin Miyan, that is Mufti sahib, sat in the meeting with his eyes closed, as if in conversation with God, and when asked to speak, said, 'Allah has saved us. Now we must start building the masjid without any delay.'

This incensed Idris Miyan, who told him, 'Build whatever you want to build. Masjid, imambara, Taj Mahal. But first, give an account of the money you had collected from everyone in the name of this case. Was the entire twenty thousand spent on a single hearing? One man saved the whole mohalla by putting everything he owned on the line, but now the credit is being claimed by fifty idle-talkers. Ashiq incurred a lot of expense in running around and gathering papers for this case. I will ask him for a break-up of all he has spent, and everyone will have to pay up.'

In the whole crisis, Ashiq has emerged not just as a hero, but a super-hero. But Ashiq is finding it impossible to digest such praise from the mohalla people. He had gone out of the house early that morning. Wahab, whom he met on the street, informed him that his father had caught Imrozwa by the ear to make him whitewash the outer walls. Ashiq's heart missed a beat. *Gaddar kahin ka'* and *'Hindu ki Aulad'*—Ashiq wants to remember these two phrases till the day he dies. If he could, he would make them write the words on his wall again, so that every time they passed by his house, the Rayyat Toli residents would recall the way they had treated him.

Right now, Ashiq is sitting with a box of sweets in hand in A.K. Rai's large room and waiting for him to come. Before this, he had gone to Pandi-ji's and then to Advocate Balram Aggarwal's house with boxes of sweets. Had Pandi-ji not sent Ashiq to Aggarwal sahib, and had Aggarwal sahib not written a letter to Rai sahib, who knows what would have happened!

After the judgement, as Advocate A.K. Rai was stepping out of the court, Hakim Ismail caught his hands and cried. When

Rai sahib consoled him, Hakim Ismail said, 'After 1947, I have seen many hard times. Each time I felt—whatever I may do, there is no way I will ever be able to prove my loyalty to this soil. This country will never recognise our troubles. We will always be seen as thieves. But today you made me feel that justice isn't extinct. I am ashamed of the doubts that came to my mind.'

As soon as Rai sahib enters, Ashiq gets up and touches his feet, and then presents the box of sweets. Rai sahib says, 'As soon as you told me about the case, I realised that the matter was political.'

'Yes, there is a leader in Aramganj, Jatashankar Sharma. This was his brainchild.'

'Yes, yes, I know. He is my cousin's sister-in-law's son,' Rai sahib says, smiling.

For a moment Ashiq is taken aback.

'We say, Satyamev Jayate. That truth alone triumphs. But truth never wins on its own. We have to fight for it. Learn to fight. When the courts reopen after Diwali, get a copy of the orders, and get the mutation done for every house. Only then will you secure the right to open your mouth before the government for things like drains and roads. There is no greater sin in this world than stupidity.'

'Yes, sir.'

'And the two thousand that I returned that day, you can give them to me now. I am not charging you. But my assistant worked very hard to gather all those documents. I am only taking what is due to him, and the cost of the driver and petrol.'

'Okay, sir, but I haven't brought the money along.'

'Doesn't matter. Give it to Parmanand at the gate whenever you are passing by. All right then, you may go now, it's time for me to rest.'

Abbu used to say, acts of goodness should be remembered till one's last breath, and bad stuff should be forgotten the next moment. Ashiq will remember all the good that has been done to him. But can he forget the bad things as easily? He has come to the shop after three days. It's Dhanteras today. The road is jampacked, and it is not easy to make one's way through the crowded rows of hawkers selling utensils and lamps and reach Two-in-One tailoring shop. People standing about on the street stare at Ashiq, as if saying, '*Waah* Mr India! The way you gave the boot to the villainous Mogambo!'

The rescue of Rayyat Toli has been the trending topic at the chowk for the last twenty-four hours. As many things are being said as there are people.

'Ashiqwa was the real game-changer. Went to the courtroom and nailed the argument. The judge was taken with him.'

'This man has Ram-ji's blessings. Because of him, even Kallan-Jumman types got saved.'

'You all are needlessly turning Ashiqwa into a heroic figure. All this was done by Advocate Rai. I have said earlier, too, that in this country no one can do anything to the Miyans. Anything that goes wrong will be blamed on the Hindus—that too, by fellow Hindus.'

It is not as if the chowk-walas aren't interested in real news. But their interest in entertainment is far greater. That's why, more than the Rayyat Toli case, another story is being passed around this morning.

'Jhantwa is going through a bad patch these days. This morning, the poor fellow was about to leave for work, when the Valmiki Nagar residents surrounded him, and began shouting that if their mohalla was demolished, his house, too, would be razed to the ground.'

'*O teri!* Then?'

Incensed, Jhantwa came out—and what did he see? Fifty people standing! No sooner had he laid a hand on a scavenger's son swinging from his gate, than someone caught him by the scruff and slapped him. Now tell me, what became of the dignity of our leader and future MLA?' Satya bhaiyya is telling the tale in his signature style.

'All the gali-walas are now clutching their bellies and laughing, saying, Hindu unity has now been shoved up the elephant's arse.'

While this sensational scene is being discussed, Alok brings in a more serious piece of news. Jagdhari Singh is very annoyed with Jatashankar Sharma. He called Sharma-ji and asked, 'Did you initiate the ruckus over Rayyat Toli?'

Jatashankar said, 'Oh yes, this people's movement came about only because of the pressure I put on the circle office.'

Gnashing his teeth, Jagdhari Singh told him, 'What a nincompoop you are! Because of your chasing after one Musalman mohalla, a dozen Hindu mohallas are now about to come under the scanner for illegal encroachment. And all these mohallas are full of my voters. Go, drown yourself in the Poorna river!'

Late Shobharam Chowdhary—multiple times MLA, and also Jagdhari Singh's mentor—had once said something that echoes in the political corridors of this town even now. 'The one who pumps the Hindu-Muslim balloon to a reasonable degree, may possibly enjoy a stratospheric ride on this air balloon. But blowing it beyond measure might not only burst the balloon, but also blow up the blower's ass.'

Such is Jagdhari's anger that he has warned Jatashankar that he must not be seen anywhere around town until the Ram Rath has passed through. Insiders say, Jagdhari Singh did not get angry on his own; the whole game was played by Shalabhmani Tripathi. That Jhantwa had been flying a bit too high. So as soon as Shalabhmani got a chance, he saw to it that Jhantwa was cut to size.

The scraps of news about his leader being beaten up, thrown out and side lined are dubbed by Kamlesh Singh as mere rumours spread by the jealous-types. 'Jata kaka is a phoenix,' he proclaims.

'He is what?'

'The "fire-in-belly" bird that resurrects even after being burnt to ashes. You won't understand such high-brow stuff.' Akhilesh and Manoj listen to their leader Kamlesh Singh, eyes filled with devotion.

'What is this, Rangbaz? A full box of sweets for Pandi-ji, and not even one kalakand for us?' Sudama catches Ashiq as he steps out from behind the transformer to go to the shop.

'I will certainly give you sweets on Diwali.'

'But those will be for Diwali. Where is the party for saving the house?'

'If you want a party, go stand outside Marwari Brahmin Dharamshala. A banquet for the poor is being organised there.'

'*Arre katua!* At least feed me two samosas.' Sudama's demand now devolves into an entreaty. Sudama's father goes from shop to shop lighting incense and lamps, and the family subsists on whatever loose change he gathers through this work. The only brother of four sisters, Sudama didn't study beyond class eight. When his father never bothered to learn the Vedic rituals of *karm kand*—in order to become a practising priest and earn some money—why would he learn? His company is such that he cannot do without liquor. He is often seen following Om-ji or Lallan, begging for a peg. Some shopkeepers like Ashiq sponsor his morning and evening snacks. This is the way this pandit's only son passes his days.

Outside Bajrangi's dhaba, Sudama is stuffing his face with samosas and chutney, when Ashiq's gang comes and whisks him away. The carrom club has been missing him. Without Ashiq, the addas for idle talk had been bereft. As soon as Ashiq Miyan

arrives, the carrom-corner on Mithilesh's veranda—kept free despite the Dhanteras rush—comes alive again. Ashiq feels as if, after years, he is returning among his own. The same excitement, boisterousness, abuses and banter. The same intimacy!

'*Arre* Rangbaz, where did you disappear? We went looking for you to the shop so many times, but you were nowhere to be found! Prem boss, too, has been looking for you.' Lallan makes a sudden entry.

'Why was Premwa looking for me?'

'You are a big gun, and he is also a big gun. Must be for some work. Come, let's go and meet him.' Lallan doesn't wait for Ashiq's reply and starts pulling him along. As he is leaving, Ashiq calls out to Hanif, 'Shut the shop, and tell your bhabhi, I will come home by ten tonight.'

There's a proverb in Hindi, '*ghoore ke bhee din phirte hain*'— even a rubbish heap's fortunes can improve someday. This proverb rings true near the Kali Puja pandal. Tall and grand, stands the pandal, reminding people of the famed Kali Puja pandals of Calcutta. In last year's Kali Puja pandal competition, this committee stood third. This year, the custodian and Member of the Legislative Council (MLC), Balchandra Saha has given them a target: 'Do whatever it takes—we must stand first this year.'

An area of over a thousand square metres has been barricaded with ropes, and hundreds of flower-pots have been lined up in rows. The whole area is lit up with tubelights. Colourful string lights blinking in patterns are being put up too. Tomorrow it will get livelier. Lallan and Ashiq go backstage. The atmosphere there is that of a green room. There are ten or twelve chairs in a curtained-off enclosure, and at some distance, a three-seater sofa, on which the president sits clad in a safari-suit.

'Come, Rangbaz, come, how are you?'

'Everything is fine, Prem.'

Ashiq is among the few from Aramganj, who can talk to Prem with such familiarity. Their relationship is old, so this can be done. Otherwise, who can talk this way to a contract killer? Prem asks Ashiq about the house, saying, that although in matters of court his hands are tied, if there is anything else he needs help with, Ashiq must tell him without hesitation.

Ashiq says that by Ram-ji's grace, everything has been resolved.

Prem then comes down to the real business. A mock weapon drill will be organised in the evening programme just before the immersion of Ma Kali's idol. Ashiq is required to perform his famous feat with lit torches in the pandal, and after that, a new dance item for the immersion procession. Something even better than his Dussehra dance, because it is a matter of Kali Puja Committee's honour.

'Let us make him dance like Madhuri Dixit this time.' A voice emerges from behind Ashiq.

Before he can turn his neck to see who is speaking, he finds himself dangling in the air. When he is put down, he realises this is Pawan Hatwal. The tall-as-a-palm-tree secretary of the puja committee is his childhood friend. These days he is a big gun, hence on the streets, he ignores him. But this is a private meeting, so he is expressing his affection for Ashiq in a playful way. Suddenly a hanger-on comes and whispers in Pawan's ears. Pawan shuffles over to Prem, and the two talk. The mood in the room turns grave.

People start moving out of the green room. There is a crowd on the street and everyone looks anxiously ahead.

'*Arre,* what happened? Is everything okay?'

'The Chandpur brothers, who had got injured in the bomb-blast in Jaipur—one of them has died. The body has arrived and is being taken for cremation now.'

'Oh my God! Will there be a curfew again?'

'The Member of Parliament, Ram Pyare Chowdhary has told the administration that they must maintain law and order at all costs, that everyone will cooperate, and a curfew must not be imposed again. Chowdhary knows that the imposition of curfew will wreck not only Diwali festivities, but Advani's programme as well. These people are just too smart.' Prem Rajbhar's statement shows that he keeps a sharp eye on local politics.

As two police vehicles pass by sounding their sirens, Pawan explains, 'The administration is getting the last rites performed at night so that there is minimal crowd.'

Soon seven or eight constables are seen coming. The body has been allowed to be put on a bier at the Aramganj crossing, from where the grieving near and dear ones of the dead man will carry it to the cremation ground about a kilometre away. Only the family of the dead man and five or six mohalla people are in this procession.

As the funeral procession passes by the puja pandal, Ashiq happens to glance at the corpse illuminated by a tubelight—fair, curly-haired, such innocence marks his face! It seems as if he's only sleeping. The loudspeaker in the Kali Puja pandal has been switched off, and in this sinister silence, the funeral procession is moving towards the crematorium. Suddenly, it seems that the procession is swelling. Several people are emerging from the lane just behind the puja pandal. They are members of the Yuva Shakti Sangh. Prem and Pawan also move forward to join the funeral procession, but the moment their eyes fall on Jatashankar Sharma, they withdraw.

The procession moves hardly twenty metres ahead, when a deafening slogan echoes in the skies.

'Khoon ka badla khoon se lenge.'

'We want blood for blood.'

This is Jatashankar Sharma, the die-hard fighter and leader. Behind him, ten more voices rend the air. 'We want blood for blood ...'

The police constables walking along swing into action. One inspector-like person tries to ascertain as to who is provoking these slogans. But the mob is already in the throes of a frenzy. The slogans are getting chanted on their own. Ajju from Valmiki Nagar points at Baiju: 'Look at that madman.'

Baiju's fists are tight, and his face is red with anger. *'Blud for blud ... Jai seeli laam!'*

Ashiq's head is buried between two pillows.

That was last night. Today is Diwali morning. But the slogan still echoes in his ears. 'We want blood for blood ...'

The minute Ashiq's heart strives to be happy, something or the other occurs to make him despondent again. The face of the twenty-year-old, curly-haired boy lying on that bier floats before his eyes. As he gets out of bed, Ashiq decides that under no circumstances will he let any despondence touch him today. In this world, good things and bad things keep happening. Today, after so long, the faces of his family members are lit with smiles. Hence this Diwali is special for him.

By tradition, lamps are lit in the shop every Diwali since Gani Miyan's time. Even in Bada Bazaar, most Muslim shopkeepers light lamps. The houses are a different matter. The Muslim houses next to those of Hindus always light lamps. But in Rayyat Toli, there is no Hindu house. Even so, three to four houses always light lamps on Diwali here. When the whole world is celebrating the festival of lights, what's the fun in wretchedly embracing darkness?

Two big earthen lamps are lit on the freshly whitewashed wall of Ashiq's house, and in the space between the lamps, the words 'Satyamev Jayate', or truth alone triumphs, are inscribed in colourful letters. These words have been etched in the very spot where the slurs 'Traitor' and 'Son of a Hindu' had been inscribed. Only blue and pink chalks have been used to write 'Satyamev Jayate', but so beautiful is Ashiq's handwriting, that the words themselves seem to be illuminated.

Shami can read, but Ayesha can't. Lamps, she is familiar with, but she does not know what's written.

'When Raja Ramchandra returned after his victory over Lanka, Diwali was celebrated. It's the same Diwali we celebrate today. "Satyamev Jayate" means, may truth and honesty win,' Ashiq explains to Ayesha.

'Just as Abbu won and our house got saved,' Shami at once repeats what he heard from his Ammi. Ayesha doesn't understand, but keeps looking at the letters on the wall.

Diwali preparations are underway full steam ahead at the chowk. Banana stems have been tied to door frames, and strings of mango leaves are being hung above the doors. Shopkeepers have collected money to decorate the roundabout with string lights. Colourful plastic buntings have been strung all the way, from the roundabout to Hari Sweets. The whole area is glittering. It's thanks to the chowk shopkeepers that the atmosphere at the chowk is joyful. Otherwise, the retired people and their sons here have small hearts, and even smaller pockets.

'Ammi … Ammi, the vehicle has come,' Shami shouts, running into the inner room. Ashiq has sprung a surprise. 'Today everyone will go and visit the shop.'

Amma refuses straightaway. 'All this is fine for the children, I won't go.' Hearing this, Zulekha Bano's face falls. Seeing this

Ashiq says, '*Arre*, if Amma isn't going, is she saying that you must also stay with her? We will be back in less than an hour.'

And so, with much awkwardness, and feeling very shy, Zulekha Bano puts on a Patiala suit stitched by Ashiq, and gets ready to go. Valmiki Nagar's Ramesh stands respectfully beside the tempo-rickshaw outside the house. He ushers her in, 'Come, bhabhi-ji.'

How many occasions have there been, when Zulekha Bano has stepped out like this with her whole family? Despite the crowded streets, the journey from their house to the shop is over in minutes. Shami jumps out and runs into the shop. The rest follow him through the shining glass door of Savitri Boutique.

'*Hai Allah!*' Zulekha is taken in by the beauty of the scene inside. Everything is shining in the tube-lit shop. Beautifully arranged salwar-suits hang in the wardrobe. Several bolts of cloth are arranged neatly on one side. Zulekha recognises the bolt from which her Patiala suit has been stitched. She can see herself from many angles in the full-size mirrors.

She feels like asking her man if the mannequin modelling the salwar-suit is prettier than her. The kids go back and forth through the two-by-four door from Savitri Boutique to Mr India. Hanif has cleaned both the shops and nicely decorated them. Tonight, he will sleep in the shop itself.

After entering Mister India, Ashiq tells Zulekha, 'Come over to this side.' In Mister India, her eyes are drawn to the big picture of Ram, Lakshman and Sita on the wall, and she can't stop looking at it. She is unaware of the fact that the 786 sticker pasted on the mirror in front of the wall is also new, and is gleaming more than ever.

'Lamps are being lit everywhere, bhaiyya,' Hanif informs.

Pointing at the row of diyas outside the shop, Ashiq tells Zulekha, 'Since you have come, light some lamps with your own hand.'

'*Dhatt*, how can I? People are watching.'

'So what? People will only say Ashiq's wife is beautiful.'

'No, no, I won't light. I feel shy.'

'You are the incarnation of Lakshmi, you light them,' Ashiq then tells little Ayesha.

After the lamps are lit, Ashiq sends Hanif out with a hundred-rupee note. Hanif observes that the old swagger is back in Ashiq's gait. Within five minutes, Hanif comes back with some firecrackers—rockets and *anar*, the flowerpot cracker— and starts looking for an old bottle to launch the rockets. But standing on the shop's veranda, Ashiq holds a rocket in his hand and lights the nozzle. The rocket shoots up. Shami claps, but Zulekha shrieks. '*Hai Allah*, don't you dare do that again!'

Ashiq laughs. 'Say that again.' Zulekha is miffed, but this derring-do makes Ashiq launch all the rockets in the same way. He then tells Hanif and the kids to go out and light the *anars*. In the light thrown by the sparkling *anars*, Ashiq sees Ghooran pandit coming towards the shop. A Muslim can never hire a Hindu as a priest, but seeing the shop-front lit with lamps, Ghooran himself enters the shop. He rings his bell inside and outside the shop, and chants some mantras in Sanskrit mixed with Avadhi. Ghooran then stands before Ashiq, reminding him of what Inderdev baba used to say:

> '*Shubham karoti kalyanamarogyam dhan-sampada*
> *Shatru-buddhi-vinaashaya deep-jyoti namostute*'

> 'Let's bow before the light that spreads good omen, health and prosperity
> Let's fold hands before the light that destroys thoughts of enmity'

Ashiq refrains from chanting the mantra, because Ghooran pandit might see it as a put-down. He drops a ten-rupee note in Ghooran's basket and calls out to Hanif, '*Arre* Hanif, give some sweets to Pandit chacha.' Hanif puts two laddus in the basket, and Ghooran pandit walks away, towards the next shop, chanting, '*Kalyan ho ...*'

On their way back, Ayesha asks, 'Ammi, why is our house not as pretty as Abbu's?'

'*Dhatt*, silly girl! That is a shop, not a house,' says Ashiq.

'She's right in saying that. Wherever a man lives becomes his house,' says Zulekha, teasing him. Her smile dimples her cheeks. This smile had been missing for the past so many days.

As the tempo-rickshaw enters Rayyat Toli, everyone watches wide-eyed. All the houses, except for perhaps two or three, are illuminated with lamps. This is not a celebration of Ram's return to Ayodhya, but of their own exile being put off. As they step inside the house, Ashiq's Amma says, 'Jumerati and Ishtiaq both came with Diwali sweets.'

This, too, has happened for the first time in the history of Rayyat Toli.

As they are about to sleep, Zulekha says, 'Can't you get a small poster like the one you have in the shop?'

'The 786 poster? We already have one in our house.'

'No, the one opposite it.'

'Why? You want to be a *kafir*?'

'May my enemies become *kafirs*. That photo is very beautiful, no other reason. If keeping a photo made people turn into *kafirs*, then wouldn't you have become one?'

Ashiq laughs heartily. When he stops laughing, Zulekha notices that Ashiq's old smile is back on his lips, revealing his gleaming white teeth—exactly like Anil Kapoor's.

24

THE LAST LAUGH

This story began on the 20th of September 1990. The calendar is now at the 20th of October. For the chowk, life might still be moving at the same old, laidback pace, but for Ashiq Miyan, life has been on a roller-coaster for the past one month. The good thing is that, like in the Bollywood movies, his story, too, seems to be heading towards a happy ending.

Today is the day of Bhai Dooj and Chitragupt Puja. Chhath Puja will follow, and with it, the season of festivals will end. The gaiety observed at the chowk from Dussehra to Chhath is seldom visible at any other time of the year. The hearts of young men ache with a sense of loss as the festive season nears its end. Once this season ends, how bereft will the streets be—without the eye-soothing vision of the lively Aramganj girls.

The Kayasths have wrapped up the ritual worship of the pen and the inkpot. In most houses, even the Bhai Dooj ceremony is over. In the post-lunch hours, men step out into the street like every day. Cassettes of fiery speeches by Sadhvi Rithambara and Uma Bharati play on a loop in Shankar's Radio Repair Centre. To remind the dozing citizens that the much-awaited Ram Rath has at last reached their town.

Lakshmikant Sahay knows that already. One after the other, he has been asking as to who among his retired friends will accompany him to Tara Pol Maidan. Verma-ji and Bhola babu refused straightaway. Durga pandit had agreed earlier, but at the last minute, he came down with a stomach ache. Finally, only Vibhuti Mishra has volunteered to go. Hung between yes and no, Madhukar Choubey, too, eventually climbs into the rickshaw when he hears that these two will buy fresh vegetables from the local *haat* on their way back.

Among the youth, Akhilesh's commitment is unwavering. He is the first to step out—not as a volunteer of the Yuva Shakti Sangh, but as an awakened Hindu patriot. Munna, too, has left on his bike. Despite the claims of Hindu unity having been shattered, many curious souls from the low-caste galis are heading for Tara Pol Maidan. But those not going are many times the number of those going. Reason being, the grand mock-arms drill being held at the Kali Puja pandal. Post this programme, the procession for immersing the idol of Ma Kali will commence.

This time, the Kali Puja Committee has sent printed invitation cards to all the leading citizens of this town. But there is much hesitation in the hearts of the upper-caste chowk gentlemen. Because among the organisers of this pandal are not just Backwards, but also 'Bhangi-Chamars' of the lowest of castes. If social mingling happens in the name of Kali Puja today, who's to say that tomorrow they won't start calling on them in their homes! Best to stay away!

Sarvdaman babu's friends nod their heads in agreement at this advice, but after he leaves, they chortle. 'His own daughter has married a low-caste Lohar, and yet such snobbery! His false pride remains undiminished. A zebra can't change its stripes, can it?'

This dilemma, though, racks only the chowk residents. No such doubts regarding whether or not to attend the mock weapon drill prevail in the bylanes of Aramganj. It is a show worth watching. One must watch it to the heart's content—what else!

The district administration, however, is on tenterhooks. The home secretary himself is taking a minute-by-minute update on the wireless. A huge crowd has assembled in Tara Pol Maidan. Not twenty-five-thousand, or fifty thousand, but one lakh odd people must have gathered there. No mean feat to gather people in such large numbers on a festival day. Advani-ji gives a fiery speech, and makes the crowds chant, *'Mandir wahin banayenge'*. There itself we shall build the temple. Youths like Akhilesh and Munna tighten their fists and, amplifying the slogan, chant on, 'There itself we shall build the temple.' The programme ends and Advani-ji proceeds to the next town. At this peaceful conclusion, the district administrator and the city SP congratulate each other.

What Lakshmikant Sahay and his friends liked best was the way Advani-ji, without beating about the bush, stated, 'Entangling the temple issue in legal minutiae is a trick that will never work. The issue of where Lord Ram was born is a matter of faith. And a matter of faith cannot be decided by the courts. If the courts stay away from this issue, they might save their honour.

'The government's policy of appeasement is amazing. Did they not see to it that the court's decision in that Muslim divorcee Shah Bano's case got overturned in the Parliament? But now, the same government is telling the Hindus, that in order to free their Ram temple, they must do the rounds of court-kutchery!

'The Hindu society is full of cowards. Had they not been cowards, would the Hindus have been enslaved for a thousand years?'

'Not cowards—they are tolerant and soft-hearted. But no more.' As Vibhuti Mishra lifts his index finger to say this, he feels as if he, too, is Advani. His missus agrees: 'The same bald head, the same grey moustache. Though your paunch is slightly bigger.' It seems, Advani has given many old men of the country a new identity. 'Moustaches and machismo', both like Advani's. Inspired by Advani, a few chowk fathers decide to end appeasement. Not of the Muslims, but of their useless sons. Radhey babu is one of them. But today, he hasn't been able to arrive at a firm decision like a real 'Lauh Purush'—Iron Man.

He still cannot decide whether he should attend the glitzy function organised by the Kali Puja Committee or not. He was roiled by a similar inner conflict fifteen years ago, when Gupta-ji had suggested, 'An English movie is running in Plaza—a very hot one, if you know what I mean. Let's go and watch the night show.' Radhey babu stepped out of the house, but turned back midway. This time, too, he decides to walk the middle path. Meaning, he will stroll up to the pandal, but not enter. He will see whatever he can from the outside. If anyone asks, he will say he is only passing by.

Every possible effort has been made by the Kali Puja Committee to be one up on the chowk's Durga Puja function. MLC Balchandra Saha is the chief guest. An arms drill like this one has never been held before in a Kali Puja function. Normally one has to wait till Ramnavami for stuff like this. Not only are they distributing sherbet among the audience, from time to time, they are even making announcements in English.

Radhey babu recognises the voice of the nutjob Om-ji, the black sheep of the Kayasth clan. Thank God! At this distance from the stage, he is safe from Om-ji, or he would have required all his agility.

Along with Bhagtu, Om-ji is the co-presenter of this show. The Valmiki Nagar residents are going gaga over Bhagtu's talent. Had there not been a great man like Pawan bhaiyya in their community, no one would have given Bhagtu such a chance. While introducing the competitors about to present their drills with spears, swords or lathis, Bhagtu mimicks the oratorical styles of legendary Bollywood characters and actors—Gabbar Singh, Mogambo, Bachchan, and so on. Watching the drills, Radhey babu is assailed by a terrible thought: 'What if all these Kurmi, Kahar, Harijan lowborns join hands and launch an attack on the chowk?'

'Ram-ji had passed by this way. Nothing bad can happen to anyone on this road.' Ashiq's words suddenly echo in his mind. But where is Ashiqwa?

'So *bainno or bhaiyyon,* shisters and bratherrs, the prize dishtribution ceremony is about to baginn. After this, the immersion procession will start. But before that, the faaainull item. Hold your hearts and brace yourselves, ladies and gentlemen, for Ashiq Rangbaz and his friends are coming—with their famous act, 'Rangbaz vs Talwarbaz.'

'Ashiq Rangbaz!' The word 'Rangbaz' echoes thrice through the surround-sound loud speakers, and a song starts playing: *'Kahan se laayi dhoondh ke ye mehboob o mehbooba, ajooba, ajooba, duniya ka aathwaan ajooba ...'* This hero, this lover, this wonder supreme/Where did you find him O pretty queen ...

A thrill runs through the crowd as Ashiq makes a hero-like entry—wearing shiny clothes, a red band tied around his head—holding lit torches in both hands. He begins by wielding and juggling the torches the way lathis are wielded on Ramnavami.

'*Arre,* Rangbajwa is looking exactly like Anil Kapoor!'

'*Garda!* He will wow everyone today!'

Radhey babu notices Durga pandit and Bhola babu standing in another corner of the pandal.

'See this! Both Gupta and Tiwari are seated inside the pandal on chairs, like VIPs. Yesterday, these rascals were inciting everyone to stay away from the low-castes.'

One by one, Ashiq, aka Rangbaz, hurls the torches four feet up in the air, and flawlessly catches them. Four sword wielders suddenly emerge to challenge him. Both sides—the sword-wielders and Rangbaz—now brandish weapons, and continue challenging one another, locked in steps of a dance, as if assessing each other's threat potential. Ashiq then accepts his opponents' challenge with the flamboyance of superstar Rajnikanth, and, passing the torches to a troupe member, picks up a sword. Sword! In hands that wield the scissors!

One swordsman charges ahead, as if he will chop Ashiq's feet off. But Ashiq jumps up high in the air and escapes. Another swordsman targets his neck, but Ashiq escapes by crouching down. He learnt these moves from his wrestler cousin, Idris. The irony is, that over the past fortnight, Ashiq has fought bare-handed.

When Ashiq moves forward waving the sword, the opponents step back. One by one, each of the four swordsmen lock swords with him. Sparks fly as metal clashes with metal. But not a scratch on anyone!

In the last round, all four swordsmen attack Ashiq together. For a moment, everyone has their hearts in their mouth. But the swords closing in for Ashiq's throat end up merely clashing with one another, and Ashiq stays unharmed even when surrounded by enemies. Then the five players freeze in this pose. Claps and whistles resound for a while in the pandal.

Word has reached the chowk that Ashiq Rangbaz is in ultimate form today, and will perform in the immersion procession. In the show today, he will present something one better than even his Dussehra act!

The procession is so well lit that every face can be seen clearly. Abeer and gulal are being flung up from trucks, raising clouds of red and pink. Volunteers are bursting crackers non-stop, making the sky sparkle the way it does on Diwali.

The immersion procession has crossed Valmiki Nagar, and is now moving towards the chowk. Leading from the front are ten to twelve women labourers, who are walking with tubelights on their heads, alongside a cart bearing a genset. On the truck that is following behind, are the officials of the puja committee and the presenter, Bhagtu Ram. Om-ji got so inebriated that he had to be deboarded from the truck after being declared 'retired hurt'. Behind this truck, another tube-lit genset-bearing cart follows. And bringing up the rear, is a flower-bedecked truck, on which sits the fearsome idol of Goddess Kali.

'From where did they get all this money?'

'From tent to crackers, all came free of charge. Who'd dare ask Prem Rajbhar for payment? Besides, the puja committee's custodian, Balchandra Saha, is a crorepati.'

'Whatever be the case, they have certainly eclipsed the chowk Durga Puja.'

The entertainment quotient of this procession has shot up due to the exemplary technical support provided by Shankar Radios. Shankar stayed up the previous night, clipping audios and putting them together in a single cassette, which is now belting out one foot-thumping Bollywood number after the other. The whole occasion is a superhit! As soon as one song ends, the next one begins, sending the dancers' energy levels soaring to the skies.

When it reaches the chowk, the procession stops at the widest part of the street, just a little distance short of Ashiq's shop. Now the item everyone has been waiting for will begin. The humdrum *nagin* dancers and 'disco' dancers are shoved aside. The thumping rock-and-roll tune of *'Bol Baby Bol'* heralds our hero. Ashiq may be an 'ashiq'—lover—by name, but today, his bearing and swagger confirm that he is a swashbuckling hero, a true 'rangbaz'.

On his head, a cap, like the one Anil Kapoor wore in the movie *Ram Lakhan*; and around his neck, a garland of ten-rupee notes that Balchandra Saha felicitated him with in the Kali Puja pandal. Look at the attitude! The same guy who talks to chachis and didis in honey-dipped tones when at his tailoring shop, is now swaggering as if he doesn't recognise anyone.

The lit torches are back in his hands. The song *'My name is Lakhan'* is playing. Ashiq is dancing just like Lakhan. From time to time, filling kerosene in his mouth, he blows out rings of fire. Everyone is awestruck. This is a tough trick to master. No one in Aramganj knows how to do it—not even Ashiq's spear- and lathi-wielding cousin Idris.

Years ago, Ashiq had seen Basant—who performed feats like riding a cycle non-stop for a full week before crowds—do it. The adolescent Ashiq was fascinated. When the cycle-show ended, he took to following Basant around. One day, in a good mood, Basant taught him the trick. 'Take a mouthful of kerosene, and, using just the right amount of force, spout it at the fire. Be very careful—if too forceful, the fire will leap right up to your mouth.

The flash-bulb of the *Deshdeep Times'* photographer pops up many times. But the flames leaping from Ashiq's mouth are several times brighter than the camera flash.

Fekan from Valmiki Nagar gets a barfi from Hari Sweets and stuffs it in Ashiq's mouth by way of encouragement. Rajnarain Singh's son, Rajkumar, swirls a twenty-rupee note around Ashiq's head, and flings it at the crowd of volunteers.

The procession is inching ahead. Ashiq feels as if the procession is not for Goddess Kali, but for his own victory. All that he had lost over the last few days, is being returned to him by Lord Ram with interest. When the procession takes a right turn at the roundabout, blood starts pumping faster through his veins.

Rayyat Toli is hardly a hundred steps from here. Look at this, mohalla people! With a shroud tied around his head, here comes the 'traitor'! He wants to scream, 'It's fine if you think of me as the son of a Hindu. Come on! Here I am! Do whatever you want now.' Ashiq wants to cock a snook at every person who has wronged him.

Ashiq whispers something in Bhagtu's ears. Bhagtu nods, and the next song begins.

Yamma yamma, yamma yamma
Ye khoobsoorat samaa
Bas aaj ki raat hai zindagi,
Kal hum kahaan tum kahaan

Yamma yamma, yamma yamma
How lovely is this hour
Let's live our lives just for tonight
Who knows where we will be after this night

'*Gajabbe tez hai Bhagtua*! Bhagtua is incredibly brilliant! What a crackling choice of music! Lyrics as blazing as the lit torches in Ashiq's hands! This feels not like some immersion *juloos,* but like a live song sequence from some movie.'

Every terrace is choc-a-block. People have been shoved to the edges to create enough empty space in the middle of the road for Ashiq to wield and juggle the lit torches from one hand to the other.

A new building owned by Shrikanth Singh stands to the right-hand side of the roundabout. Its half-basement has godowns. A corridor with six shops has been built eight feet above street-level. Shrikanth Singh himself lives on the top-most level.

Constructed after demolishing his old house, this commercial-cum-residential complex has been christened 'Singh Arcade'.

The shopkeepers as well as the houseowners are watching the show intently, when there is a power outage. The owner of Prakash Studio immediately replenishes the genset with petrol and tugs at the starter rope. With a sputter and a clatter, the corridor lights up again. The song blaring from the loudspeaker changes. This is from Amitabh Bachchan's latest movie.

Itne baju, itne sir, gin le dushman dhyan se
Harega woh har baazi jab khele hum ji-jaan se

All these arms and heads, let the foe count them all
Every bet he will lose, when we wager it all

Ashiq's form now is worth seeing. Every gesture of his embodies the lyrics. Every little muscle on his arms can be seen moving, as if eager to wager life itself. His eyes are full of defiance, casting a challenge at all foes. But who is Ashiq's foe here? No one from the chowk. And now, maybe no one in Rayyat Toli either.

Gani Miyan, his Abbu, was right in saying, 'Even the worst man is good inside.' Enmity, rage, hatred. Such meaningless words. No. No one is Ashiq's foe. He is a man who can only be loved. What will anyone gain by treating him as an enemy?

The song ends. Within five or six seconds, a new one will begin. Holding the lit torches in both hands, Ashiq stands at attention—waiting. As soon as the new song comes on, every muscle in his body will come alive again, to enact the sentiment of the lyrics. Fussu moves closer to Ashiq, holding up a bottle of kerosene. Ashiq fills his mouth, and Fussu backs away to stand at a distance, like the twelfth man in a cricket match. Ah! Looks like the new song has started! *'Khoon ka badla khoon se lenge … Jai Seelee Laam …'*

Before anyone can register this sudden cry, a huge ball of fire comes rolling. Such a big ball from Ashiq's mouth? No. Ashiq hasn't blown this fire. He himself is inside this ball now. A tornado rages in the two-metre radius from the point where Ashiq is standing. The people watching from the terraces register the horrific incident only when screams rend the sky.

In the doorway of Prakash Studio, Baiju stands trembling. Another cry—a vile mix of shock, fear and excitement—spurts out of his mouth.

'Bllud for blludd ...'

It takes a few bewildering moments for Prakash to realise that sneaking in somehow, the fellow tossed a petrol can at Ashiq. A full three to four litres of petrol. Now only flames leap up from the spot where the show was going on. Wild, red flames—intent on swallowing everything up.

Sometimes, as a story is being written, the nib of a writer's pen splinters on its own. The final few words etched out in drying ink fight for breath, like a fish gasping out of water. Silence that suddenly devours all noise is the most terrible thing in this universe. That silence now spreads across the chowk. Beyond that, what's left to say?

In a story inching towards a climax, bewilderment like this might seem like a dramatic ploy on the part of the writer, I don't deny that. A writer might insist a thousand times that he has no idea how the story will end, but no one ever believes him. I am not claiming that I did not know how this story would end. If you recall, I had said right at the beginning that every wrist watch—whichever wrist it may be strapped on—is a time bomb. My error was that I got so engrossed in telling the tale that I forgot that the hands of the watch had inched this close to the timer.

The time bomb exploded and now only a stunned silence prevails.

The night passes somehow, and morning dawns. No one remembers when a morning like this was last witnessed in Aramganj. Except for two or three shops, all the others at the chowk stay shut. Police patrolling extends from Rayyat Toli to the Kali Puja pandal. People on the chowk talk in hushed tones about the night's incident.

'A woman labourer carrying a tubelight on her head got skinned alive by the fire. She will not survive. Three other women are badly burnt. All have been admitted to Ramlal Modi Hospital. Fussu's right hand is charred so badly that the bones are visible. Chunnu was lucky. When his hair caught fire, someone smothered the flames with a cloth. Even so, the singed hair is stuck to his scalp. Harendra Yadav, Lallan, Pradeep and Baldev also got burnt, but only slightly.'

'What's the update on Ashiqwa? Does he stand a chance?' This dejected question elicits no reply.

The panic and scurrying after the night's incident called to mind the aftermath of a terrorist attack. All those out on the streets ran for their homes. Or were dragged in by their brothers and fathers. The only ones left outdoors were those participating in the immersion procession and the victims. That's why, no one can say for sure what exactly happened after Baiju flung the petrol can. Using bits of information gathered from various sources, everyone is trying to reconstruct the story.

'Had anyone else been engulfed by the fire, Ashiq would have jumped in at once, risking his own life to rescue them. But how can the one who is on fire pour water over himself? By God, the way he was flailing—two steps forward, and four backwards—it looked as if, draped in fire, Ashiqwa was still doing breakdance.'

'What happened then?'

'Fire draped over his body, Ashiqwa moved towards Sheetla Mandir. You remember how he had once saved Peetambar's boy from drowning by jumping into the step-well? Even when his body was on fire, his mind was in perfect order. He knew exactly what he needed to do. But see his luck—he crashed into Ojha-ji's kiosk and collapsed. The flames kept devouring his body. People filled up bucket after bucket with water from the handpump on the road and splashed it over him. Finally the fire was doused after Alok got a blanket from somewhere and wrapped it over Ashiq.'

'He must have already died by then.'

'No, no, he kept muttering some words, again and again. Ayesha, hospital ... and God knows what all. The doctors were amazed that a man burnt to such a degree could utter anything at all. Such a braveheart! They say, those who are strong-willed, respond better to any treatment. The burns need to be protected from infection. If the doctors manage to arrest the infection, he might even get well. But even then, it will take a long time.'

Everyone knows that Satya bhaiyya's words are half lies. But today, his words seem to have a divine ring to them. As people listen, they hope and will that his words come true. That somehow, Ashiq recovers and returns home. The news arrives in the next hour—Ashiq will be home by evening. Not from the hospital, but from the mortuary.

Yesterday itself, by midnight, the doctors had declared him dead. The police had quietly sent the body for a post-mortem. Now the post-mortem is over, and his last rites will be conducted under tight security.

Kamlesh Singh and his followers ensure a lockdown, by chastising the owners of the few shops still open for business. After all, Ashiqwa had been a part of the chowk since boyhood. They owed him this much at least. All the leaders, workers and volunteers involved in the Kali Puja procession would have been implicated in a police case, and tangled in endless rounds of inquiries and court proceeding, but Balchandra Saha used his political clout to save their skin by wheeling and dealing with the higher-ups in the capital. But what will become of Baiju?

The shopkeepers thrashed him soundly after the incident, and locked him inside Prakash's studio. But somehow he escaped and then fell down the railing. Some say that Prakash's brother pushed him; others say, he fell down, trying to escape. He is in the hospital with a head injury. There's no telling if he will recover or perish. The police report says that he is of unsound mind, hence the whole thing is being treated as an unfortunate accident, and no FIR has been filed. For the first time ever, the Kali Puja organisers and the Yuva Shakti Sangh members are seeing eye to eye on a matter. Everyone is of the opinion that nothing would be gained by pursuing this further; it would only exacerbate the tension between the Hindus and the Muslims. This information is vouched for by Nirmal Jain, the journalist.

There is substantial police presence in Raiyyat Toli today. Several Muslim leaders have come and left. Ashiq's close friends are nervous about going to his house. Even so, setting fear aside, Mithilesh has come. Mithilesh watches his dear friend's body being brought in—tied up in a bundle like some object—and set down in the courtyard of the house.

When the unbearable sound of women crying rises from the house, he goes to stand under a tree in Imli Maidan. Then comes the thought, that in such a volatile atmosphere it might not be safe to stand alone like this. So he returns and stands quietly on the margins of the gathered crowd. Evening falls. It feels as if everything is shrouded in a black, bleak grief.

The children are nowhere to be seen. Maybe they have been sent to someone else's house in the neighbourhood. Zulekha's teeth are chattering. The women surrounding her are trying to push water through her lips with a spoon. When she regains consciousness for some moments, she cries out—'Told you not to … didn't I … that you'd get burnt.'

The men bathe the body and wrap it up in a shroud. When they are about to depart, Amma starts muttering, '*Ai* Zulekha! Babua is going to the shop—why haven't you packed his tiffin yet?' Ashiq's sister Parveen, and Idris's wife, Zainab, hold her tightly. The minute the bier is lifted, Ashiq's younger sister, Shabana breaks down. 'Bhaijaan is leaving … Bhaijaan is leaving …'

Amma rushes out. 'Stop! Let me at least put a little black dot on my Babua to ward off the evil eye. He's my only son … take him in a fitting manner … ' The sobs take over. Amma gets adamant. She must see her son one more time. When everyone fails to hold her back, she is brought out. She stands near the body as the shroud is lifted from Ashiq's face. Amma keeps staring for a long time. 'When he has already been set on fire, why not also wrap one *Ram-nami chadar* over Babua …' Idris's wife Zainab pulls Amma to her chest so that her words get muffled and no one hears them.

After all, what answer can be given to Amma's question. When Rambhakt Ashiq has already been cremated like a Hindu, why not cover him with a Ram-nami chadar as well for his last journey?

The funeral procession is going past Inderdev Pandey's doorstep, where Ashiq would pause for a few minutes every day on his way back from the shop. But today, it is beyond his capacity to stop. 'The path to Ram is paved with hardships,' Inderdev Pandey would often say, and Ashiq would keep reminding himself of it. But now, who will say these words, and to whom?

In simple words, what Inderdev Pandey said meant: God is the name given to all that is good and auspicious in human beings. His disciple, reduced to a lifeless body now, goes past his door in silence, carrying his God within him. Did the God within also turn to cinders with him? It is said that good or bad, pure or sinful, everyone must die one day. But to die like this! There must be some limit to destiny's cruelty.

On that gloom-bedecked street, the funeral procession moves under police guard. The crematorium is on the right-hand side of the road that leads to the Poorna river. A densely wooded, rocky path towards the left leads to the kabristan, the graveyard for Muslims. This graveyard doesn't fall under any Waqf board. These days, most Muslims use the walled graveyard in the north of the city. But Barkat Miyan suggested that Ashiq should be committed to earth in the place where the rest of his clan is buried.

The windows of all the double-storeyed houses on the chowk are open. People are peering down from their terraces too. Compared to other days, there are hardly any people on the road. As the *janaza* goes past the Two-in-One tailoring shop, Manoj observes that the Anil Kapoor poster on its shutter too looks gloomy. They have moved only a few steps ahead, when a loud wail is heard. As if someone is doubled-up with grief. This is Basanti chachi. Her laughter, her rage, her grief, all are like this—sudden and intense. Who will keep an account of the scenes witnessed in the houses on the chowk on the cursed night of the immersion procession? Abha didi was almost paralysed. And now, as the funeral procession goes past her house, she shuts herself inside a room. The same room from which she would see the vultures.

The grave has been dug. Apart from the residents of Rayyat Toli, some seven or eight people from Aramganj have joined the funeral. Ashiq's landlord Triveni Mishra stands in a corner with Nirmal Jain. Akhilesh and Munna from the Yuva Shakti Sangh are also present.

Aramganj Chowk's Rangbaz and Rayyat Toli's Misir—having atoned for countless treacheries—now lies in his grave. Kamruddin, who is reading out the namaz-e-janaza, announces, 'Gentlemen, all those who want to have one last look at the *marhoom,* late Sheikh Nizamuddin Wali Ashiq, may do so now, so that the ritual of consigning him to the earth may begin.' Ashiq's childhood friend Pawan Hatwal peers at him and says wonderingly, 'Look at his *ishtyle. Saala,* he is still teasing everyone.' So saying, he crumples to the ground. Prem Rajbhar hugs him tight, but five minutes later, he himself is seen crazed with grief, kicking again and again at a tree trunk. This is the contract-killer Prem, who has taken countless lives with blades and pistols.

By the light of Petromax lamps, Alok peers into the grave. The expression on the charred face is the same. Neck slightly bent, mouth open, it seems as if Ashiq is laughing.

The grave is now covered with planks. Holding Shami in his arms, Idris Miyan makes him throw a handful of earth over the grave. All the others present follow him in throwing fistfuls of earth. Rambhakt Ashiq now lies in the very jungle where, in his boyish imagination, Ram-ji had arrived to spend his exile, after walking past the chowk.

'*Sukh ke sab saathi, dukh mein na koi*'

After this sad tune, Bhagtu's voice echoes once again past midnight. '*Jeena yahaan, marna yahaan/iske siva jana kahaan ...*' People feel as if the words are a cry from Ashiq's heart:

> Here I lived, I perished here,
> Where will I be, if not here?
> Call out to me, whenever you care,
> I will linger on, forever here.

25

THE STORY ISN'T OVER YET

Ek tha raja, ek thi rani
Dono mar gaye, khatm kahani

There was a king and a queen
Both died, thus ends the scene

My grandma would chant this ditty to shoo off the kids pestering her for a story. Had it been any other story, I too would have said the same thing. After the 'king' and the 'queen' die, what remains? The story should have been over, but that is not how things panned out. Sometimes the story does not end; it becomes immortal after the hero's death.

This was Ashiq's aka Rangbaz's story. I was merely the teller of this tale, at best holding the 'Power of Attorney' for Ashiq Miyan, and hence had the authority to tell it on his behalf. But now the true heir has arrived, the man I mentioned on page one of this story. Today, on the 30th of January 2020, after alighting from the Hyderabad flight, this man has checked into Hotel Capital Heights. After dumping his bags there, he has been cruising around town in a sedan.

When we lived in this town thirty years ago, India was locked in the cage of a mixed economy. Today, people are free to peck at the offerings of a liberalised economy. Its impact is visible in the deluge of malls and business centres that has overtaken the town. Aramganj has changed so much now that the vestiges of the old town have to be hunted for.

The car is slowly cruising along the road leading from Rayyat Toli to the chowk. A shiny new building stands in one corner. The ground floor has a showroom for motorcycles, and on the upper floor is the office of the town corporator, Kamlesh Singh.

Here I need to stop. It's hard to imagine now, but once, on this very piece of land, Gopal the cobbler's hut had existed.

On the 20th of October 1990, at Aramganj Chowk, a fire had claimed Ashiq. Two months later, on a cold December night, a similar fire had risen up while the town lay nestled in deep sleep. Gopal's hut had been set ablaze. Gopal was often seen standing, bucket in hand, with a pleading expression on his face. In a place where even drinking water wasn't within his entitlement, who would have rushed at midnight to douse the fire engulfing his hut? By morning, nothing except a heap of ash remained. Not even bones were found. The late Om-ji would often mock Gopal in passing, 'What will become of you, Nepal?' Haplessly caught between the Hindu and Muslim settlements, Gopal was seen as a low-caste cobbler by the Hindus, and as a Hindu by the Muslims. What became of him?

Some say that while his handicapped wife perished in the fire, Gopal had managed to rush out of the burning hut. Still, the expression *'Gopal zinda hai'*, Gopal is still alive, hardly sounds as exhilarating as the phrase *'Tiger zinda hai'*, Tiger is still alive. Years later, someone spotted him begging at the Howrah station. There are as many stories as there are people. But the truth, beyond all these stories, is that today Kamlesh Singh is the owner of the land on which Gopal's house once stood. People say, just as well, at least a Hindu property has remained with a Hindu. The desolate house belonging to Inderdev Pandey, too, has been redeemed by some businessman from Marwari Tola. The peepul tree tied with countless prayer-threads still stands there.

The car is now moving out of Rayyat Toli's narrow lane and advancing towards the chowk. Rayyat Toli, too, has changed a lot. Most houses there are made of brick and cement now. A year after Ashiq's death, his Amma, too, passed away. After that, selling her portion of the house to Idris Miyan, Zulekha Bano left for her maternal home in Phulwari Sharif, Patna. The remaining five-seven years of her life were spent there. A small mosque now stands on Imli Maidan, built as per the wishes of Mufti sahib, that is, Kamruddin Miyan. Sheikh Nizamuddin Wali Ashiq's name, too, is etched on a platform built on this ground.

But a far greater transformation is seen on the chowk. The trend of combining two or three houses to erect a huge commercial property has changed the entire 'geography' of the place. Buildings with glass facades and marble lifts now grace the chowk. A few old-style houses too remain. These belong either to the naturally contented type of characters, or to households where there is no one left in the family to chase a builder to get the redevelopment done. Triveni Mishra's house, too, has changed into a four-storeyed complex. A retail store of a big brand stands where Two-in-One tailoring shop used to be. The visitor from Hyderabad has told his driver to halt the car outside this retail store. Now this man, past thirty-five, but very fit, stands on the road outside the store, smoking. He has a thick moustache, a light beard, and is wearing sunglasses. Blowing rings of smoke, he looks thoughtfully at everything.

This man has come to Aramganj after decades in order to write the last page of this story. When his looks and mannerisms match those of a character out of some web series, shouldn't the ending of his story, too, be likewise? Full of suspense, tension and drama? Is it possible that his father's death turned this man into a cold-blooded murderer, and after having smouldered in the fire of revenge for years, he is now about to do something that would chill the whole town to the marrow? Such an end would doubtlessly make the story thrilling and sensational. But I don't have the permission to do so. Being just the teller of the tale, I can only tell you what is true.

Don't go by his looks. This man cannot finish even one sentence without laughing. His real name is Shami Sheikh, but among his friends, he is known as 'Rangeela'.

Ashiq's son is a step ahead of his father in his spirited outlook. Battered by the vagaries of time, he has written his destiny with his own hands. Hailing from a clan of tailors, this guy now works as a senior manager in a well-known IT company in Hyderabad. A voracious reader, Shami is carefree, open-minded and friendly.

In his college days, he had bought a book of stories by Premchand from a second-hand bookshop. In it was the story of a Lucknow lawyer called Rangeela babu, 'the colourful one', who fancied Urdu poetry and spouted couplets. Rangeela babu was someone who, instead of grieving over the blows of a cruel destiny, kept cocking a snook at fate.

In the story's climax, Rangeela babu, after having faced the trauma of losing his nearest and dearest ones, is busy with the preparations for his only son's wedding. But instead of the wedding procession, he ends up taking part in his son's funeral procession. He does not weep at this heart-rending blow of fate. He guffaws, as if challenging God, *try doing something worse, I am not going to change.*

Shami had pasted his favourite dialogue from the story above his study table. '*Live brazenly in this world. The more they hit you, the more you twirl those moustaches brashly. The real fun is in keeping your spirit intact, even when under the executioner's foot.'*

In his student days, Shami was fascinated with this character, Rangeela babu. He spoke of this story so often, that his friends started calling him 'Rangeela babu'. Later it got shortened to the cooler 'Rangeela'.

Apart from having an amazing sense of humour and an open mind, Rangeela is also unpredictable to a great extent. It's rare to find such a blend of traits in anyone's personality—a devil-may-care attitude on one hand, and a deeply philosophical bent of mind on the other. This explains the magnetic pull Shami has with people. He often says, in order to survive, one has to brazen it out. In a way, walking the path of truth requires impertinence and audacity, and a man with audacity often finds himself all alone, while thousands look contemptuously at him from the other side. Blogging is Shami's hobby. He reads a lot, and to communicate his thoughts to the world, he blogs. His father was immolated in the middle of the chowk, and the world kept asking the eight-year-old exactly what had happened. His traumatised, heartbroken mother, too, passed away one night in her sleep. He was brought up by his mother's family, almost like an orphan. His ordeal didn't end there. His only sister, Ayesha, was married off, but died at the age of twenty-two in childbirth. Despite all this, Shami is content with his life, because he is 'brazen'. He published this account of his brazenness on his blog, and it went viral. This story opened the doors to his past.

One day, Shami received a message on Facebook messenger: 'I keep reading your posts. You may not know me, but I knew your father very well. I would love to meet you once.' Shami read this text many times over. His heart had not beaten so wildly even when the most attractive girl in office, Linda Fernandes finally said yes after making him wait for a long time.

On Sunday morning, he was in Banjara Hills, a locality in Hyderabad where top-ranking government officials have their bungalows. A servant respectfully ushered him into the drawing room. Shami's gaze kept flitting, from the paintings on the wall to the Facebook profile on his phone, from which he had received the message.

He has many fond memories of his Abbu. It was he who had told him that Spiderman was more powerful than Ali and Bajrangbali. Even today, Spiderman is his favourite cartoon character. Such stories keep floating in Shami's memories; but what of his father's story? Shami has no particular interest in finding out because there are hundreds of stories about him, not just one. The story that Shami's Ammi, Zulekha Bano, had told him is one story. On the other hand are the stories he heard from people while growing up in Patna—stories in the form of questions and conjectures.

'Might have been a good man, but his company wasn't good. When thieves and rascals are your mates, the outcome can never be good. Something must surely have happened, or why would anyone throw petrol and burn someone down just like that?' Shami still remembers Bilqis mami whispering to the woman next door. That's why, even by mistake, he never discusses his father's death with anyone. He knows that the lanes of the past are an intricate maze—one may enter it easily, but the way out is hard to find.

Shami deliberated for a full two days over the invitation received on Facebook, and finally with great difficulty, persuaded himself to grapple with his past. His thoughts were interrupted by the sound of footsteps. Before him stood a very gentle-looking lady of about fifty. Big-eyed, a bindi on the forehead, and wearing a cotton sari. Shami hesitatingly greeted her, 'Namaste ma'm.'

'Hello! I hope finding the address was no trouble ... You write so well on your blog!'

'Thanks, ma'am.'

The woman was observing Shami closely, making him feel awkward. She sensed his discomfort. 'Shami, this world is very small. I found out whose son you are from your blog. I am your bua, your Abbu's rakhi-sister.'

This was Sarvdaman babu's rebel daughter, Puja, who had eloped and married a low-caste boy, and because of whom rounds had been openly fired for the first time in Aramganj. Puja's husband Dileep Vishwakarma, an income tax commissioner, was posted in Hyderabad. Shami knew nothing about Puja. Puja, too, was seeing Shami for the first time. The link that could possibly have brought them together had snapped thirty years ago.

'You look exactly like your father,' Puja said.

'My mother, too, used to say that.'

Then Shami told Puja about himself. Apart from his wife Linda, there were two children, Fidel and Tulip, in his family. After living in Hyderabad for twelve years, Shami had decided to emigrate to Auckland in New Zealand.

After opening up somewhat, Shami finally asked Puja the question that had been roiling inside him. 'I wanted to ask you something. What exactly happened to my father? Meaning, the man who immolated him—what was on his mind?'

Puja's face clouded over. After a long silence, the answer came from Dileep Vishwakarma, her husband. 'Some questions never find an answer. Many good people have to die without any reason. The reason behind the deaths of people like your father is a deliberately or unintentionally created environment. The one who threw the can of petrol at your Abbu was a dimwit. The real offenders were the people who created such a hateful environment. The air at the time became so toxic, it incited a dimwit to commit such a heinous act.'

'The environment is no better now,' Shami said.

Dileep Vishwakarma sighed and said, 'Your father seems to me like the hero of a Greek tragedy. When I came to Aramganj, I got acquainted with him. I knew him for only two years. But I haven't forgotten him. Anyone who came into contact with him felt indebted to him in some way or the other.'

Her husband's words reminded Puja of something. She got up and went inside. When she came back, she had a transparent plastic file in her hands. Dileep Vishwakarma took the file from her, and looking at Shami, he said, 'In the toughest time of our lives, that is, while eloping from home to get married, your father forced me to take twelve hundred rupees from him. Thirty years ago, how much would a tailor in a small town have earned, and how big his heart must have been, to give someone so much money!'

Dileep was overcome with emotion. Steadying his voice, he said, 'I had kept this money aside, to repay him, but the "incident" happened before I could do that. But see how destiny works. We met you unexpectedly. If you'll allow me to give you this money, it will bring me some kind of closure. I will, of course, always be in Ashiq bhai's debt.'

'My father is still alive.' Shami came back home screaming, astonishing Linda. Thrice he repeated the same words: 'My father is still alive. My father is still alive. My father is still alive!'

Thirty years. Meaning a little more than a quarter of a century. Long enough to completely change the world. The Berlin Wall got made and then demolished in less than thirty years. India got divided on religious lines, and India and Pakistan were formed, and in less than thirty years, Pakistan, too, split into two. The three-hundred-year-old Babri Masjid was demolished, and in less than thirty years, the construction of the 'historical' Ram temple began. Lal Krishna Advani, who had cautioned the courts against getting involved in the dispute, 'enjoyed' in his own lifetime, the spectacle of the same courts meting out 'justice'. Thirty years is truly a long time. In this span of time, a lot gets made and unmade. But the world of Shami's Abbu has remained intact so many years after his death.

People don't even remember big leaders with such clarity for so many decades after their death. When Shami touched the yellowing hundred-rupee notes, he felt as if he was touching his father's fingers. Dileep Vishwakarma's words kept ringing in his ears. 'I will, of course, always be in Ashiq bhai's debt.'

'It seems I still owe him some debt from my past life. Maybe it is to be paid off this way,' Abha had told Puja after some probing. Abha Asthana, meaning Ashiq's didi from the chowk, who was Puja's bhabhi by way of being neighbours in the mohalla. Abha was the second such link, after hearing of whom, Shami decided that he must take a peek into the lanes of his past.

It has been six years since Abha Asthana's husband passed away. Her only son, Guddu, is settled in Singapore. But Abha isn't willing to go and live with him. The reason being Baiju. For thirty years, Ashiq's murderer has been living a cursed existence.

Baiju's matter remained inconclusive. No evidence was found to indicate whether Baiju had fallen off the railing, or whether he had been thrown off it on the night of 20 October 1990. He spent two weeks in hospital, and when he returned, he had changed completely. He had been dim-witted earlier, but now he seemed to have completely lost the capacity to comprehend anything. He had acquired a permanent limp. Though he mostly stayed mute, he would burst into tears from time to time for no apparent reason.

A commercial building stands where Baiju's ancestral house used to be. Residential flats have been built on the upper floors. Legally, Baiju was entitled to half the property. However, his uncle gave him the small room next to the generator room, outside which the ironing man plies his trade in the basement of the building.

Till the uncle and aunt were alive, Baiju got to eat what was cooked in their house. Now, no one from his family remains in the building. During the day, Baiju lies on the veranda of the shops built below Abha's house. Rain or shine, Abha Asthana sees to it that four chapatis and some sabzi are put before him everyday. Sometimes he rings the call bell on the first floor. When Abha opens the door, Baiju just stands there mutely. Which means he wants something to eat. Seeing Abha, a few others from the chowk also give him food from time to time. But the official duty to feed him is Abha's.

'Earlier I felt repulsed by him. The idea that, had he died in the hospital itself, it would have been better, haunted me. When he came back, I saw the neighbourhood children pelting stones at him for fun. Slowly, pity got the better of me,' Abha had told Puja once.

This compassion turned Abha Asthana from a homemaker into a well-known social worker of the town. She began reading up on differently-abled children and people with special needs, and started working to help them. Thanks to her efforts, today, a school for such children exists in the town.

Shami has been roaming in Aramganj since morning in the manner of a foreign tourist or a documentary filmmaker looking for research material. In a very detached manner, he is trying to ascertain his father's true story. He notices that most Rayyat Toli women are in burqas. He does not remember his mother ever observing purdah. The passage of time does not always imply progress. Time turns backwards too.

After passing through Rayyat Toli, Shami arrives at his Abbu's friend Mithilesh's place, and then at Alok Kant's.

Ashiq's carrom partner Alok, who had carried Ashiq's bier on his shoulder, occupies an important post in the town's civil administration these days. Hugging Shami, Alok, too, says what Puja had said. 'You look exactly like your father.'

Alok Kant is probably the only person left in Aramganj who had witnessed the incident of 20 October 1990 with his own eyes. Shami wants to know why and how his father died. Alok, however, isn't keen on talking about Ashiq's death; he is eager to talk about his life. Shami comes to know for the first time that his father's nickname was Rangbaz. He himself is known to his friends as Rangeela. The calculus of fate works in curious ways.

Hearing about Shami's career and family life, Alok's face lights up the way a family elder's would. Then he suddenly inquires, 'When everything's going well for you in India, why have you decided to settle in New Zealand?'

'Chacha, I had heard from Ammi that my Abbu's final days were spent hunting for property papers and doing the rounds of courts. He had to prove that the ancestral house in which he had lived all his life was indeed his. Now I will have to prove that this country is mine. A person cast out of his house can probably build another one. But what can a person do when banished from his country? I am scramming before matters come to a head.' Shami chuckles as he says this, and Alok's face falls.

A weird thought haunts Alok's mind. He wants to tell Shami: Do you know what changed in my life after your father's death? I could never touch tandoori chicken again, because, to this day, I remember the stench rising from his charred and convulsed body. But all Alok can do is give Shami his blessings.

However, Abha Asthana didn't hold back from telling Shami that after Ashiq's death, she couldn't bear stepping into any tailor's shop in the mohalla. Ashiq's Abha didi is now sixty-five years old. Puja had told Abha about Shami. Abha had also spoken to Shami several times on the phone after that. Now she is restlessly waiting for him to come to lunch.

'The same smiling face.' Abha Asthana repeats this observation every ten minutes. Shami observes that whenever she says this, her eyes get moist. Reading this moistness, Shami keeps thinking, if only Abbu had been here, and I with him, in this town.

Then he thinks, even if he was here, what would have happened? Back then, some crazy person set him on fire. Today, every second person is behaving like Baiju. It's quite possible that news channels would have dubbed my father as a terrorist who immolated himself to escape being caught.

Shami remembers Shadab. The shy twenty-three-year-old Shadab started his career under Shami. Shadab would often pass the phone to him when his father called, and the voice from the other end would say, 'You alone are my beloved son's local guardian.' Shadab had gone to Meerut on leave, promising he would get *gajak* for everyone on his return. But he could not return. Hit by a police bullet, he had died right in front of his home.

The newspapers said that among those killed while 'rioting' against the Citizenship Amendment Act and the National Registry of Citizens, was the 'rioter' Shadab Ahmed, an engineering degree-holder. This was the turning point after which Shami said yes to Linda's old idea of emigrating to New Zealand.

The day passes swiftly. The January sun begins to set as early as six p.m. Shami repeats his demand. 'Please let me meet him once.'

Abha says in a pleading voice, 'Let it be, son, what will be gained by meeting him?'

Shami laughs and replies, 'Nothing. I just want to see him in person. Trust me, I won't make any trouble. You don't even have to tell him who I am. In one sense, I made this trip to find closure. So I don't want to leave any loose ends untied.'

Abha half-heartedly calls out to the girl working in the kitchen. 'If Baiju is sitting downstairs, fetch him.' The girl goes down and returns upstairs after a while. An emaciated man slowly pulls up behind her, holding on to the railing. He must be around fifty, the hair from the front of his head is all gone, his cheeks have caved in, the veins on his forehead are prominent, and he has a few smallpox scars on his face.

Is this the man who haunted Shami's dreams? This man doesn't have the face of a murderer. Going by his clothes and mannerisms, his condition seems a tad better than a beggar's, but worse than a daily-wage labourer's. The man has come up and is standing quietly by the door.

Abha Asthana asks him, 'Where were you yesterday? Pushpa kept standing with your food for so long.'

'At a bedding.'

'Whose wedding?'

'Yestelday it waj my bedding.'

'*Arre waah!* What all did you get in the wedding?'

'Watch, scootal, umblella, TV, motol-caal.'

'And the bride?'

'I will get the blide latel.'

Abha is talking to Baiju in all seriousness. Shami is quietly watching this exchange.

'Come on, it's time for you to have your lunch. And don't leave the polythene bag in front of the shop, or Murari will thrash you one day.'

Baiju holds both his ears, and is about to bend down to do squats, when Shami gets up and walks to the door.

'Do you recognise him?' Abha asks Baiju.

Baiju stares at him wide-eyed for a few moments, and then bursts into tears.

'Don't be alarmed. He does this every time he meets someone unfamiliar.'

'This is my brother's son, my nephew,' Abha explains to both Baiju and Pushpa.

Hearing this, Baiju clicks his heels to salute Shami. Abha says, 'Okay, Baiju, you may go now.'

But Baiju keeps standing there and, without saying a word, extends his palm towards Shami. Despite his mental incapacity, he knows the value of money.

'What do you need money for? Go away from here,' Abha scolds him. But by then, Shami has taken out a hundred-rupee note. Baiju literally snatches the currency note from Shami's hands, and, without meeting his eyes, limps down the stairs.

Suddenly, Shami's head starts to reel. He feels like he's going to fall, but somehow plonks down on the sofa. Seeing him like that, Abha gets nervous. 'Son, are you all right? I told you not to do this. Pushpa, get some water, quick.'

Shami opens his eyes after a minute, and says with a laugh, 'Don't worry, I am okay. I just need to go down for five minutes.'

'Why? What happened?'

'I am sorry. I am a smoker. It has been a while since I had my last cigarette, that's why my head is swimming.'

'Go into that balcony. No one uses it,' Abha says, pointing in the balcony's direction. Perhaps she fears that Shami might go after Baiju.

Even after taking in long drags, Shami's anxiety doesn't subside. What sort of emotional crisis is this? Earlier, he was plagued by the fear of finding out something about his father that he wouldn't be able to stomach. And now, when most people of this town have given witness that Ashiq was a unique person, and by every measure a great man, Shami's mind is filled, not with his Abbu's thoughts but with that of his killer. He has watched many documentaries in which the victim's family forgives the killer. Shami had this idea, that before moving to New Zealand, he would do one good thing. He would embrace his father's killer, and tell him he has forgiven him. But Baiju did not give him the opportunity.

The Rangeela babu style of twirling the moustache, after being battered and defeated by life, sounds grand; but what if your father's murderer comes and stands before you? Even if mentally unsound, a killer is a killer.

Friends have needlessly put me on a pedestal. I am no Rangeela-vangeela, just a bigmouth of sorts. I don't have the guts to look the truth in the eye. That's why—first I kept my face turned away from my father's past, and now I am leaving the country forever.

Shami lights one more cigarette, and for a long time, stares expressionlessly at the balcony wall. Suddenly, a macabre thought occurs to him. That his arm is around Baiju's neck in a vice-like grip, and he is squeezing it with such force that Baiju's eyeballs pop out, fall down, and bounce like marbles on the ground. Then he smashes them under his shoes. Won't it be possible to come here again tomorrow, and somehow lure Baiju downstairs itself, and ...

He has never had such a violent thought before. What has come over him? Only this morning he came to know that Jatashankar Sharma passed away a month ago. Had he been alive, Shami would have definitely gone up to him and, holding the flame of his lighter close to his face, told him, 'Try bearing this— not for long, just for ten seconds—and imagine what my father went through when he was burnt alive.' The bastards who drilled such hatred into the fragile mind of someone like Baiju certainly don't deserve forgiveness.

'Man harbours the delusion that by forgiving someone, he is doing them a good turn. But the truth is, one needs to forgive in order to release one's own self from the prison of terrible memories. There is anger inside you because of what happened to your father. But try thinking about Abha aunty once. She has no direct relation with either the one who was killed, or the one who killed. Still, she feels strongly for both. It is easy to hate evil, but very tough to become good oneself, in the truest sense of the word.' What Linda said on the phone this afternoon echoes in his ears.

'Tea is ready,' Pushpa calls out to Shami. Shami returns to the drawing room. Tea is on the table. Abha is in the other room. Shami opens his bag, which contains notepads, envelopes and papers of all kinds. Shami takes out a pen and starts writing. Abha comes out in the meanwhile. As soon as the tea is drunk, Shami stands up. 'I'll take your leave now. Have a morning flight to catch. But before going, I have to fulfill my mother's wish.'

Abha is surprised. 'But you said your mother is no longer alive.'

'Yes, but the wish is an old one, and will have to be fulfilled.' Shami touches Abha's feet, and leaves.

Ammi would keep repeating to him, that as per the new trend, the residents of Rayyat Toli had stopped reading the *fatiha*—the opening verses of the Holy Quran—on Shab-e-baraat. They said, when this custom wasn't followed by Arabic Islam, why must they follow it? 'But you must go at least once, and read the *fatiha* at your father's grave.'

Shami's upbringing in the maternal household left nothing wanting in making him a true believer. He is well aware of all the rituals and customs of Islam. But what he often tells Linda is also true—'For all practical purposes, I am an atheist.'

Shami is headed to the final stop of this trip. After getting his car parked some distance away, in the New Market parking lot, he is now moving, with a small bag in hand, towards the deserted area which once served as a graveyard. The mission is spiritual, but the thoughts running through his mind are of this world.

On his visit to the old house in Rayyat Toli this morning, his father's cousin Idris Miyan made a fitting point. 'Whatever it may be, the time is always right. We often pray for the bad times to pass. But mostly, we have no way of knowing that in the times to come, we will mourn the passing of even these bad times. We had been afraid when Babri Masjid was demolished; but now we are much more afraid. It won't be surprising, if in the coming days, the situation will worsen to such a degree that our future generations will start referring to these times as good times. It is just as well that you are starting a new life in another country. Even the Prophet migrated, went on *Hijrat*. Wherever you choose to live, may you be happy.'

Walking on the stony path now, Shami is thinking, everyone prays for our happiness, but is it so easy to be happy?

Linda often says, 'Your zest for life sets you apart from the rest.'

Zest for life and nonchalance are parts of his personality. Hence, even if he wants, he cannot appear depressed. But the fact is, whatever happens outside, does impinge on one's inside. Before he can decipher how or when, he finds himself surrounded by these alienating shadows lengthening all around him.

Before this, Shami has never had to remind himself of his religious identity while talking to anyone. But now, as soon as he opens his mouth, he gets the feeling that everything will be seen and understood only in the context of his identity. When Shami lost a few close friendships to this new socio-political climate, he decided to refrain from openly discussing things that others disliked. But when the Supreme Court verdict on Ramjanmabhoomi came, the promise Shami had made to himself was broken, and he wrote on his blog, 'The grand temple of Maryada Purushottam Shri Ram is being built by bringing down two structures. One of them is in Ayodhya, and the other is in Delhi. I never saw the first structure, and have no emotional attachment to it. But the essence of my identity depended on the second structure. It was a guarantee of my security. When that itself has collapsed, what is left for the likes of me?'

Walking on the uphill path littered with stones, Shami feels that his *Hijrat* has begun. Going elsewhere, in search of better times, is *Hijrat*. But can anyone guarantee that the reality of Paradise will match the Paradise of one's dreams? Also, which part of the world can be said to be totally peaceful today? The country that Shami is going to settle in, is counted among the foremost of developed, cultured and law-abiding countries. But is it not true that a few months ago, some crazed fellow had opened fire on people praying in a mosque there?

We can choose only our decisions, not the consequences that follow. Did migrating from Mecca to Medina make the heirs of the Prophet happy? For the sake of maintaining peace, Lord Krishna left Mathura and went to Dwarka. But soon, Dwarka, too, was soaked in the blood of his own clan, and then claimed by the ocean. Shami is not going elsewhere in the hope of bettering his prospects. His heart right now has an emotional void, which is beyond hope and dread. A deep void created from the acceptance of his fate.

Emerging from these thoughts, Shami casts a glance ahead. The thorny bushes and absolute silence confirm that his destination has arrived. A dust-storm in the afternoon had seemed to portend unseasonal January rains, but thankfully, now the weather has cleared. The path is clear in the moonlight.

Shami is now standing at the location specified by Sajid bhai—an old cement bench before a neem tree. Shami's Abbu is resting in the spot right in front of that tree. Two huge rocks standing there for ages mark the place. Thankfully, the overgrowth here is not as dense as it was along the way.

Shami sprinkles rose water on the ground, then spreads rose petals all over. Though he has lit a candle at the grave, Shami feels that angels, in the form of countless fireflies, are themselves casting light on his father's sacred soul.

Shami begins to read the *Surah Al-fatiha* in a resonant voice.

> *Bismillah-ir-rahman-ir-rahim*
> *Al-hamdu li-llah-i rabb-il-'Alimin*
> *Ar-rahman-ir-rahim*
> *Malik-i yaum-id-dinIyaka na'budu*
> *Wa iyaka nasta'in ...*
>
> In the praise of the all-beneficent, merciful Allah
> The Lord of all worlds, to whom, all praise belongs
> O Master of the day of retribution
> You alone we worship
> To You alone, we turn for help ...

Hearing the echo of his own voice in the wilderness, he feels as if Allah is indeed listening to him. After reciting the *Surah Al-fatiha*, Shami recites the four *kuls*. After finishing the *Aayat-al-kursi*, the Throne verse, he thinks—what else is left? He does not remember the verses of *Darood-Sharif*, so he searches for it on his phone and reads it out. Now comes the time to offer a *dua*, a prayer for his father.

'*Ya Allah, grant forgiveness to my father, Sheikh Nizamuddin Wali Ashiq, for all his errors and wrongdoings. Grant him freedom from all troubles in his grave. Grant my father a place in Paradise.*

'Ya Allah, fill all our lives with thoughts as bright as my father's thoughts. Grant us a life like his, but never give such an unfortunate death to anyone. Ya Allah, may no child in this world live without the shade of his father's protection upon him, the way I walked through this life bereft of my father's protection.'

Going beyond the established rituals of seeking blessings, and asking for *dua* at the grave, Shami continues talking to Allah Miyan with whom he has nothing to do in his daily life. After seeking blessings for his father, he asks for blessings for his mother, for his sister Ayesha, and for others in his clan.

Nothing of his Abbu's now remains in the Rayyat Toli house. Sitting on the bench in the graveyard, Shami feels as if this graveyard is now his Abbu's house. He opens a pack of cigarettes and then stops. How can he smoke in front of his father? Then he laughs at himself. From whatever he can make of his father, he knows that Ashiq Miyan would never have stopped him from smoking in front of him.

If you know a person well, then even after dying he does not die. He can talk to you as he would have, had he been physically present. Right now, Shami is talking to his father with the same informality. He is swinging from his father's shoulders, his father is telling him all the stories he used to tell when Shami was a kid. Suddenly, he feels as if his Abbu is saying, 'Where were you all these days? And now that you have finally found me, why are you leaving me and going elsewhere?'

After an hour, Shami gets up from the bench with a heavy heart. Walking back in the moonlight, he feels as if his Abbu is walking beside him. Suddenly by some magic, outlines of Ram, Lakshman and Sita's figures become visible in the clouds above. His Abbu used to say, 'This was the way Ram-ji had passed through.'

Startled, Shami stops in his tracks, gazing at those bright outlines in the sky. Is something still left undone? He turns back to the grave, and raises both his hands in prayer to seek a *dua* once more.

'*Ya Allah, grant forgiveness to all those people whose crimes are responsible for my father's death. Shield Baiju from worldly troubles. Grant the favour of filling Baiju's mind with light and his heart with peace. Aameen.*'

Now, nothing else remains to be done. While walking back from the grave towards the road, he looks at his phone. There are five missed calls from Abha Asthana. Only friends with such love in their hearts must have held back his ancestors from going to Pakistan. He calls back immediately.

'No, bua. Nothing got left behind. That envelope is for you. I forgot to tell you. There is a cheque inside ... yes, of one lakh rupees ... you fill out the name.

'No, bua, please don't say no. You must be spending a lot on Baiju's upkeep. Accept some contribution from me as well. Please invest the rest in the school you run.

'Please take care of yourself. I am going next week. Linda and the kids, too, are going with me. What if we don't like it there? We will come back then. What else?' So saying, Shami laughs out loud, and the minute the phone disconnects, starts sobbing like a child.

Dew has begun to fall from the cold sky. Shami wipes his eyes. The time has now come to bid a final goodbye to his Abbu. The thirty-eight-year-old son kisses the picture of the thirty-two-year-old father on his phone's screen, the way his father used to kiss him once. The photograph of the chowk's top rangbaz appears more joyous and life-affirming than ever. And it seems that walking towards the dense forest via Aramganj, Ram, Lakshman and Sita, too, have put aside their tribulations for the moment, and are smiling beatifically.